CAPTURE DEATH

CAPTURE DEATH

THE KURTHERIAN GAMBIT™ BOOK 20

MICHAEL ANDERLE

LMBPN

DISRUPTIVE IMAGINATION

Copyright © 2017 Michael T. Anderle
Cover by Gene Mollica and Sasha Almazan
https://www.gsstockphoto.com/
Internal Artwork © 2017 Michael T. Anderle, Drawn by Eric Quigley

LMBPN Publishing
PMB 196, 2540 South Maryland Pkwy
Las Vegas, NV 89109

Version 2.2, March 2023
eBook ISBN: 978-1-64971-587-6
Print ISBN: 978-1-64202-053-3

THE CAPTURE DEATH TEAM

Beta Editor / Readers

Bree Buras (Aussie Awesomeness)
Tom Dickerson (The man)
S Forbes (oh yeah!)
Dorene Johnson (US Navy (Ret) & DD)
Dorothy Lloyd (Teach you to ask...Teacher!)
Diane Velasquez (Chinchilla lady & DD)

JIT Beta Readers

Sarah Weir
Kimberly Boyer
Joshua Ahles
Micky Cocker
James Caplan
John Findlay
Kelly O'Donnell
Larry Omans
Paul Westman

Veronica Torres
John Ashmore
Thomas Ogden

Thanks to our JIT Readers for this Version

Dave Hicks
Diane L. Smith
Timothy Cox (the myth)
Deb Mader
Rachel Beckford
Peter Manis
Veronica Stephan-Miller
Mary Morris

If I missed anyone, please let me know!

Original Editors
Stephen Russell
Lynne Stiegler

This version edited by
Lynne Stiegler

**Thank you to the following Special Consultants
for CAPTURE DEATH**
**Jeff Morris - US Army - Asst Professor Cyber-Warfare,
Nuclear Munitions (Active)**

CHAPTER ONE

QBS *Shinigami*, in Space, Location Unknown

The darkness was enveloping. The woman was transfixed in her nightmare, and the raw emotions roared out of the darkness and pummeled her body. She twitched, half-frozen, half-thrashing, against unfathomable pain as her raw nerves reacted to her subconscious agony.

WAKE UP, BETHANY ANNE! TOM yelled through their link.

His friend continued to flail, unable to hear his screams as he sought to locate the places he could try to take over her neuro-transmissions.

She was beating the hell out of the bed.

>>This mattress is going to be sub-optimal after this.<< ADAM commented.

You mean, it's going to be *fucked*, TOM corrected.

>>You seem to be using more of Bethany Anne's colloquialisms lately.<<

Yes, I'm cursing a lot more, TOM admitted. **After this long as her closest organic friend, she has rubbed off on me. I like to think I've provided a modicum of restraint and mathematical understanding in exchange.**

Bethany Anne's arm slammed into the bulkhead behind her head and dented it.

Well, shit. TOM mentally ground his teeth. **I hate this.**

>>**What?**<< ADAM asked.

BABA YAGA, WAKE YOUR ASS UP! TOM yelled through their connection.

The thrashing slowed over the next minute.

>>**That is rather confusing and disconcerting.**<< ADAM noted.

No shit! TOM sighed. **I'm concerned we are losing her, ADAM.**

>>**She is still there, TOM, but based on my research into multiple personality disorders, she isn't a classic case. She** *chose* **to switch to Baba Yaga, for better or worse.**<<

Yeah, you can do all the research you want, but we need to catch these seven Kurtherians, or I could lose my best friend.

>>**Her mental waves are coming out of REM, so she will be with us in just a moment.**<<

What the hell just happened? Baba Yaga's red eyes flicked opened and she looked around, taking in her room before speaking aloud. "Shinigami, turn on lights twenty percent." The cabin's lights came on and she looked at the bulkhead, then her fist. "Ohhhh, that left a mark."

I'd say.

"Still wondering what happened." Baba Yaga turned over and looked around the room for additional damage before she made an ugly face. "This mattress is trashed."

>>**That is an understatement.**<<

I'd say you probably produced the equivalent of a nuclear explosion in the Etheric. If you had been on a planet, it would have been a challenge to hide the effects. I've no idea what it did throughout the dimension.

Baba Yaga reached down to the end of the mattress and

started rolling up what was left. "Shame the mattress didn't come with a warranty."

You aren't listening to me.

"I'm listening, TOM," Baba Yaga admitted as she stripped off the ripped sheets. "I'm just not *responding* to you. That's different." She padded out of her cabin, carrying the remains of her mattress and linens. "Teach my ass to thrash around with claws on a cloth mattress."

"We aren't on a planet, and there are probably no Kurtherians within a hundred thousand miles at the moment." She took a right, and five steps later, there was a place in the wall to shove the ruined mess so the ship could consume the debris and recycle it. She walked back to her cabin. "So, what's the big deal?"

TOM's voice came over the speakers. "If you don't handle the reasons behind these nightmares, you are going to scream loudly enough for something nasty to find us."

Baba Yaga chuckled as she stepped back into her suite. "Like what, some creature large enough to eat our ship?"

"Yes, that's a possibility."

Planet N'Var, Non-allied Space, Industrial Shipping City of Cleerk, Two Blocks from the Spaceport

The alien had three legs, three eyes, three tentacles coming out of his head, and a nose about three feet long. The three eyes looked from Leath to Leath.

And counted *seven*.

"No way," Jermom shook his head. One of his tentacles waved above his head, pointing at the Leath in front of him. "I cannot hide you, Levelot."

"Why not?" asked Levelot, the prime Leath of the Phraim-'Eh Clan, as she looked down at the alien. "Our coin is good, even for someone like you."

The alien looked across his desk at the prime Leath in front of him, then one of his eyes slid quickly to the left when two hushed voices hissed at each other under the hood.

From the *same* Leath.

All three eyes focused on Levelot. "I know who you are." His other two tentacles lifted as they pointed to the seven aliens in front of him. "You were the gods of the Leath."

"Then you should know to fear us, you insufferable little slug," The male Leath who had introduced himself as "Behome't" snarled.

"I know why I fear the Witch of the Empire. She has killed many, including your people. Why should I fear you more when it is obvious you are running from *her*?"

Behome't ground out, "We run from no alien. We are—"

Levelot cut him off. "Looking for a place to rest for a moment. Our people decided they would like to try another way, and after we allow them the chance to live with their decision for a year or two, they will again be receptive to moving forward on the path which—"

A tentacle went up in a "stop" motion. "Won't happen. You will be dead, and so will I." He looked at the aliens. "Do you have any idea what the Witch of the Empire did back on Alchemist 441?" There was no recognition in the Leath's eyes as Jermom turned his head and spat into a dish on the floor before turning back.

"Tell us." Levelot pulled her robes tighter. "Let me understand why you fear this one being so much."

"Me?" Jermom chuckled. "It isn't just me, Levelot. If the Empress sends her Witch after you," his tentacles pointed at them again, "and yes, she *has* sent her after every one of you, you either find a way to disappear forever or you die when she finds you."

His tentacle stabbed a couple controls on his desk and a video screen blinked into existence in an orange frame, displaying a newscast showing a bunker of some sort. Black smoke billowed into the green sky as blue flames licked the air. "This was a group of Skaines that got in the way of some of her Rangers. They called the Empress last year, and she sent the Witch."

A tentacle stabbed the hologram. "This was a very heavily defended base that most police would have negotiated with, or called in an airstrike or kinetic round to deal with."

"Kinetic wouldn't have worked," Levelot murmured. "You can see the berms and support effort."

Jermom eyed the Leath; she wasn't as clueless as he had thought. "You're right, it wouldn't have."

"So," Levelot looked at him, "how did she rain fire on their base and destroy it?"

Jermom shut down the newscast. "From the inside. It blew up from the inside and there was only one survivor, a child, and a recording of the radio chatter as they tried to find and kill the intruder."

"How many did she have with her?" Behome't asked.

Jermom looked at him. "Was I stuttering?" he asked. "There was *one*! The Witch herself." He turned his head and spat once again before turning back. "That's why you seven are wanted criminals that even *we* don't want to touch. You are the walking dead, and you aren't nearly scary enough to stop the Witch." He cursed for a moment. "It's been what, somewhere around a hundred and fifty years since the humans took over the Yollins? In that time, only the Leath have stood against them, and that was for the greater portion of that time. But," one of his tentacles stabbed down on his desk before he used it to point back at Levelot, "this is the important part. *You are running from them!*"

Silence descended on the room as those in front of Jermom absorbed what he had said.

"There is no information that cannot be helpful." Levelot turned to her right. "Terellet, it is time to separate."

The Leath who had spoken to itself in two voices looked from Levelot to the alien and back. "Now?"

"Yes." Levelot turned back to the alien, whose eyes were

growing larger. His tentacles had frozen in the air. She smiled, "You are trying to move and have now figured out you *can't*." The Leath female leaned over the desk and spoke softly. "Baba Yaga may frighten you, but she isn't the scariest thing in the universe, Jermom. Unfortunately, you will only be able to enjoy this knowledge for the next few moments while your body becomes the new home of our dear friend Gorllet."

The Leath known as Seventh of the Seven stepped around the side of the crowded room and walked behind the desk. She took off her robe and folded it, laying it on the table.

"Goodbye, Gorllet. May you make this transfer successfully." The Leath sat down and reached around the alien, turning its face toward hers.

"Goodbye, Teret," the same Leath mouth uttered, albeit in a darker and more sinister voice. "I hope you recognize how patient I've been while you hosted me. I will endeavor to remember your graciousness."

"So it shall be," she remarked, again in a female voice as she leaned forward to place her lips on the alien. Her body started convulsing.

Levelot turned away from the transfer. It would either be successful and they would be eight, or it wouldn't and they would most likely be seven again, but without the burden of a mentally unstable Kurtherian.

The math didn't work out when the imaginary number she had to introduce for Gorllet was in the calculations.

The symmetry was flawed.

As glass broke behind the desk, Levelot looked at Behome't and Torik. "We need to do something about that Empiric Witch and her people." She took a deep breath, "Or we will never be able to rest." she admitted as she exhaled.

<u>QBS *Shinigami*</u>

Baba Yaga halted in her room, her eyes narrowed in concern as she thought of her comment. "Shinigami?"

"Yes?"

"Are there creatures that can eat this ship?" the ink-black woman asked.

"Of course," the EI admitted. "Didn't you know this?"

"Well," Baba Yaga thought about the answer as she resumed walking through her outer room to her bedroom and past her bed to find a new set of linens, "I guess I'd heard rumors, but I never thought about running into one of the beasts." Her voice was muffled as she stuck her head into a storage chest. "Are there any around?"

"None that we can register," the EI admitted.

Baba Yaga straightened from the chest and tossed the new set of linens on the bed, then walked out of her bedroom, through her suite, and into the hallway. She stopped and looked down the hallway in both directions. "Where are the spare mattresses?"

"Deck two, supplies area. There are only three," Shinigami reminded her.

Baba Yaga started down the hallway. "Remember to resupply when we dock somewhere that can provide a decent product. I don't want some lousy lumpy mattress," she grumped as she took the stairs down a level. She jumped down the last couple of steps and continued along the hallway. "How many large things are out there?"

"Are you asking about organic creatures?"

"Yes," Baba Yaga answered as she strode toward the supply area.

"Do you want to know everything that is large enough to hurt this ship or just those species which can survive in the cold of space as well as hurt this ship?"

She ran a hand along the bulkhead in thought. "Cold of space and hurt this ship."

"There are over twenty-two confirmed organic-type creatures

which could hurt this ship. There are a few that can move through space, and others which tend to congregate in one area."

"And do what?" Baba Yaga asked as she stepped through the supplies room's door. She looked around the large room and found the rolled-up mattresses, then grabbed one before heading back toward her cabin. "Dock me the cost of this."

ADAM ignored the command. She had already paid for everything.

"Do we have any research on these behemoths?" she asked as she stepped through her cabin door and walked to her bedroom. She slid off the wrap that kept the mattress rolled up and grabbed the sheets, then laid the mattress down and started making the bed. "You would have thought the future had a better solution for sheets than...sheets," she muttered.

>>**There are multiple types which allow you to use the product and eject it into space, where it will disintegrate in time.**<<

That's not necessarily better, ADAM, just more convenient. What happens if a ship hits one of those items that was tossed out? Baba Yaga asked as she tucked in the first sheet.

>>**The mathematical chance of that happening is rather small.**<<

I'd rather not be the first to explode a ship due to my laziness.

"There are," Shinigami replied to her earlier question, "twelve separate confirmed engagements between organics and ships. There are hundreds of suspected encounters that lack proof."

"What proof do we have?" she asked as she tossed the pillow on her bed. A video popped up on the wall to her left, and she took a moment to sit on her bed. "Wish I had popcorn."

The view on the screen was of space, and there were three ships. One looked like a warship about half the size of the *Arch-Angel II*, but it obviously was not as advanced. It had been hurt, but not too badly. One of the two smaller ships had been broken in half.

Baba Yaga stood up and stepped closer to the bulkhead screen. "Is that a *bite* out of that ship?" she asked softly.

"Yes. This is a confirmed attack that occurred a decade ago, some twelve systems away. The ship with the bite taken out of it was a mid-range transportation vessel, which issued a request for help. The two warships belonged to a Tulet group that was in-system. The smaller warship didn't do well; it got too close to the creatures. The battleship was able to pummel the creatures from a distance, and the report says two died, but seven disappeared."

"Son of a bitch!" Baba Yaga waved a hand. "Turn it off. I'm a believer."

TOM's voice came on. "Just like that?"

"Yes," she admitted as she sat back down on her bed. "There is no reason to ignore it. I don't know why I wouldn't believe there could be creatures that used space like our oceans back on Earth."

She turned toward her nightstand. "Now, let's figure out our future steps."

CHAPTER TWO

QBBS *Meredith Reynolds*

Lance nodded to Admiral Thomas as he sat down with a cup of something akin to coffee in his hand. Team BMW plus Tina, Jean Dukes with three of her team, and six Yollin specialists in Gate technology surrounded a large table.

"Thank you, everyone. I appreciate you being here," he started. "Use your tablets if you want to know who is who. I've hated the 'Go-around-the-table and introduce yourself' thing for nearly two hundred years. Technology has improved, so use it." He turned to the woman sitting four chairs to his left. "Jean?"

Jean Dukes nodded. "It's going to take us a while to pull that oversized Gate out of the Leath system."

"No choice," Lance replied. "We got it as part of our war reparations, and I'm not leaving a back door like that anywhere. In fact," he tilted his head toward Admiral Thomas, "I don't know if I want it here in the Yollin system either. If we can hide that big sumbitch and keep it safe, we need to do that."

"With what?" Jean asked. "The *Meredith Reynolds* is the biggest gun we have."

Lance nodded to Team BMW. "We're starting large-scale

production of the BYPS setup. Let's plan on using those, plus we need a dead-man switch on the Gate. I'd rather blow it up than give someone a straight shot back to Earth."

Bobcat spoke up. "Can we perhaps *not* blow it to shit and gone?" He flipped his hand over and back. "I've seen the requirements to build another of its type, and while not unique, it would make a banker pucker their butt to have to write another check like that."

"I've seen the cost just to move it," Lance agreed, "and that is a pittance compared to the actual effort to build one of those behemoths." He turned to Jean. "Do we have an EI ready for the Gate?"

She shrugged. "ArchAngel II says we don't need a true AI on that fucker, so yes. I'd have preferred to chat with ADAM and TOM on the subject, but I understand that the few comments we get back from them consist of 'Give them time?'"

Lance nodded. "Yes. Their comments are, 'She's safe, she hasn't found the Seven, and she hasn't destroyed a planet...yet.'"

"Not exactly the most comforting message," Admiral Thomas grumbled.

"Yet brief and accurate," Bobcat tossed in.

"This isn't a Baba Yaga meeting," Lance's eyes narrowed at the humans in the group, "so let's focus. We don't need to give our Empress a reason to concentrate on this project herself, so this Gate needs to be moved safely, effectively, and quickly." He looked down at his tablet, his eyes narrowing at a new number.

"Meredith," he continued, "is this new projected time to move the Gate accurate?"

"Yes, General," the station operations EI replied. "We have done the numbers, and it will take..."

"Decades." Lance sighed. "Less costly than building, but more than I'd hoped."

"Not much we can do," Admiral Thomas conceded as he looked at his tablet. The rest of the people around the table started doing the same. A couple of the Yollins had their heads together. Arguing over something to do with the update, he figured.

"Okay, as Dan would say if he were here instead of on Leath, 'Grab some bricks and start slamming some nuts until someone figures out a solution to make this happen a little," he looked at his tablet once more, "no, a *lot* faster.'"

The teams worked on options for another thirty minutes before Lance called for a stop. "Get with the main team liaison and work through the communications group. Bart, Jean, Bobcat, and team, please stick around."

It took five minutes for everyone to finish up their last few questions with each other and step out of the meeting room, but soon there were only seven of them.

"Okay." Lance looked down the right side of the table, which held Bobcat, William, Marcus, and Tina, and then back up the left with Jean and Admiral Thomas. "We need to deal with getting that big-ass circle here faster."

"It's not going to be 'snap your fingers' fast, Lance." Admiral Thomas looked him square in the eye. "Can't fight physics on this."

"Not worried about a little time, but I'm sure as hell worried about *that* much time."

Bobcat scratched his cheek. "I'm sure we can cut it...maybe in half at least. But," he pointed a finger up, "we need time to mass-produce enough of the BYPSs to surround a planet and seed them in Earth's system on likely routes. We can't build them fast enough to leave here in ten years anyway."

"When we get Bethany Anne back, I'll let her deal with that issue," Lance replied. "That's up her alley anyway."

"Anyone got a system that needs to be cleaned up?" Jean asked. "She seems to like to straighten out systems. I suggest we give her nothing but a ride and drop her off, then we all get to bet on how many months it will take her to sort out the world."

"I would give her weeks," Tina popped in.

"Less than two," Bobcat replied, smiling at Tina, who was thinking about the bet.

"Not too much to clean up in the Empire anymore since the Rangers have been working so hard," Marcus commented. "I've heard that even Tabitha is bitching about being bored."

Jean leaned forward. "That's true, I've heard the same. I understand Barnabas is actually eager to find a new criminal organization or two."

Lance tapped on the table. "Focus, people! Tabitha isn't our problem at the moment." He sighed. "I'm personally hoping that Bethany Anne will focus on getting to Earth and securing that area. It would be nice if there was a Michael at the end of the trip." He looked around, a small smile playing on his lips. "Might as well wish for Santa Claus to swing our way, too."

"Well, if this were a romance story, we would get our happily ever after," Jean told him. "All by the end of the first book."

"How the hell do you write one book about a love that spans over a hundred years and finish it with a happily ever after?" William asked. Everyone turned to look at him, and Jean raised an eyebrow. "Love is ephemeral." William snapped his fingers. "It's here one moment, gone the next." He smiled and waved a hand when he noticed everyone staring at him. "Uh, forget I said anything."

Under the table, Tina squeezed Marcus' leg and nodded in their friend's direction. Marcus looked at her and then at William, who wasn't paying attention, and then back at her again. He leaned over to whisper, "What?" in Tina's ear.

Tina rolled her eyes to the ceiling as she squeezed his leg again. She loved her man regardless, but sometimes he was annoyingly clueless.

"The ability of romance writers aside," Lance continued, eying Jean, who smiled back in reply, "this is real life, not a book. Let's assume we won't have the power of Michael to bring Bethany

Anne home to us. Once we get her back, we need to have something exciting for her to do."

"That doesn't involve taking over another race?" Admiral Thomas asked.

"Assuming she gets the Kurtherians?" Jean added.

"I pray she doesn't find any *more* Kurtherians," Lance heaved a sigh. "Let's hope Baba Yaga doesn't burn any worlds in the process."

The rest of the meeting was over in five minutes, and Lance said his good-byes to Jean, whom he hadn't seen in a couple of weeks, and Tina, who hadn't been at the last meeting involving the three amigos.

He walked out of the meeting room and picked up his Empress' Guards as he headed back to his own quarters. Once they passed the military guard post, which protected many of the suites for those in the higher-ranking jobs on the *Meredith Reynolds,* his security team retired to their own barracks as he walked toward the suite he shared with Patricia.

After he stepped in he removed his tie and tossed it over the couch, then called as he walked into the bedroom, "Pat?"

He thought he heard a muffled noise so he followed it back out of the master bedroom past his office and down the hall to the guest room at the end.

Where he found his wife with her head under the bed.

"Problems?" he asked as she pulled her arm and head out from under the bed.

"Yes!" she exclaimed, a bright glint to her eye. She raised the hand that was holding a small object in triumph. "Jean's granddaughter Nickie was over last Tuesday and was playing in here. She left a toy behind and has been complaining to Jean ever since."

"I just left Jean," he jerked a thumb over his shoulder, "not fifteen minutes ago." He scrunched his face. "Where was I when she was here?"

"You were out flying around and discussing where the new hidden R&D locations could be located with Bartholomew."

"I remember." He stepped out of her way as she went around him and headed toward the living room.

She waved the item over her head. "I'll get this back to her later. The ladies are going to get together."

"To gossip?" he asked, a smile on his face as he followed her.

She did not slow down, nor did she turn around as she set the little toy on the counter. "Stop smirking, and stop looking at my ass."

"But—" he started.

"No butt," she countered.

"I wasn't saying b-u-t-t," he clarified as she turned around. "I was saying 'but I wasn't smirking.'"

She eyed him. "You were smiling."

His smile cracked his face. "Exactly!"

She put a finger in his chest. "You didn't argue about where your eyes were."

He stood a little straighter and put a hand on his chest. "That is because I am strategically smart enough not to engage in an unwinnable argument."

"Uh-huh. Then why are you harassing me about gossip?" she asked. "You know we are there to catch up on everyone's families."

"Because I'm positive there is gossiping." He raised an eyebrow in question.

Patricia kept quiet.

"And I like to keep you engaged. I'll know I'm seriously in trouble when you don't care if I compliment you or anger you."

"The opposite of love isn't hate—" she started.

"It is indifference," he finished as he put his arms around her and kissed her forehead.

Her face was pressed against his chest, so her voice was a little muffled against his shirt when she continued, "You have the ability to make me go from pissed off to happy in two seconds, so I think you are still safe, General Reynolds."

"Good," he told her as he reached up with his right hand to play with her hair. "I'd like to think I haven't bored you yet."

"See that you don't." She patted his side. "There was a pool boy on L3 who looked appetizing."

Lance chuckled. "There aren't any pools on L3," he told her. "That's the level for waste and trash."

He waited a moment for her to check with Meredith to make sure he wasn't lying before she spoke.

"Oh." A moment later, she changed the subject. "Anything on Bethany Anne?"

He kissed her one more time before he stepped over to the counter and picked up the toy, which was a replica of the original *ArchAngel*. "She sure was a pretty ship," he commented sadly, remembering how she had looked in Earth's atmosphere. He set it back down and walked to the couch.

"No," he admitted as he sat. "She has done a damned fine job of dropping off the face of reality."

"Nothing from Nathan?" She stepped into the kitchen and pulled out two beers, opening the tops and going back into the living room.

He reached up for one. "Thank you."

She looked down at him. "Who says both of these aren't mine?"

"Feeling lushy tonight?" he queried, looking at her with a patient face and leaving his arm still outstretched.

Patricia eyed him before handing him a beer. "You're lucky I don't turn one of these over on your head."

He accepted one of the beers. "Thank you, and I was never in any danger."

"Oh?" She sat down on the opposite couch. "What makes you say that?"

"While you wouldn't hesitate to drown me," he winked at his wife, "you wouldn't soak the couches in beer."

She raised her beer in a toast. "Damn right. I can get *you* in the shower easily, but these babies? Not so much." She ran her hand over the couch pillow. "It took me two years to get these finished."

He nodded. "Would have been faster if you hadn't wanted this shade of purple."

She shrugged. "I thought they dyed the plant fibers to make the fabric, I didn't realize they grew the plant with the color in the fibers already," she agreed. "Now stop dodging the question."

"No, nothing from Nathan's contacts. It's like someone is scanning them and pulling the good stuff out."

"Or maybe there is just nothing there to find?" she asked.

He pointed his beer at her. "That's probably the truth, but we just don't have anything to go on. How probable is it that the white-haired Witch of the Empire can hide forever?" He shook his head as he took a swig of his beer. "She will eventually leave clues, I'm sure."

"Yes." Patricia nodded. "Lots of dead Kurtherian or Leath bodies. You will just have to follow a trail of skeletons to catch her."

"Let's hope they are the Kurtherians," Lance admitted, his eyes a little distant.

"You worry she has gone too dark?" Patricia asked.

Lance stared into the liquid in his bottle for a moment before looking up into Patricia's eyes. "Honey, I trust Bethany Anne with all my heart. However," he chewed on his thoughts, "we have enough from ADAM and TOM to know that isn't who we are working with right now."

Patricia stood up and walked around their coffee table to sit next to Lance and grab his available hand. "She will come back to us, Lance."

"I hope you're right, honey," he admitted, still looking into the depths of the liquid. Hoping he didn't find his daughter's dead body on some foreign planet.

All because he hadn't seen the strain they had placed on her for so damned long. He sighed before taking another sip of his drink. No one in real life was a superman or woman, and he should have known that.

And now he knew his daughter's limits.

QBS *Shinigami*

Baba Yaga turned toward her little nightstand and picked up a tablet. "ADAM, have you finished the research for the planet Devon and Lerr'ek?"

"Yes, Baba Yaga," ADAM answered. He had tried calling her Bethany Anne before, but the result was a tongue-lashing that caused even his Etheric-based brain to hurt. "I have gamed over seven hundred and seventy-two thousand, six hundred and twelve different scenarios depending on who is elevated within the political infrastructure on the planet."

Her red eyes glanced at the ceiling. "Spill it. I'm not feeling very patient."

You are never patient, TOM quipped.

Back to the doghouse with you, she told him.

Seriously? TOM asked. **Well, shit. One minor acknowledgment of the truth, and you throw me into the doghouse again.**

What a fucking whining alien you have become. And who is teaching you that language?

The noise in Baba Yaga's ears confirmed TOM's incredulous disbelief.

Hey, I cussed when we met, and you didn't change how you spoke.

There must be a certain amount of familiarity before it becomes commonplace.

Are you saying that you fought the good fight for a hundred-plus years, and now *you have decided to cave in?*

TOM thought about this for a moment, wondering where her logic trap was hiding. **YEeessssNNnoooooPeerrrrhaps?**

Baba Yaga snickered. *Wuss. You won't commit to an answer.*

Why do human parents not allow their children to play with certain others?

That isn't simply a human thing, Baba Yaga countered. *I've seen multiple alien races forbid it. Except those who are hive-minded, since that is their thing.*

You didn't answer my question.

I'm giving myself a moment to find your trap, she conceded.

TOM snickered in her head.

"So," she answered aloud. Bed now made, she left her cabin and headed toward the bridge. "Human parents don't allow their children to play with certain others so they aren't a bad influence." Baba Yaga entered the bridge and sat on her couch. It started molding itself to her, elevating itself and becoming a flight chair.

The video monitors angled up from beneath, giving her additional options for input.

Shinigami had learned that Baba Yaga liked to use all the forward monitors, including the three that were at her own seat and those from the seats to her left and right. This provided sufficient capacity when working problems with the three of them.

An AI, an alien, and EIs as her teammates.

"However," Baba Yaga continued after belting herself in and selecting screens for her views, "if I remember correctly, it is the older and wiser beings who should be capable of not succumbing to a bad influence. You out-date me by a thousand years or more."

She turned her head to prepare the second monitor to discuss issues with ADAM in a moment. "Plus, you stuck your scrawny alien ass in me, so you forced me to be stuck with *your* influence."

"I was bored," TOM told her through the speakers. "And I've lasted for over a hundred and fifty years, so give me a fucking break."

Baba Yaga looked up, her red eyes dimming as a smile curved on her face. A moment later, her eyes opened in shock. The lights reflected off them, and her laughter could be heard throughout the ship as she cackled and slapped the closest thing to her in glee.

"Please stop pounding on the monitor arm. You could break it," Shinigami requested. Baba Yaga stopped whacking the monitor arm, but she continued laughing and instead thumped her own leg.

"Oh…my…*STARS!*" She sucked air in and reached up to wipe away a tear. "That was fucking *PRICELESS!*"

TOM paused a second before answering, "Glad you enjoyed it. I'll be here all night."

Her chuckles died down. "You've used that before, and I *will* get to helping you, but not just yet." Baba Yaga swiped her hand across the second monitor and started pushing virtual buttons.

"I'm not in a rush," TOM admitted. "I was trying to make the funny last a little longer."

"Oh! Well, let me get with ADAM first. Look through his seven hundred and seventy-two billion…"

"Thousand," ADAM corrected through the speakers.

"Whatever. Once you pass a couple hundred, it's all the same to me," she muttered. "I file them all under 'too many.'" She looked up and started reading the latest report from Lerr'ek. Her eyes jerked back and forth and up and down so quickly an observer might have believed she had a muscle tic, or worse.

A ping sounded to her left, so she looked over, and her eyes narrowed. She slid her finger up the screen to read the information. Pursing her lips, she asked in a normal tone, "Shinigami, is the information related to N'Var accurate?"

"It is as accurate as Nathan's contacts believe it to be."

"What are the chances Nathan and his team have seen this information yet?"

"None," the EI answered. "I've pulled that data out of the stream."

"Okay, put us on a heading for N'Var. Fast as we can safely get there."

The stars in the forward view started turning as the ship smoothly accelerated on a new heading. "We will Gate in thirty-seven minutes," Shinigami informed her.

"Understood." Baba Yaga nodded. "ADAM, are there any options that allow us to support Lerr'ek without going to Plan Number Two?"

"There are four individuals who straddle the line on having done good for others while making their way up the political ladder on Devon. Lerr'ek is going to have to work with these people, but to date, none of their negotiations have been in good faith. He has not taken any actions against those in power. He has, however, had to play a high level of defense to make sure none of the accidents killed him."

"'Accidents' is a euphemism for 'kill him and make it seem an accident?'" She asked.

"Yes."

"Okay, tell Lerr'ek I appreciate all of his efforts. Let him know I'll be on my way to Devon soon and to just start the whispers, but leave my name out of it. I don't need Stephen thinking he can tag me there. Also, tell Lerr'ek that if Stephen asks, I haven't spoken with him."

"Understood, Baba Yaga." The EI's voice went quiet.

>>**Won't Stephen be upset?**<< ADAM asked.

Stephen knows the HR rules for Lerr'ek, so he will understand. Lerr'ek will be okay as long as he doesn't upset me. Telling Stephen that Baba Yaga is coming to Devon would **absolutely** *upset me. Before you ask, I'm not against the social outcasts on Devon. Many of them are just trying to make ends meet. But the dregs of the worst are working their way up the political ladder. I can't let that group get too far on my planet while I'm gone.*

So who *are* **you against?** TOM asked.

Fucktards.

"But first," Baba Yaga hissed aloud. "Let's see if these juicy rumors on N'Var are my *prey.*"

CHAPTER THREE

<u>Devon System, QBS _Shinigami_</u>

"Transit completed. We are a standard distance away from normal traffic lanes," Shinigami stated as Baba Yaga checked the information streaming in through the data taps the ship had started grabbing as soon as they could reasonably connect.

ADAM was doing his best to burrow through their security. "Not the worst security," the AI told her through the speakers. "Some of this will take me a while."

"Three hours before we can be in N'Var's atmosphere at the highest rate of approach," Shinigami announced.

Baba Yaga had already explained that the highest _safe_ approach speed was too slow. Shinigami didn't ask anymore.

"Very good," the ink-black woman answered as she unclipped herself. "I'm going to the armory." Two of the video monitors disappeared under the flight couch as she slid from the extended chair.

Two minutes later, she walked into the armory and looked around. "I think today we will go for the crimson armor with a black hood and cloak." She stripped off her normal clothes and laid them to the side, and grabbed an under-armor suit that sealed magnetically up the front. Too bad her actual Under Armour® suit had disintegrated decades ago.

After donning it, she took a few minutes to carefully place the armor on her body one piece at a time. She hissed a moment later. "This shit was easier with a helping hand or two," she mumbled.

"You can always reach out and ask for help," TOM quipped. "I'm sure there are a lot of people who would love to help you get armored up."

"I don't know if you are being facetious or really trying to help, TOM." She grunted as she locked the last part of her armored top and pulled her neck opening left and right to get her armor to sit right on her shoulders.

"I live to serve," he replied.

"Still no clue, you annoyingly obtuse and opaque alien symbiont," she commented as she pulled on a holster set and grabbed her Jean Dukes Specials. Finally, she grabbed her *Star Wars* hooded cloak and walked back to the bridge with it in hand.

Two hours later, the ship was silently slicing through the atmosphere, the clouds twisting in the trail of the black ship as it flew toward the City of Cleerk, which was a quarter of the way around the planet.

It was just turning to evening and would be dark in Cleerk soon.

Baba Yaga's favorite time of the day.

Planet N'Var, Non-allied Space, Industrial Shipping City of Cleerk, Spaceport Air Traffic Control Room

It was the middle of the second shift, almost dusk, and Baylot was staring out of the air traffic control tower windows into the distance. A movement caught his attention, and he turned his head to see a craft at a distance sliding through the city's airspace.

Not abiding by the laws where it was flying.

He spoke over his shoulder as he kept an eye on the ship. "What craft is flying in Quadrant Five-Three-Seven?" A moment later, Radar came back with, "No ship is in that quadrant."

Baylot's eyes narrowed in annoyance. "Bistok shit," he mumbled and reached over to grab a heads-up display helmet. Dropping it over his head, he dialed up the magnification and searched for the ship. Sure enough, it was sliding between a set of buildings.

He reached up to tweak the magnification a bit more and the HUD popped the black ship into stark relief. He could see it well enough to identify a sigil on the wing. "Got you," he whispered.

"Sir?" a voice called behind him. Baylot put up his hand to forestall any more inquiries as his eyes narrowed in on the sigil.

Then he swallowed and pulled off the helmet.

"Did you find anything?" Radar asked, curious.

Baylot shook his head. "I didn't find shit."

No one noticed his hand shaking when he put the helmet down. He turned back and nodded to Radar. "My mistake," he told her as he stepped out of the office. He could almost feel the Witch's eyes on him as he walked toward the washroom.

Planet N'Var, Non-allied Space, Industrial Shipping City of Cleerk, Bar

The captain of the local law enforcement squad scratched his head as he looked at the destroyed office.

A young voice spoke. "He isn't here, but the people in the bar say he didn't come out." A second Queegert, its three tentacles drooping to the ground, told the cop, "He said he would be here."

"Your uncle isn't the best citizen in the city," the law officer mentioned to the young Queegert.

"Save me the lecture, Captain D221," the little female answered, one tentacle flopping up, then lying back on the ground. "I'm aware Uncle Jermom isn't the most law-abiding

Queegert, but to me, he was a good guy. He said he would be here and wanted to talk to me, so he would have been here."

The officer looked around to see if anything else made sense to him. He knew seven Leath had come into the building to speak with Jermom, but what he didn't have was any understanding of what had happened to the boss of this establishment.

He hoped the few patrons outside who were being questioned had some clues. He had just turned to the side when the smaller Queegert next to him started to shiver.

Captain D221 turned when the officer he had placed outside the room started walking in backward. "Greth, what are you doing?" he asked, annoyed. "I told you to stay outside."

Greth had his hands up and started to turn sideways, and the captain saw the black-cloaked alien who had a weapon stuck in Greth's face. A Shrillexian like Greth should have taken the drawn pistol as permission to kick this alien's ass. "Who are you?"

The alien ignored the captain for a moment and spoke to his Shrillexian officer. "Do I have your undivided attention?" the alien hissed in a scratchy voice, "or do I have to knock the shit out of you before you'll listen?"

Greth's eyes focused on the barrel of the Jean Dukes Special between his eyes. He had always wanted to see one of the fabled weapons, but up close and in-between his eyes was not how he had wished his first in-person demonstration to occur. "I bow to your skill, Witch," he told her. "Do you promise you are here to help and not kill?"

"I told you that already," she hissed, her eyes red under the cowl. "So long as my quarry is not here, or I'm not impeded if they are, I will leave peacefully." She looked around the room.

A blink of the eyes and the pistol was gone. Both of her hands were now hidden in the folds of her cloak, but the captain had already noticed the armored fist holding the pistol.

Now it was his turn to stare at the black face framed in white hair hidden under the cowl of the robe. Her glowing red eyes looked him up and down. "Youuuu," she smiled, sharp teeth showing, "are part android."

She walked up to him and reached for his face and D221 slapped upwards to knock her hand away, only to look down in surprise when her other hand caught it and held it tight. "Don't be stupid," she hissed. "I'm not here to hurt you. I just seek knowledge."

"What knowledge are you going to get—" he started to argue when the tips of her fingers touched his forehead.

\>>**I didn't know you could connect to androids.**<<

I didn't know I couldn't, she replied. ***There is no try, there is only do.***

I **cannot believe you just said that**, TOM interjected as he helped her navigate the connection between the organic brain and the android connections. *Nice* **piece of work here,** he commented as they slipped into the brain. ADAM picked up the connection and started his own efforts.

Captain D221 *was* part android. His organic body had been partially destroyed some years back in a manufacturing plant explosion when he had been working the second shift under-cover to figure out who might be stealing from the company.

When he woke up several weeks later, his body had been grafted with the implants, including an upgraded computational cortex right behind his forehead.

I am here, an alien's voice spoke into his mind.

\>>**As am I.**<< another voice added. >>**We will only review that which is pertinent to this investigation, Captain.**<<

Captain D221 was barely into his first bit of shock when his memories ran in front of his eyes as if he were watching a video.

Seven Leath? the first voice queried his brain. Then everything he had looked at in this room and outside in the bar flashed through his mind.

"Damnnnn," she hissed and pulled her hand down. "Those fuckers were here and I missed them."

The captain put a hand to his forehead. "What have you done?"

The hooded figure knelt to look the female Queegert in her three eyes. "I'm sorry to tell you your uncle is dead."

The captain started to place a hand on the Witch's shoulder, but jerked it back when he heard, "Don't!" Or had he imagined it? Either way, without touching the alien, he asked, "Why do you say that?"

The female Queegert asked at the same time, "They took him?"

She nodded to the niece. "Those seven Kurtherians held the Leath people under their sway for decades. They stole bodies to keep themselves going. I don't know why we don't have another body on the ground here."

>>**Bethany Anne, there is a positive confirmation. Jermom walked out of here with the seven Leath on the video security backup.**<<

The police didn't try to look at it?

>>**The local stuff was wiped. The backup is a tiny stream copy, easy to track if you are looking for it. The security on the other side was pitiful.**<<

Baba Yaga thought for a moment. *They must have shrouded those minds in the bar.*

TOM interrupted. **One of the Leath was probably housing two minds in one body, and now they have split back into eight.**

"New information." She looked back at the Queegert. "Your uncle's body is hosting a Kurtherian. I'm sorry, little one, but that isn't your uncle anymore."

She stood up and looked over her shoulder at the cop, her eyes flashing a warning. "Stay out of my way if you don't want more deaths on your hands, Captain."

With that, she stepped around the shorter alien and nodded to the Shrillexian. "Another time," she told him as she swept out the door.

He looked at his captain. "Tell me we aren't going to try and take her down."

The captain looked at his patrolman, surprised. "You don't want to fight her?"

The Shrillexian jerked a thumb toward the open door. "No, and I don't wish to jump off a mountain and go *splat* on the ground either. There is no valor in proving yourself an idiot, or going to an ignoble death by stupidity."

Baba Yaga removed her hood as she stepped through the bar area. A couple of the patrons stared at her as she passed them.

As she left the bar, she heard a policeman's audio announce they had a positive hit for Jermom.

She took off, running hard to make sure she got there first.

CHAPTER FOUR

>>**Turn left!**<< ADAM shouted on their connection.

Baba Yaga, arms pumping, turned the corner of the street and bit down a curse. The buildings in Cleerk were constructed of some sort of porous stone, often gray with occasional streaks of green or black running through them.

Ahead of her, the street became a sort of bazaar of temporary shops and shoppers. Street lamps and lights on the buildings provided more than enough illumination to cast everything in a bright glare.

Baba Yaga looked up and pushed off her right leg, jumping about fifteen feet and then crunching down on the street.

"*Gott Verdammt*, ADAM!" she huffed. "Change the fucking weight on this stuff!"

>>**A little notice that you were about to jump would have been helpful**!<< he shot back.

Baba Yaga's second thrust produced the result she had been looking for as her armored body flew above the heads of the shoppers and merchants. The buildings rose three and four stories.

She kicked off the first building and showered those below

with the small pebbles her armored boot dislodged as she jumped across the street high enough to just barely clear the roofline.

"*FUCK!*" she screamed when she noticed the roof she was about to land on was made of some sort of glass.

Baba Yaga disappeared into the Etheric before crashing through it.

Turning to her right, she moved forward fifteen steps in the amorphous fog and then peeked out. Taking another step, she dropped to the roof of the building on the right of the one whose roof she had almost crashed through.

She landed on her feet and took off running again. "Where *is* that bastard?" she yelled as she dodged a couple of pipes that protruded through the roof.

Dammit, running through the Etheric with this new armor was a bitch!

>>**Two blocks to the right and one up,**<< ADAM replied.

"Pay attention to my weight!" she commanded and took two steps. She caught the edge of the rooftop with her right leg and pushed as hard as she could to catapult herself across the street toward a red building that was in the correct direction.

Fortunately this building was a story lower, and she knew it had a solid roof. Her cloak fluttered behind her as she landed on her left leg and kept running across the building, then jumped up about twenty feet to the roof of the next building.

A quick kick and she rebounded off a stone wall, then landed at the edge of another roof, arms windmilling to make sure she didn't slip off and 'do a Tabitha' four stories down.

Her head flicked back and forth. "Where is the little fucker?" she hissed in anger.

You know, TOM took a moment as she looked around to find Jermom, **it would be possible to save the uncle**.

"What?" she replied. "I thought you said if a Kurtherian took over the body like that, they got rid of the host."

In the long term, yes, but it probably hasn't been long

enough. Jermom could still be in there, screaming as the Kurtherian keeps him down.

"Well, how the fuck are we going to pull a Kurtherian out of him? Or can we kill the Kurtherian inside?"

Best chance is to get the Kurtherian to come out.

"How?"

Not sure. Tempt them using their sense of superiority. He or she will want to move to a better host than they have now.

"You want me to find a tempting host around here?" She put a hand on her waist. "We could get one or both of the aliens killed."

Technically the uncle is going to die anyway, but I wasn't suggesting we use a random stranger as the bait.

It took her a microsecond to realize what TOM was suggesting. "No fucking way!" She started jogging down the roof. "You want me to use my own body so I can have *two* Kurtherians duking it out?"

I'd rather think that there is no way another Kurtherian can beat me.

"How sure are you of that?" she asked, her eyes scanning the street below as she continued moving along the roof.

Not terribly, TOM admitted. **That is why I'm not saying we should absolutely do this.**

"If you fail, that fucker will have my body. I'll die, and you along with me." She caught sight of a Queegert and zeroed in on it as it wove through the bodies below. "That would end my revenge and breach my promise to save my people. Is one random alien criminal worth that?"

>>**Confirmed! That is Jermom.**<< ADAM interrupted.

Baba Yaga eyed the building across the street, then she took two quick steps and jumped, angling like a billiards shot to the walls a bit ahead of her quarry. Her foot was tilted as she stiffened her leg right before slamming into the building, and she twisted to her left as she dropped down from above. "Look out below!" she growled as all sorts of aliens looked up in surprise.

Gorllet, Eighth of the Eight, was relishing his new-found freedom. As a passenger in Teret's body, he hadn't gotten a chance to use the senses, so he was enjoying the sensations, smells, and other...

Shit. He looked down and wrinkled his nose. "What a dirty world," he spat in disgust.

While this alien's body was somewhat simple, he rather liked the three eyes. It allowed for broader spatial awareness.

Pretty handy, he had just decided when he caught the action above his new host. He stopped in his tracks and flicked up the three tentacles to block the rocks that started showering down on him as an alien dropped to the ground yelling a warning.

His middle eye opened in surprise as the alien landed in front of him. The well-lit street backlit the alien, whose white hair was floating around her head.

What surprised him the most was that she spoke Leath.

"Where are your brethren?" she hissed at him as he took in the armor. If this was to be a gun battle, he was woefully unprepared.

Good thing it wouldn't be.

She pulled a pistol and casually shot him in the leg.

PAIN!

Gorllet fell to the side and grabbed his leg as she walked toward him. He hadn't been prepared to deal with the body's reaction, but now he shut down the nerve transmitters so the pain wouldn't overwhelm him.

Blessed relief! He stared at the alien as she squatted next to him, her pointed teeth bared in the reflected light. "Hurts like a sono-fabitch, doesn't it?"

"I've had worse in life," Gorllet replied as the pain diminished.

Unfortunately, his body wasn't going to operate too well at the moment.

Wits, it would be.

"Not recently, I suspect." She pushed on his wound with her pistol barrel, but he felt nothing. Two of his eyes looked down at what she was doing, and one kept looking at her. "In fact, the theory is you were a ride-along with one of the seven Leath that were seen leaving. Since you can't seem to feel pain, I'm going to assume you are one of the Kurtherians I'm searching for."

He sneered. "You are the Witch. I will..."

The vicious slap rattled the shit out of his vision and his head swung violently to the right. He shut down more pain connections as agony exploded in his ear from her slap.

She finished his comment, "Not do a damn thing or I'll kill your host, and then you will die when I burn the body."

Gorllet was refining the calculations for this situation, taking care to review the permutations, when she continued speaking.

She pointed a finger at his body, then at the ground next to him. "You will come out of this host."

"Why?" He looked around at the locals, who had stopped to watch.

He could hear someone from local law enforcement working to push his way through the crowd.

"I'll feed you so much pain, me shooting your leg will feel like ecstasy."

"You will kill the host at the same time," he replied with a glint in his eye. "Where will that get you?"

"Satisfied you are dead," the alien replied. "He obviously wasn't a good citizen since your people knew about him."

Behind the two of them, a police officer finally made it through the crowd. "Get back!" the Shrillexian demanded as he took in the two figures on the sidewalk, the stones all over the street, and looking up, the large chunk of rock missing from the wall above them. "You with the pistol! Set it down or I'll..."

Baba Yaga shook her head for a moment. "Just my luck Eddie the Ignorant was the first one on the scene," she hissed to herself as she looked down at Gorllet. "Don't you go anywhere," she commanded before her head turned like a gun turret to look at the newly-arrived cop. "Officer, keep these people back or I'll send you to a new dimension."

The officer's eyes narrowed as he reached down and pulled his pistol. He was lifting his arm to aim when the white-haired alien disappeared.

"Where did she..." He stepped forward, and Baba Yaga appeared behind him. He was able to twist halfway around before she shoved him off his feet.

This time *he* disappeared.

Baba Yaga took three steps and resumed her squatting position near the Queegert. "There, now I've got some more time to play with you."

>>**Would you stop messing around? I'm showing five more cops only half a block away.**<<

This fucker is going to tell me where his people are.

How are you going to make him do that? TOM asked. **We can't force him to speak, and killing him inside the body would kill the host.**

Who said I had a problem with that?

Rather "Michael" of you to say that, Baba Yaga.

Perhaps he had the right of it, TOM, she spat back. *My patience has grown thin.*

No, your pain has grown too much, TOM argued.

>>**Can you connect to Jermom's senses?**<< ADAM asked the two.

"What?" Baba Yaga asked aloud.

"I didn't ask anything," Gorllet replied, confused for a moment before he smiled. "You aren't alone!"

The red eyes flared as the lips parted to show her sharpened teeth and she leaned forward, her right hand reaching for his

MICHAEL ANDERLE

forehead. "Well done, Kurtherian. That was your one hint that your future is about to be horrible. Welcome to hell…"

Gorllet watched through Jermom's eyes as the fingers touched his forehead. It was a tiny intuitive leap for him to switch from using the eyes to sensing along the links Gorllet had connected to his host to find his synapses and nerve fibril heads connected by the alien just a moment before he started screaming.

The Witch had found him, and now he was on fire.

The amount of pain being sent up his connections threatened to overwhelm him, but pain had been his constant friend for decades. What he received, he sent back in spades. He struggled to keep his wits as he withstood the attacks and looked for an opening to go back up the channel to attack her. If he could grab her consciousness, he would be able to transfer from this body to hers.

Through his pain, Gorllet kept internally focusing on finding the weak link, the forgotten thread he could use to move up through the host's system and back to her. His laugh was maniacal, evil, as he realized he could end the war right now.

Let's see who bends first, Witch!

Captain D221 was expecting carnage as he made his way through the crowded streets. "Move aside!" he yelled as he considered ways to try and direct the innocents away from the fight.

He really didn't want to have a gun battle with an armored vigilante from another star system who was hell-bent on finding self-determined war criminals infesting the criminals of his city.

The paperwork on the destruction and death would take him a month.

Elbowing aside the last citizen in his way—some sort of alien with four sets of green ears and a yellow bump on their back—he stumbled into the cleared area to see the Witch.

36

He assumed Jermom was the Queegert on the ground. She must have shot his leg since there was blood. Both bodies vibrated, their eyes closed and her hand on his forehead.

He made sure not to get near his gun.

A short Torcellan touched his arm. "Are you looking for your officer?" The captain looked down, his eyes narrowed in confusion. The Torcellan pointed toward the Witch. "She pushed him and he disappeared."

D221 turned to stare again at Baba Yaga and Jermom. "Of course she did." He grabbed his comm and clicked a switch. "This is Captain D221. Keep the civilians away from the two on the ground." Releasing the call button, he nodded to another of his officers, who was making his way into the opening. "Get everyone to move back. We don't know what's going on with these two!"

He turned to the crowd and started yelling for them to give the officers more room.

He sure hoped Baba Yaga didn't have any explosives on her body.

Gorllet found a link back through the connection to the alien's mind and thrust his consciousness into it. Traveling past Jermom's synapses and through the connection, he followed the path into the alien.

FINALLY!

You're mine now, human! he crowed as he read her lineage from her mind. He was able to get some information easily, but it was proving difficult to dig deeper.

He didn't notice that the path back to his body closed behind him.

I don't think so, a new voice snarled, interrupting his efforts.

Who is this? He was mentally looking for the new traveler

when pain spiked into him. This wasn't like the pain from earlier; this was assaulting him in an area no other alien should be able to attack.

He had been hit through a Kurtherian *Etheric* connection.

Gorllet screamed in pain and frustration as the attacks continued hitting him, not allowing him time to get his bearings. He turned to flow back into his own body to get away.

That was when he found out he was blocked from moving back into his old host.

Welcome to Hell, the voice told Gorllet. **I'm your guide, Thales of Miletus. You may call me Death.**

Gorllet screamed in frustration, then pain, and then his consciousness ceased to exist.

Captain D221 saw a couple of the crowd cover their mouths and point to the bodies, so he turned back, only to see Jermom's mouth open and a large worm-looking creature start to crawl out. It stopped moving while it was still partially in Jermom's mouth.

A few moments later, Baba Yaga started shaking her head and pulled her hand from Jermom's forehead.

She looked down at the worm and made a disgusted face, confirming in a hoarse whisper, "I've got to pull that out?"

D221 looked around to make sure the citizens didn't move closer.

He watched as she grabbed the worm and pulled slowly, the emerging body growing longer and longer. "Oh God, this is gross!" she muttered. "I'd better get triple-time pay for this shit." Her other hand reached over to grab another portion, and she continued to pull the creature out.

D221 hoped it was normal for this Witch to speak to herself.

She tossed about a body-length of worm off to her right side and shook her hand, flinging viscous fluid off her gloves. "Oh my God, I'm so burning these gloves." She continued bitching for a moment before grabbing her right fingers with her left hand and starting to pull the glove off, "I know I can't burn them, but I swear there'd better be a way to clean them or your ass is grass, TOM."

She finished pulling her glove off and cupped her hand, and a moment later, a red ball started forming above her palm. When it had grown to about the size of her head, she tossed it onto the worm that was now slowly wiggling on the street.

The sizzle of burned flesh was immediate.

Baba Yaga jumped up and put an arm over her face. "Oh, the SMELL!" Then, looking around, she ordered, "Someone get Jermom a doctor." She looked down at the quickly shriveling black worm and murmured, "That's going to leave a mark" to herself before she turned to gaze at the captain.

"Captain D221?" she asked. When he nodded, she flicked a hand toward the Queegert. "Jermom should be okay."

He nodded. "How about my missing officer?"

She smiled—not a very reassuring sight, as he would later write in his report. The Witch took a step closer to him. "I'd move a bit to your left."

The captain took a step. "No, two more of those tiny things." She watched him step twice more. "Good." She disappeared, then his officer appeared and stumbled right past where he had been standing a moment before.

She didn't reappear immediately and his Shrillexian officer looked around, caution in his eyes. "Where is the Witch, sir?" he asked, recognizing his boss.

A moment later, a gun was tossed out and bounced across the ground.

Right after that, the Witch reappeared, holding the ammunition cartridge in her hand, and eyed the Shrillexian with annoyance on her face. "Are you ready to act reasonably, or am I going to have to stick my size seven-and-a-half boots up your ass?"

The captain looked at his officer. "Be respectful," he told him, a stern expression on his face.

"Don't have to tell me twice." He nodded to the Witch. "Can I have my weapon?"

"Of course, but if you aim in my direction, I'll assume you wish to become a target." She turned to the captain, keeping the officer in her peripheral view, and pointed to the dead worm. "One Kurtherian, dead." She pointed to Jermom. "One Queegert, alive." She pulled the hood back up over her head as those around them started pointing up. "I'm leaving. That bastard didn't know where his people went."

"Off-planet," the captain replied. "We traced them a few minutes ago."

"Well, that pisses me off," she ground out as she looked up. "My ride is here. Take care, Captain." She smiled at him, her white teeth glistening in the light that made it under her cowl.

"Why don't you…" he started, but she had vanished. He placed a hand over his eyes to block the light and saw what looked like a ship hovering above the buildings. A moment later, the ship gracefully started moving up and turning to its left in the air before it disappeared, accelerating into the dark quickly enough to seem like it was there one moment, gone the next.

He sighed. "Come to the office and help me with the paperwork." He looked down at the Queegert and wondered what kind of person gave a shit about a criminal on an out-of-the-way planet like N'Var.

He looked at the burned worm. She could have destroyed his body anytime she wanted to and saved herself the trouble of trying to keep Jermom alive.

He looked at his officer, who seemed to be settling down. "Next time you see her," he nodded his head in the direction her ship had taken, "how about you don't pull a weapon?"

"No shit," the Shrillexian agreed. Then remembered who he was speaking to. "Sir," he finished. He wouldn't need either a battle or the Shrillexian medicine to calm his urges for a while. Being alone in that white milky dimension had taken care of his fighting needs, and frankly, that bitch was scary enough to give him nightmares.

CHAPTER FIVE

QBBS *Meredith Reynolds*

Lance scribbled his signature on the tablet and handed it back to Cheryl Lynn. "No," he told her, his frown evident, "I don't know where she is. You'll have to deal with the requests for interviews, like I do."

Cheryl Lynn eyed the General with absolutely no humor in her eyes. "And how do you propose I do that? Use a hologram?"

He snorted. "I wish. Wait," he looked around before leaning closer, "is that an option?" he asked, his voice low.

Cheryl Lynn shrugged as she considered his question. "Should I check into it?"

"Hell, yes!" Lance leaned back and raised his voice to normal. "That all?"

"Yup," she answered, turning around and waving the tablet. "I've got permission to rule the galaxy now."

She stopped suddenly, her facial expression horrified as she looked back at Lance. "Forget I even said that." Her eyes scanned those near Lance. "I don't want it!"

"Damn," he muttered with a straight face, "so close."

She smiled and turned toward her office as Lance and those with him headed toward the military shuttle bays.

John Grimes leaned over. "You don't want to leave my cousin in charge of the galaxy, Lance."

Lance looked sideways at him for a moment, and John shrugged before he continued, "Okay, *I* don't want my cousin in charge of the galaxy. I love her, but ruling idiots isn't a skill she has."

Lance slowed down as Eric walked ahead of them, a smile on his face as he went to check out the shuttle. "Hell, ruling idiots isn't a skill most people have, but *manipulating* idiots is." He nodded toward Cheryl Lynn's office. "She can manipulate idiots with the best of them."

"She claims it comes from raising teenagers," John told him. He caught Eric's thumbs-up, then nodded for Lance to enter the shuttle. "All clear, so let's get this zoot-suit boogie going," John told him as the small group of support staff started up the gangway.

The voice of the pilot came over the speaker system, causing Lance to raise an eyebrow at John. He shrugged and replied, "Said he wanted to come back to the front seat because he didn't trust the 'young'uns' to ferry around the most important man in the Empire."

"That's probably because he thought he might get the job if I croaked," Lance retorted as he listened to the pilot.

"This is your pilot, Paul Jameson. Everyone needs to hold the hell on because you are riding the Empress' Express. We brake for no one." There was a pause before he continued, "I didn't come out of retirement to dither, and we got clearance." His words filtered through the ship as they lifted off the bay floor and slid through the forcefield that kept the atmosphere inside the *Meredith Reynolds*. They were only a few feet outside before the shuttle made a sharp downward turn and sped away.

Lance noticed the divergence from standard flight path protocols. "He isn't taking any chances with us, is he?"

"Nope," John agreed. "I'm sure he filed about twenty different flight plans."

"And none of them was the real one," Lance surmised. He pressed a button on his armrest and started to lean back. "Shame they said we couldn't use *ArchAngel II*," he commented as he pushed his hat down over his eyes.

John smiled. "Well, *technically,* they provided the specifications for the ship you had to travel in. It just so happens *ArchAngel II* is bigger than that specification."

Lance moved his hat far enough over that one eye could stare at John. "Did I just hear a change in the plans?"

"There was no change of plans, not exactly." John murmured into a microphone on his lapel before looking at the General. "We are going to take a taxi from here to the meeting system, bypassing the normal gates, and then we will have the same taxi bring us back."

"We can only arrive in one ship…" Lance stopped speaking for a moment and thought back to his last communication with Admiral Thomas.

His eyes narrowed as he looked at John. "That ass is shipping this tuna can inside the *ArchAngel II* to Gate to somewhere close, isn't he? Then we pull out and close the final distance while *ArchAngel II* waits for us?"

"Got it in one," John admitted. "A whole bunch of us want to make sure no hairs on your head are damaged." He paused for a moment. "Well, except those you pull out yourself."

"Folks scared of having to become the figurehead while Bethany Anne is out?" Lance asked, the smile under his hat evident in his voice.

"Hell," John answered, "I'm just scared of what Baba Yaga would do if I had to let her know her father was dead."

Lance's smile slowly faded as he considered the possibility

that worlds might go up in flame and he shook his head. "John, she wouldn't do that."

"No," John agreed. "*Bethany Anne* wouldn't."

The two men chose to look out their respective windows, each lost in thought as the shuttle raced to meet the looming Leviathan-class superdreadnought in space.

To head to the first meeting that could change the futures of trillions of people and whole solar systems.

If they were willing to play nice, that is.

Marquer's World, Independent System, Allied with the Zhyn

Lance looked down at the purple-hued world crisscrossed with yellows, oranges, and the occasional green. The oceans were greenish-blue, but the clouds, at least, were white.

Thank God, Lance thought to himself. *Otherwise, it would have been a damned Escher painting brought to life.* Lance turned to look at John, who was sitting next to him. "I can't get over just how different these worlds can be."

"Not exactly Earth," John admitted, "although I believe the reason for that down there is the color of their star. Something to do with the red frequency." He shrugged. "It was over my head. I've never cared too much about colors." He nodded out the window of their shuttle. "Although I have to admit that is a little much. Purple ground? That is just seven different types of wrong."

Paul Jameson's voice came over the speakers. "This is the captain speaking. Please be aware that everyone should keep all body parts inside the craft at all times. If not, I suspect any limbs will be violently ripped off and you will bleed out in mere seconds." There was a click and a moment of dead air before he came back. "Sorry, I've been told that was an inappropriate safety message. I told the EI to go fuck itself. Now we're having a discussion about crassness. Apparently, telling an EI to do something anatomically impossible calls into question my ability to think rationally. As we land this little ship, I'm going to allow you to suffer along with me. Please enjoy the landing show brought to you by yours truly, the long-suffering pilot."

There were a few chuckles from behind Lance when, sure enough, Paul piped in his conversation with the shuttle's EI.

"No," Paul clarified, "I did not mean that you should *literally* go fuck yourself. I'm aware that you have no body with which you could accomplish the act."

"Then why would one say something so base and illogical?" the EI asked. Lance judged its voice to be somewhere between polite and confused.

"Because it allowed me to explain, in what I thought were no uncertain terms, that I didn't care to hear your subjective opinion on my safety instructions to the passengers."

"Have you considered the research which explains that describing violent results to humans can, and often will, stress them out?" the EI retorted. "Further, should something actually happen to this vessel, they would then be in a less-than-optimal mental state for working to support themselves and others to get through the emergency?"

There was a momentary pause before Paul came back, his voice sounding confused. "Whaaat? We have a full complement of military and other civilians in high-stress occupations who eat emergencies for breakfast and shit surviving-for-dummies books by mid-afternoon."

The shuttle's EI immediately replied, "I'm sorry, but that comment makes no logical sense. I know of no organic bodies that can consume an emergency in any of the seven definitions, including those which were brought along with the original Empire founders from Earth."

This time there was a longer pause before Paul sighed and his voice, full of exasperation, replied, "Shuttle B-Seven-Two-Five?"

"Yes?"

"Go fuck yourself!"

The shuttle landed on the secured field, and John and Eric worked the outside security before Lance was allowed off the craft.

Lance walked a bit stiffly since he was wearing advanced malleable armor under his clothes. John and Eric had donned their dark-red armor, which immediately told anyone who was paying attention to the Empire which group they were part of.

Even though the Empress wasn't here, her stamp would be noted. She would be at the talks in spirit, which was Lance's intent.

"Think we will get attacked before or after we check in?" John asked Eric. The two stayed close to Lance, who was striding across the tarmac. No one had met Lance at the shuttle, which was fine with him.

However, he would use that little fact later during negotiations. Power plays annoyed him, but that didn't mean he didn't understand them.

"Savants," Eric suggested. Lance looked over his shoulder at the Empress' Bitch as Eric kept watch around them. With his helmet on, Lance couldn't see his eyes inside the faceplate.

"Do what?" Lance asked. "Was there a question to go along with that word?"

"Just thinking," Eric replied as his head pivoted left, then right. "We have all sorts of savants in the Empire. Why don't we see which ones we could use effectively and put them together on teams? I know we usually form a team around a particularly capable person, but what would happen if you brought together savants who complemented each other?"

John remarked as his head turned to the left, "Eric keeps his wits about him by allowing his subconscious to play. It's safer to record his comments and come back to them later. It's something he picked up from..."

John's head jerked right to watch a floating vehicle making its way toward them. It slowed down when John knelt and brought his Jean Dukes pistol up, pointing it at the ground in front of the oncoming craft.

He wasn't aiming at the aircar...yet.

It slowed to a crawl.

It was the size of a large van back on Earth, aerodynamic, and a ghastly shade of red to his eyes.

Rather like a muddy pink.

The van angled to stop about twenty paces away on the tarmac, and two clear plastic-looking doors slid to the side midway.

A female Ixtali appeared and stepped to the tarmac, and John slid his pistol back into his holster as she nodded to him. "Hello, John Grimes. It is a pleasure to see you again."

John just nodded and returned to scanning the field.

Lance couldn't tell too many Ixtalis apart. He hadn't interacted with them much when Bethany Anne had helped them decades ago.

This one, however, he did know. "Pleased to meet you, Senior Legate Addix." His gruff voice was never pleasing, so he hoped the translation sounded better to her.

Each proffered a small bow to each other and she replied, "And a pleasure to meet you, General Reynolds of the Etheric Empire. I apologize that it took us so long to come out to your ship. I needed to get rid of two others who wished to politic with you on the ride back."

The Empress' Bitches went over to check out the vehicle.

John stepped into the van and inspected the inside before nodding for Lance to come aboard. He turned to Addix but she waved Lance forward, so he stepped in. Eric waited for Addix to join them.

Eric motioned to John. "Inside, outside, or on top?"

"On top," John replied.

Eric nodded and pushed off, jumping easily to the top of the van. The three inside heard the *clump* that marked his landing.

Then a couple deep clicks.

Addix turned to John. "He will be all right up there?"

"He's locked on," John replied, his facemask reflecting her rather spider-like face back to her.

Although John had interacted with enough Ixtali to recognize a few of them, he always used the translation HUD to help him figure out what their various mandible movements meant.

Addix provided directions to another Ixtali in the front of the vehicle. "We are going to go closer to your ship, as if we were waiting for another person to emerge. That will allow me enough time to explain the dangerous and infested waters of this meeting to you."

"I would appreciate it." Lance looked around. The van had seating areas against all four walls, although a couple of the seats wouldn't work well for humans. He raised an eye at one that looked like a torture device—a long cone with a point on the top, which was about a foot taller than the other seats. He wasn't sure what kind of alien needed a cone up their ass, but it wasn't him.

He took a seat and raised an eyebrow to Addix. "This van is clear of recording devices?"

"Yes," Addix confirmed, moving her robes around to allow her to sit down as well.

Her four arachnoid legs were revealed as the robe rose a foot off the ground. "Thank you for attending this meeting. I know the Empire would like to move forward into a new agreement with other societies, planets, and systems, but most fear you. Now that the Leath have been beaten and you are requiring them to dismantle a fair amount of their military infrastructure, there are many who wonder what the Empire will do with all your advanced ships."

"Protect ourselves," Lance grumped. "It seems every time we try to be left alone, some alien group or another either tries to attack us or subvert us or asks for protection from other bullies."

Addix nodded her head in understanding. She was old for an Ixtali—damn near ancient. She suspected that her extended life was due to something the Empress had done to her, whether because Bethany Anne appreciated the support Addix had provided in years past or wanted a voice supporting the Empire on the council, she had no idea.

"I am not much longer for this life, General Reynolds," Addix gave him a slight bow of respect, "so I pulled in all my favors to be the representative for the Ixtalis to this conclave of peoples."

"That sounds ominous," John muttered. He became aware that both Senior Legate Addix and Lance were looking at him. "Shit! Sorry, I didn't realize I could be heard."

Lance turned back to Addix. "You are doing this for Bethany Anne?"

"No, for your people," Addix replied. "However, while I am very appreciative that the Empress is not here for political reasons, I would have wished to see her one last time and person-ally thank her for how she has helped my people. I am doing what I think best to return the favor."

"How so, and why is the Empress not wanted?" Lance asked.

"The Empress is impatient, and these events require the patience of the gods." Addix seemed to be resigned to endless negotiations.

John chuckled. "That leaves you out, Lance." Lance turned to stare at him again. "What? Oh, speaker still on?"

This time Lance was sure there had been no mistake. "John, would you like me to elevate you from diplomatic security to *diplomat?*"

Inside his facemask, John's smile disappeared, and just a hint of sweat started on his brow. "No, no, I'm good. I'll just turn around and make sure no inappropriate comments come out again."

"Good." Lance watched John retreat before he focused again on the Ixtali Legate. "As John mentioned, I'm not the most patient, either."

"We know, General Reynolds, but it would have been very difficult to get anything done even if the Empress had said nothing." Addix's spidery black hands rose to the sides of her head. "The Empress' hair starts to float and her eyes glow red when she gets emotional. I can only imagine what might have happened if someone said something disrespectful to the Empress' people."

He nodded his understanding. "It would have been hard to negotiate if she kept killing the negotiators. However, she wouldn't have killed them without reason."

Addix leaned forward. "General Reynolds, the whole point for some of the stronger people, such as the Noel-ni, to be here is to try and anger the other side. If the Empress had attended, half of the other groups would be dead or relegated to another dimension. The Empire would be at war with many peoples just because she didn't understand the tactics of a particular group. I don't think that is what she wants, is it?"

"No." Lance sighed, knowing that a few decades back, Bethany Anne might have been able to weather the annoyance of being at one of these meetings.

But not anymore, or at least not now.

Addix continued, "There are many who are very supportive of your effort to deal with an upset Empress. Many know you will have to weather her displeasure when you get back for the disrespect of her being requested not to appear."

If you only knew how she would have jumped for joy if she even had a clue. Lance couldn't get ADAM to tell him whether Baba Yaga was paying attention to anything happening in the Empire during her absence.

"She isn't in a good spot emotionally at the moment," Lance started, but Addix interrupted.

"Exactly!" Her mandibles tapped in extreme concern. "It would have been very hard for any of us to speak truth if that truth might have upset the Empress." Addix leaned back in her seat. "How could some of the negotiators lie? And they *will* lie since it is part of their negotiation efforts. The Empress would have called them on their… What is the human word? 'Bullshit?'"

Lance nodded and chuckled, and thought it funny that human euphemisms were being seeded throughout the galaxy.

She continued, "Their *bullshit* would be pointed out and not allowed. They cannot help themselves, or at least some of them cannot. The Empress will be there in spirit, but this first conclave of the peoples would have been a bust if the Empress were present."

Addix stopped speaking for a moment and glanced around. The van was parked next to the shuttle, and she gazed at it before turning back to Lance.

"I must inform you of these realities. We Ixtali have excellent information networks, and we want to share our knowledge with you—not as a condition of anything, but to prepare you for reality as we see it."

Lance pursed his lips and raised an eyebrow. "Okay."

She lifted one of her arms and pointed toward the small city to which they would go soon. "They are going to make it a prerequisite that for an Etheric Federation to come into existence, the Empress will have to step down."

Lance was quiet a moment. "That is going to be a serious stumbling block," was what he answered aloud, but internally he thought, *No shit!*

There was no damned way Bethany Anne would agree to rule the Federation, even if they begged her to.

She was done. Emotionally she was spent, and she needed her own form of vacation that didn't have an end in sight.

He rather wished she was in contact, though.

Addix continued, "There are many who are willing to concede the Empire should have the biggest seat at the Federation table since it will have most members, but if the Empress were still in power..."

Lance's eyes narrowed as he considered what she might be getting at. "Addix, we aren't going to roll over so someone can neuter us," he told her.

Internally he was already making plans for the future.

CHAPTER SIX

QBBS _Meredith Reynolds_

When Ecaterina stepped into the medium-sized meeting room, there were quite a few people present. Nathan entered behind her and angled to her left to approach Scott and Darryl, who were grabbing some snacks.

Ecaterina walked around the large wooden table and took the chair next to where Tabitha was already sitting. She spoke quietly as Tabitha turned in her direction. "Tabitha, you can't blame yourself for the situation."

Tabitha raised an eyebrow, a small sardonic smile playing at her lips. "I guarantee you," she swept a finger around the room, "pretty much every one of us believes that we are guilty."

Ecaterina looked down at the table and shrugged. "Okay, I can understand that, and logically I know that we all had our roles to play." She paused for a moment, thinking back to the last time she had seen her friend. "Bethany Anne always seemed to be on top of everything. She was the rock that never moved."

Tabitha shrugged. "All of us are suffering, Ecaterina. It has been a long time since we left Earth."

Tabitha's eyes flitted around the room from person to person as she continued her thought. "Some of us are in long-term relationships that help us cope. Some of us have enjoyed a weekend, a month, or even two-month-long flings, depending on our jobs or our needs."

Ecaterina raised an eyebrow at Tabitha.

Tabitha rolled her eyes. "I haven't had a weekend fling in a long time!"

Ecaterina smirked, then elbowed the Ranger. "Whose definition of 'a long time' are we using?"

A small smile played on Tabitha's face as she bit her lower lip. "I always use my definition, of course." She winked at her friend. "I am well aware that there are at least four systems where a weekend fling is equivalent to approximately thirty-seven minutes of Earth time."

Ecaterina raised an eyebrow. "Are you sure that you are not a lawyer? You seem to be very precise with your syntax."

Tabitha shrugged. "It's my programming background. When you type words into computers, they must be very specific." She reached up to tap her head. "Plus, once you get trained in logic, and how to weave in and out to make a computer do your bidding, it is very hard to put down."

The ladies were interrupted by Barnabas' striding into the room. "Okay, everyone, let's grab some refreshments and sit down." He jerked a thumb over his shoulder. "Darryl and Scott have some updates to provide so that we can try to figure out how to find our Empress."

Barnabas walked over to the refreshment station and took his own suggestion, grabbing a drink before stepping over to the dark wooden table and sitting on Tabitha's other side. He nudged her with his left arm and she pushed back, grunting with effort.

"What have you been eating? You're as heavy as a ship. Didn't I tell you to stop with all those carbs?"

Ecaterina shook her head as she watched Tabitha try harder to push Barnabas. Barnabas had grasped the table with one hand and had wedged one foot against the floor to help him stay put. Tabitha, however, had come six inches out of her seat in her attempt to push Barnabas. "Dammit, how many times do I have to try and make my point with you?"

Barnabas chuckled. "Young one—"

He didn't get another word in before she erupted, "Young one? I'm damn near two centuries, you old fart!"

Ecaterina moved her chair farther away to give her friend more room.

Tabitha faced Ecaterina and used her back to start pushing her chair against Barnabas, and the next thing Tabitha knew, Barnabas had grabbed the back of her antigrav chair and flung her away from the table toward the wall. A small "Shit!" slipped out of Ranger Two's mouth before she swung her legs around and used them to brace her feet against the rock wall before she slammed into it.

There were chuckles in the room as Tabitha pushed off the wall to slide back toward the table. She stuck one foot down and tapped the floor, turning her chair in half a circle to slide gracefully back into her slot. She leaned toward Barnabas, who likewise leaned a little toward her as her eyes narrowed. "This isn't finished!"

Barnabas raised an eyebrow. "I never thought it was." He nodded and smiled as he leaned back in his chair, adjusting himself while he looked around the table.

He was in the middle, with Tabitha and Ecaterina and then Nathan on his left. On his right were Bobcat and William, and on the other side of William was Peter. Darryl, Scott, Frank, Barb, and Stephen rounded out the attendees.

Barnabas nodded to the people across the table from him. "Okay, let's get this meeting going. Darryl?"

Darryl nodded to Barnabas as he took a swig of water, then set the bottle down and looked around the table. "Since John and

Eric are with Lance at the meeting, Scott and I took the time to see if we could find any rumors related to Baba Yaga—"

Bobcat interrupted, "Any success?"

Darryl shrugged. "It depends on your definition of success. With a character such as Baba Yaga, there is more rumor floating around out there than truth. In fact, with so many parents using Bethany Anne's alter ego to scare their children at night, it is almost impossible to find any fire amongst all the smoke."

Frank, to Scott's left, furiously wrote in his notebook as Darryl continued.

"Out of the countless number of tips we received, we believe only two of them were accurate. Given Bethany Anne's new ship, the only solid clue is the occasional picture with the rather iconic vampire on the side. I'm surprised she hasn't covered that up."

Frank looked up from his notebook. "I imagine she is either consciously or subconsciously providing us clues to her whereabouts."

Barb turned to ask her husband, "What do you mean, 'subconsciously?'"

Frank took his pen and tapped it against his lips for a moment before he answered, "Remember, Baba Yaga was originally supposed to be an avatar for Bethany Anne so she could go out amongst the people and accomplish operations while keeping the Empress herself out of the action."

Barb nodded. "Okay, I get that."

She was very aware that sometimes you had to lead her husband to the next point or Frank would continue explaining until everyone grew old and became dust.

"In hindsight, it is obvious Bethany Anne prefers to be active and out in the field." There were a few chuckles and snorts around the table.

Frank moved his head left and right, and a small smirk played on his face. "Okay, all of us here knew that back on Earth. Unfortunately, we *forgot* that salient fact."

The mood of the table had darkened a bit, so Barnabas reminded them, "Folks, there shouldn't be any self-blame here. Trust me when I tell you that Bethany Anne is just as responsible for the situation as the rest of us. This isn't about us failing her or her failing us. We are a team, and we will find and bring our friend back. She will need our support when she gets here because she will be just as harsh on herself as you are being on yourselves."

Frank nodded to Barnabas before continuing, "Bethany Anne is a responsible person. With her change to Baba Yaga, I believe she is—in her mind—shirking a responsibility due to grief. This has been exacerbated by how many years she has been forced to stay on the throne. However, Bethany Anne is still operating as her alter ego and has been for a significant amount of time, so my point related to subconscious was whether *Baba Yaga* is delivering the hints." Frank turned to Scott and Darryl. "Or is Bethany Anne providing the hints from underneath Baba Yaga's persona? We still need to figure this out, but you can bet that at some level, she will be providing us clues," he turned to Barb, "to let us know that she is still alive, at least."

Nathan asked from across the table, "Did you guys have any trouble with being recognized?"

Scott nodded as Darryl answered, "Yes. I am not sure how much the recognition caused us to receive—or not receive—tips."

Scott added, "Some of those space stations were so large we could have been at the same place as her at the same time and still not run across each other. I was shocked by how big some of those floating cities really are."

Tabitha nodded her head in understanding.

Stephen remarked, "In my opinion, we need to send a new group out, one that isn't as well recognized as you two."

Barnabas looked at his brother. "Are you offering?"

Stephen nodded. "She is my Queen. My liege, until the end."

Peter was across the table from Stephen. "No one would recognize me. I wasn't in the news nearly as often."

Stephen raised an eyebrow.

When Tabitha spoke up from the middle of the table, everyone's head turned to look at her. "I'm going." Barnabas started to say something, but she jammed her hand over his mouth. "What Barnabas was about to say," she changed her voice to mimic her boss, "is that it would be a really good idea for Ranger Two to accompany you, considering you two don't have as much experience walking amongst the people as yours truly."

Barnabas gently pried Tabitha's hand from his face as she glared at him. "Amazingly enough, she is right."

Tabitha looked at him in shock. "I am?" As he nodded, she indicated the people around the table. "I have witnesses!"

Barnabas told her laconically, "You would be right more often if you didn't go off half-cocked all the time."

She smirked, and he shook his head before turning toward Bobcat. "What ship should they take?"

Tabitha started to speak, but before she got a word out, Barnabas' finger was in her face. Her eyes narrowed, trying to focus on it.

He looked at her. "Not a word." He left his finger there for a moment, and when she opened her mouth to bite it, he flicked her nose and pulled his hand back. Tabitha put both of her hands over her nose and tried to muffle the squeal of pain.

Bobcat turned to William. "What about the *Scamp Princess*?"

William shrugged. "What about Ricky Bobby's new research vessel?"

Bobcat started nodding in agreement. "That is a ship she doesn't know with an AI who has been trained in fighter tactics."

William continued, "It has hidden armament in case Ricky Bobby needs to fight, but it is predominantly a scouting vessel."

Bobcat finished, "With some of the latest technology we could stuff into it." The two men turned to Barnabas.

He shrugged. "Will Ricky Bobby do this?"

"I don't see why not," William replied.

Bobcat added, "He just wants to get away from everything for a while. That will probably break Julianna's heart, but she will have to understand. After his isolation for so many decades, he needs time to decompress."

"This isn't exactly a moment to decompress," Ecaterina pointed out.

This time it was Barnabas who provided insight into her observation. "Actually, it might be good for him to work with a few normal people in a low-key operation before he goes out solo into the great unknown."

"Besides," William tapped his stylus on the table, "Ricky Bobby appreciated Bethany Anne giving Julianna her blood after their first battle."

Nathan spoke up. "Bad Company's spy network can filter out a lot of the smoke. We are pretty good at that. Why don't we give you the most obvious locations to check? Hopefully it will save you from the difficulties Darryl and Scott just had."

"That is a good suggestion." Scott looked at Tabitha. "Trust me when I say that just mentioning Baba Yaga will get you one of three responses."

Darryl put up a finger. "Abject fear."

"Cluelessness." Scott put up two fingers.

"Myths that are far from reality," Darryl finished, putting up three fingers.

Tabitha shook her head as she listened to everyone. *Achronyx, make sure you keep the engines warm,* she sent to her ship.

Marquer's World, Independent System, Allied with the Zhyn

Militarily neutering the Etheric Empire was *exactly* what Lance suspected most of the other powerful groups wanted.

He continued his discussion with the Ixtali Legate.

"We don't trust many out there with the ability to create a Federation of equals. Our goals are to integrate our commerce and support each other with the ability to negotiate with words instead of force. However, there will be no moving forward with an Empire that has lost both its rank in the Federation and its military."

"I am aware," Addix replied after a moment, "that humans came into our area of space as warriors. Many people believe you incapable of putting down your weapons, but this is your legacy, not mine, to determine."

Lance thought about the different ways to deal with this concern and hated all which came to mind.

If he were in their shoes, would he trust a Federation member that was the eight-hundred-pound gorilla? He needed a way to give them what they asked for without giving them what they wanted.

"There is one last thing you might not be pleased to hear," Addix informed him as the van doors closed and the vehicle started the trip to the conclave.

When Lance heard the final request, he wished he could find his daughter and rip her a new asshole.

Gott Verdammt! He wasn't sure if she had *known* this was coming, but he suspected she might have foreseen the possibility.

If she had?

Then no wonder she was off searching for Kurtherians.

It would take Lance the whole conference and another week and a half to simmer down and realize there really wasn't another person for this challenge if *he* wanted a Federation to exist for the Etheric Empire.

He was *fucked.*

Two weeks after his meeting with Addix, Lance smiled to himself in the bathroom mirror as he got ready for work after his shower.

He *was* the right man for the job, and working with his daughter for so many decades had honed his skills at subterfuge to a new level.

The other species wanted to play politics? Well, they would learn to *never* fuck with the Etheric Empire in that arena.

Because no one could be more devious than he was. He would work to make this Federation better and safer for humanity, for the Yollins, and for those who had signed on when the Etheric Empire was just an Empire, not the Etheric Federation.

Everyone else who wanted to play games had better learn that you never fucked with a Reynolds.

The daughter *or the father.*

CHAPTER SEVEN

Above Planet Devon, QBS *Shinigami*

The planet arrayed beneath the ship looked like a black and white diamond in the middle of black velvet cloth. Baba Yaga gazed at the viewing screens on the bridge. "I didn't realize how large the city was the last time we were here."

I believe you and Stephen were discussing Nathan's contact, TOM replied.

Baba Yaga tapped her lip. "Yes, but I would have remembered a city *this* large."

Shinigami interjected over the speaker system, "We did not actually show anything on the view screens as we approached last time. I did not have enough experience with security to confirm whether they could hack anything of mine until we connected with the spaceport."

Baba Yaga shrugged. "Oh, that makes sense. Well, as the Mistress of the Planet, it's time that I get busy one way or another."

Deciding whether to give up the title? TOM asked.

"No." She looked at the tall structures jutting from the morass of buildings below. "It actually excites me to realize that the infrastructure from hundreds of years of effort is ready to take it to the next stage." She turned around and headed toward the armory. "Time for the Mistress to get dressed and meet her people. Shinigami, take me to the location on the planet where we intend to build the military spaceport."

>>**It is not a very large planet.**<<

Baba Yaga nodded in agreement as she walked down the passageway. "I think I am done trying to go large. Baba Yaga is happier dealing with just one small planet and making a difference. You know how it is—I would rather be a large frog in a small pond than a small frog in a large pond."

>>**As opposed to being a large frog in a large pond?**<<

Baba Yaga pointed at the video screen inside the armory when she walked in. "Right there! Shinigami, take us through that canyon and make a couple passes around this location. I think we can do some terraforming right here to hide even more ships and activity from space." She tapped her lips. "We are going to need a justifiable reason why this planet is unimportant."

>> **Well, you could try erasing the knowledge of the planet. You could make the planet have a reputation so horrible that people stay away from it, but it will be impossible to accomplish much unless it is in the vested self-interests of a lot of people to hide the facts.**<<

Baba Yaga nodded in agreement. "I think you're right. It's almost like I would need to accomplish all three at the same time. We would need to implement software updates to ships that arrive here and try to selectively delete any information they put into the ship's computers before they leave."

>>**Do you have any idea how *difficult* that would be?**<< He sounded a bit shocked at her suggestion.

She started donning her armor. "Yes, and that is why I'm going to leave that task to the most experienced artificial intelligence I know."

>>**Wait a minute, how did I get involved in this?**<<

She locked her armored waist-piece in place. "Who said I was talking about you?" she asked, grabbing the midriff piece.

>>**Well, if you are *not* talking about me, tell me what other artificial intelligence you believe has more experience?**<<

She grabbed her armored jacket and pushed her right arm into the sleeve. "None. I just wanted to know what made you think I was talking about you," she replied, swinging her other arm into the sleeve and lifting it to settle on her shoulders before she started to lock it in place.

>>**Because I am the most experienced artificial intelligence you know, that was the most logical conclusion.**<<

"What is going to happen when you find an artificial intelligence who is superior to you?" Baba Yaga questioned as she grabbed her armored pants and locked them to her waist, then started folding the armor around her legs and locking the pieces into place.

"You know there is a fairly good chance we will eventually meet quite a few who are," she remarked. She marveled at how the suit showed no seams when she was finished with the latches.

ADAM used the speakers this time. "What *should* happen? It won't be any different than me meeting a different alien species." There was a pause before he added, "I suppose."

Shinigami informed her over the speakers, "I am finished with my research. I have enough topographical information to support the next stage of development at this location."

Baba Yaga grabbed her weapons and left the armory, and she heard the door close behind her.

It took her a little while to walk back to the bridge and then to her couch, where she slid into her pre-conformed captain's chair. "Take me into the city, but choose a small landing spot out of the way. I don't want it known that I'm here yet."

>>**I am not sure that is possible without hiding the ship. Remember, the last time we were here, Shinigami had to fight off a lot of cyber-attacks. It would not take long for hackers to**

realize the fingerprint of the defense if they attack you again. <<

Baba Yaga thought about it for a moment while reclining on her bridge chair. "Let's see if we can purchase a small landing spot with a warehouse to park inside. We will not connect to the world's communication network until we have a suitable security program in place. It should block any fingerprinting of our defense measures."

Shinigami told her, "This will require at least an hour to accomplish."

Baba Yaga nodded in understanding as she checked a few screens before touching a button that moved them away from her. "That's fine, I'll just take a quick nap. Wake me when you're done."

No sooner had Baba Yaga said this than she got comfortable, turned her head to the side, and closed her eyes. Her white hair fell across her face, blocking out the slowly dimming bridge lights.

Planet Devon, Older Warehouse Area Outside the Main City

Baba Yaga kept the hood of her cloak around her face as she stepped off the ship.

It had taken close to three hours before Shinigami's research into the right location had been completed. Then the right palms had to be greased to help the paperwork flow, but finally, all legal documents were in proper order. Once that was accomplished, *Shinigami* was able to land and move into the warehouse.

Both Shinigami and ADAM calculated it was safe to do this in the early morning light with the ship's cloaking engaged.

The shadows still cast by the tall buildings to the east would keep the rather run-down warehouse district shrouded in shadow for another half hour.

>>**Should I tell Lerr'ek that you have arrived**?<<

No, I'm going to get the pulse of the city before I find him. Just locate him to the best of your ability.

As she stepped out of the large warehouse, the three-story-tall doors closed behind her, eventually clanging shut as she waited. Baba Yaga looked around and sniffed the air. The smell of cutting fluids and some sort of petroleum product seemed to be the main components in this blue-collar area. Her own building had office space for a business.

It was exactly what she wanted. "It's dark, it's out of the way, and I can hide." She wrapped her cloak tighter as the thin atmosphere made it harder to breathe, and she coughed.

"This atmosphere needs to be fixed," she mumbled as she strode down the long street between the different warehouses. She had probably walked a mile and had only seen three organics before ADAM directed her into one of the entrances into the city's interior.

Most of the city was comprised of enclosed spaces. Underground areas had been carved out of the rock, and the large buildings above ground were constructed from local stone, metal, and glass, or high durability plastic. They occasionally towered high above her.

Before she walked inside, she watched the air traffic. A few personal ships flitted through the buildings, and one or two large commercial bus-type transports waded between the buildings.

She wasn't sure if it got busier later in the day.

Underground it was a different story. She was jostled many times as huge crowds surged along the different walkways and through tunnels going who-knew-where. She just kept walking and enjoyed the feeling of anonymity.

"No wonder the prince wanted to switch places with a commoner," she mumbled. "It feels more alive…"

"NO!" a voice yelled, and her head whipped around to locate the sound.

"You could just protect yourself," she grumped. She now

heard a *clang* and some struggling, so she pushed through the crowd. She had almost passed the correct tunnel entrance when she heard another cry. She turned quickly and was rammed in the side by an alien that looked like a large purple centipede.

Bouncing off in surprise, she took off down the hallway leaving the alien bitching at her in something even her translation couldn't figure out. She realized the sounds had been amplified in the tunnel. The altercation wasn't very close.

She bounded up two levels of stairs into a large, darker cavern and kept climbing as she studied the mechanical contraptions inside.

"What *is* this shit?" she asked, jumping up another flight of stairs.

>>**Probably the core air and liquids systems for a skyscraper above us.**<< Adam replied.

She stopped at the top of the third flight, where the metal grating stretched at least two hundred yards down the side of the cavern and then turned a corner.

Inside her hood, her mouth dropped open in surprise.

Someone shouted, "GIVE IT BACK!" and then she heard a high-pitched scream of frustration. There were three regular-looking aliens punching a small Shrillexian, who had covered his head with his arms.

A package dropped to the ground as the Shrillexian stepped back. He didn't notice a fourth alien, a Torcellan with a pipe, ready to clock him over the head when he could get a good lick in.

The Shrillexian went down with a *thump* when the opportunity presented itself to the Torcellan. He looked at the downed Shrillexian, pipe in his hands, before dropping the pipe. It banged twice before it rolled off the gangway and dropped three flights to the rock floor below, clattering around down there for a moment.

The Torcellan, his almost albino humanoid appearance

making him easy to recognize, placed a hand over his mouth and gagged. He then shoved himself past the others, who had been staring at him, and ran toward the staircase she had just come up. She moved into the darker shadows as he sped by.

He didn't have a good color to his face, to be fair to him, she thought.

She hoped he found a washroom in time.

The others helped up an older two-legged Yollin female. One of them handed her the dropped package.

None of them noticed Baba Yaga slowly slide in behind them. "You did good," Baba Yaga hissed aloud.

The three aliens turned in surprise to gape at the dark-cloaked person in the shadows, the *whoosh* of the nearby air-pipes the only thing breaking the silence as they pondered whether they needed to try and protect themselves once more.

"You may leave." Her hood nodded toward the tough on the ground. Her eyes narrowed as she noticed something wrong. "I will take care of him."

"Why?" asked a medium-height alien. Mustard-yellow skin and high cheekbones were just two of the attributes that made him different from the typical bipedal design of a lot of aliens.

That, and the fact that his skin looked reptilian. So far, he hadn't stuck a foot-long tongue out, and she was grateful for that.

Because…gross!

"I want a word with him," she replied as she gestured for them to move along. "And you need to give *all* of the lady's stuff back to her." She pointed to the older Yollin woman. "Check your bag."

The mustard-skinned leader's eyes narrowed. "Who are you?" he asked, his hand settling near his waist.

Baba Yaga started chuckling, and her dark raspy voice was not pleasant, no matter how good the translation efforts. "I'm the Mistress of the Planet," she whispered, "and you will obey." She lifted a hand, and a blue sphere appeared. Lightning arced and snapped off the sphere to different parts of her arm and fingers.

It crackled louder than the whoosh of the air-pipes, so it captured their attention. "Or you will die."

"Here!" A gray alien behind the snake shoved a couple additional items into the Yollin woman's hands and started running, and a second later, the other alien followed. All that remained were the snake-looking leader and the Shrillexian on the ground.

"Pull that weapon," she nodded toward his hand, "and I'll make your Shrillexian friend here take your dead corpse to the nearest trash disposal unit." She released the globe and it hovered in the air before slowly floating in his direction, moving a few feet a second.

A moment later, his eyes opened wider as it grew in size. When the arcing blue sphere had traveled half the distance between her and him, he took off running. Baba Yaga waved to the woman to leave. "I'm going to have a discussion with the one on the floor." She turned to nod toward the staircase. "May you have a better morning."

"Thank you," she replied, nodding as her mandibles clicked in appreciation. She slowly sidestepped toward the main walkway, and as she turned to hurry down it, she called back over her shoulder, "May the Empress live forever!"

Baba Yaga waved a hand negligently. "Yada-yada, Empress forever," she hissed as she took two steps toward the Shrillexian. "You can get up under your own power, or I can use pain to help motivate you."

"It's not like that didn't fucking hurt." The Shrillexian turned over, groaning while reaching up to gingerly touch his head. "That wasn't in the plans."

"I suspected not," Baba Yaga replied, looking down the hallway. She wondered if the Torcellan had relieved himself of the contents of his stomach in public. She turned back to the Shrillexian. "You heal quickly, so stand up." When she casually flicked her hand, a small blue flash of electricity arced between it and him, and little spiders of electricity crawled quickly over his body.

"OWWW!" He rolled away from her, then pushed off the ground and jumped up. His feet came down one in front of the other, prepared for an attack, as his hands came up to protect himself or punch.

He hadn't needed to bother, since she hadn't moved.

"You are better than this!" she hissed, her voice dripping with scorn. "Shrillexians are a proud people! What are you doing working with con artists?" She jerked a thumb in the direction the others had fled. Stepping closer, she pulled down her hood. "What is your name?"

The Shrillexian was annoyed. He had been ready to deliver a beatdown to the stranger just a moment before, but now he took an involuntary step backward.

He tried to talk, but nothing came out. His shoulders slumped, and he took a knee, head bowed. "Keitphet."

"Keitfet. Keitfel. Ceatput… Fuck it," she hissed in annoyance. "I'm calling you Keith. Stand up." He did so as she watched him. "Now, attack!"

He jumped at her, raising a hand to slam down on her head and kicking out with his left leg. She slapped the kick out of the way and jabbed her left palm into his chest, knocking him backward. He slammed into the metal walkway and rolled.

He reached out in time to grab the rail that protected people from falling off, but both his legs went over the side.

Keith worked himself back onto the grating before standing up once more. He resumed a fighting stance but moved no closer.

"Good," she hissed, walking toward him. "You are still willing to challenge me." She stopped ten feet in front of him with her hands hidden in the sleeves of her robe.

He put his hands up. "I need to move this needler behind me on my waist, I'm not going to use it on you." She nodded, so he reached back and slowly brought it around with his right hand.

MICHAEL ANDERLE

He looked down before slowly flicking off the power button and shoving it into his waistband. "Rather be shot in the ass than in the front," he told her. "Truth to tell, I'd rather not be shot."

"How very unShrillexian." Baba Yaga stepped closer. "You never answered my question. Why are you with those con artists?"

"I need to fight," he answered.

She blinked twice before she asked, surprised, "You do this so they will beat you up?"

"No," he admitted. "Every third con, I get to be the hero and take them out. They are allowed to fight back when it's their turn to be the thief." Keith shrugged. "I make up for the beatings at that point."

"Why don't you have a job?" She looked around. "Perhaps not here." Turning back to him, she continued, "Why aren't you in a mercenary group or working as a bouncer or training fighters? I have to believe a Shrillexian who can heal himself if you kick his ass is worth hiring."

"Doesn't work that way." He placed a hand parallel to the ground at the level of his head. "No one believes a short Shrillexian is a good hire."

"It isn't the size of the dog in the fight, but the size of the fight in the dog," she grumbled.

"What's a dog?" he asked.

"You." She waved him forward. "Come with me. You will be working in one of my companies." She started back toward the stairs. "You will be happy to know the HR Manual only has one rule."

They went down the three flights of stairs and out into the main traffic tunnel, which was less congested than before. Three blocks later, he finally spoke again. "Um, what's the rule?"

She didn't slow down as she answered, "Don't upset the Mistress of the Planet."

CHAPTER EIGHT

QBBS _Meredith Reynolds_

Eric said goodbye to John after the two of them dropped off their armor and weapons for a complete check with the R&D labs.

Nothing had happened during the General's political meetings, but Jean was paranoid. She would be checking everything for enemy effort, especially nano-spy devices and digital attacks.

It was damned good to be home.

There was a tag on his HUD, and he checked it out and smiled. The boys had come over for the monthly dinner.

He picked up his speed so he would arrive soon after dinner started. Gabrielle wasn't one to move the time she served dinner, so you had to move your ass to get there on time.

"Meredith," he subvocalized, "please make sure I make all available transits and open the doors for me."

"Is this another 'Operation Get Eric Home Quickly?'"

"Yup," Eric agreed and amped up his speed. He cut through two parks and jumped up three floors on one occasion to crawl over a wall. That surprised two lovers, who had thought his shortcut would be a safe place to make out.

"Sorry about that!" Eric told them, smiling before he disappeared.

The young woman looked at her boyfriend, whose mouth was open. "Arthur, who was that?" she asked. He turned to look back to her, a twinkle in his eye.

"You know," he told her, pulling her closer to him with a smile playing on his lips, "you've always said you only had eyes for me."

"Sure," she answered. "I've said that for two years now."

"Well," Arthur nodded toward the hallway where the man had just disappeared, "that was proof you meant what you said."

She frowned. "I'm not sure if I should hit you or be happy."

"That was Eric Escobar, one of the Empress' Bitches, who is married to Gabrielle Nacht, Stephen's daughter. A close friend of the Empress. I know a couple of women who would jettison their husbands if someone like him were to smile in their direction."

"Yeah, but he isn't *you*." She leaned in to kiss Arthur harder.

Eric made it home just as Gabrielle set the last side-dishes on the table. She turned and winked at him. "I figured if I made the rice, you would walk a little faster."

Before Eric could say anything, John Michael piped up, "Dad, Mom had Meredith show a map of the station with a blip for you."

Gabrielle turned to her son, eyes narrowing.

Stephen Michael reached over to grab the Spanish rice. "Personally, I was hoping you might be a little late so I could have your portion."

"Keep it up, Steve." Eric kissed his wife and pulled out his seat at the head of the table, "and I'll take all of the rice for myself, including," he picked up his fork and reached to his left, swiping some of the rice his son had just placed on his plate, "all of yours."

"We have two grown men for sons," Gabrielle commented as she sat down, "and when the three of you get together to eat, it's like I have three boys again."

"We are what we are, Mom." Stephen passed the bowl of rice to his dad. "You should roll with it instead of fighting the inevitable."

John Michael grabbed a steak before passing the platter to Gabrielle, who passed it to Eric. He turned to his father. "So, did you kill anyone?"

Stephen rolled his eyes.

"We call it an 'after-action report.'" John elbowed his brother. "You diplomats should learn a trick or two."

Eric took a steak and made sure he had plenty of rice. Gabrielle's eyebrow rose at the fourth spoonful, so he placed it back in the bowl. "Nope."

"Maim?" John Michael asked.

"Nope," Eric replied.

"So, it was quiet at the meeting?" John asked, a little surprised.

"Oh, hell, no," Eric answered before taking a bite.

"That's what I keep trying to tell All-Testosterone-and-No-Brain-Cells next to me." Stephen elbowed his brother back. "Diplomacy is chess with major repercussions."

Eric looked up from eating to see all three looking at him. "What?"

Stephen asked, "So what happened?" The other two nodded their agreement with the question.

"Um." He scratched his chin. "The General wanted to kill some of the groups by the end. They want to gut the Empire of our military so that 'we can all be equal.'"

John was talking with his fork. "Why the hell would we do that?"

Stephen answered, "It's pretty much a requirement. Otherwise, everyone will continue building their own militaries, and eventually someone is going to be bored or need to focus the people elsewhere so they'll attack. It's better to try to keep everyone pretty equal."

John Michael shook his head. "Uncle Lance won't let that happen."

Stephen Michael shrugged. "Well, unless he wants another war right now, I'm not sure what choice he has."

Gabrielle replied, "You will find out that you always have options, Stephen."

Stephen Michael shrugged. "I can't think of any, and I reviewed the archives with Giles."

Gabrielle's eyes narrowed. "He's doing *digital* archaeology?"

John Michael and Eric glanced at each other and smiled.

Stephen Michael continued, "Not really, but he was grounded for ninety days by Uncle Lance a month ago after he stole one of the unused Pods to check out an area on Yoll."

John Michael stopped before he stuck his fork in his mouth. "He stole a Pod?"

Stephen Michael replied, "Technically, he took it without proper authorization. Since he had his father's okay, Meredith allowed him to use it."

Eric was cutting his meat. "How did he get Frank's permission?"

Gabrielle answered, "Barb said he was vague on one of his questions to his dad, but then told Meredith to parse the recording, so she didn't question the approval."

Eric chuckled. "You'd think Meredith would learn."

Gabrielle shrugged. "Apparently even an EI can be charmed."

Stephen Michael shook his head. "I've heard the women talk. It would take an alien to be safe from that guy's smile."

Eric started reaching for the rice again but stopped when Gabrielle looked at him. "What?"

She shook her head. "Go ahead. I have another bowl in the warmer."

Stephen turned his head in the direction of the kitchen. "Are you serious?"

"Yes," she replied. "Go get it. I can see from your dad dumping the rest of the rice on his plate that we will need it."

"Damn right, we'll need it," Stephen muttered as he stood up to grab the extra.

Eric put the empty bowl down. "Giles is a good guy, but he has too damned much of his mother and father in the wrong proportions for his own good."

There was a moment of silence as Stephen Michael retrieved the rice. When he had returned, John Michael changed the subject. "So, we had a special assistant in training today."

Eric noticed his wife's eyes narrowing before he turned to his son. "Oh? Do I know this person?"

Stephen placed half the bowl of rice on his plate as he spoke. "She's about a hundred and…" He looked up. "What do you weigh lately, Mom?"

She tapped her finger on the table several times before answering, "Enough to kick your ass, my impertinent offspring."

"You always taught us to be straight talkers," he replied.

"No," she answered, "Straight shooters. Apparently I didn't provide enough motivation for self-preservation when I taught this to you."

John Michael came to his brother's defense. "I'd say you gave Uncle John's granddaughter a reason to work harder."

Stephen Michael added, "You know what they say."

John Michael looked at his brother. "There is nothing bigger than a Grimes' ego?"

Eric disagreed. "That's their youth, not their genes."

John Michael changed his tune. "Okay, that pride cometh before a beatdown by Mom?"

Stephen thought back to all the training his parents had

forced on him whether or not he wanted anything to do with martial arts.

And for him, that had been heavy on the "not."

"That must have been funny."

John Michael nodded. "Oh, it was. Let me tell you about..."

His mother interrupted, "Let's not rehash a friend's embarrassing lesson."

Stephen Michael asked, "Why not? You always told Aunt BA when you kicked our asses."

She shook her head. "That was different. That was two close friends chatting, not telling the whole group."

John Michael seemed a little embarrassed. "Soooo... If someone maybe surreptitiously took a video of the fight and posted it to our squad's website?"

Gabrielle didn't miss a beat. "That would be bad, and that person should immediately pull it down."

A moment later, Eric pulled out his tablet. "OUCH!" He squinted. "That had to hurt. Oh, she's pissed off now." He shook his head. "Yeah, that's not going to go well." There was a loud *thump* from his tablet's speaker. He looked up at his wife. "I haven't seen that move since..." He looked up at the ceiling before returning his gaze to the tablet. "Have you ever done that to me?"

She shook her head. "I was using some techniques I played around with in the eighties."

Eric's face scrunched up in confusion. "The *nineteen*-eighties? Which martial art?"

Everyone turned to look at Gabrielle, who cleared her throat and picked up a napkin. "The seventeen-eighties."

Stephen Michael leaned forward. "How old *are* you, Mom?"

She shook her head. "Not saying a word. Have you tried asking Grandpa or Uncle Barnabas?"

Stephen Michael made a disgusted face as he stabbed a piece of meat. "Yes, but then Uncle Barnabas erased my memory."

Eric looked at his son. "He did?"

Stephen Michael scratched the back of his head. "Well, he *said* he did. How is one supposed to know?"

For a moment, everyone focused on eating before Gabrielle spoke again. "Okay, there's something I need to tell you, and it might not be pleasant."

Stephen Michael turned to his right and whispered loudly enough for those in the next suite to hear. "Dad, what did you do?"

Eric shrugged. "I haven't been back long enough, so I don't think it was me this time."

Gabrielle's eyes now had a faint red glow. Stephen Michael pointed at Eric, who was already pointing at his son.

Gabrielle shook her head. "Like father, like son." She pushed her chair back a bit. "The Empire is changing, and it's time that we all make decisions for our future. I know that you two are happy with your jobs, and I'm happy for both of you, but I'm thinking that I am ready to spread my wings again."

John Michael smiled. "Are you going to beat up more people?"

Stephen Michael nodded to his right. "Like Dad?"

Gabrielle patted Eric on the arm. "I like to talk about how I kicked your dad's rear in the past, but I know he has been going easy on me for the last thirty years."

Eric was staring at her, mouth open.

Stephen Michael reached for the rice. "Yeah, Dad, all it takes is watching you and Uncle John go at it to realize you always let Mom off easy."

John Michael grabbed a bowl of Yollin corn. "Mom always says that because you love her, you can't hurt her."

Eric considered. "Well, that's true."

John Michael reached for butter. "So tell us again how Mom had to drag you back from the edge of the pyramid when all those Leath were trying to get up the sides?"

Stephen Michael added, "And how Aunt Bethany Anne allowed all the weapons to get crunched when the columns fell?"

Eric chuckled. "Let's not revisit history. That was before you were born."

Stephen Michael shook his head. "Hey, we were there."

John Michael added, "Just not fully formed."

Eric pointed his fork at his sons. "Guys, Mom's important announcement?"

John Michael looked across the table. "Sorry, Mom."

Gabrielle nodded acceptance before she continued, "I think it's time I put away my apron."

John Michael stared at her, surprised. "Holy shit, you *are* going to kick some more ass."

Gabrielle glanced at Stephen Michael, the one who preferred discussion over almost anything else. "Stephen?"

He thought for a moment before answering. "It's who you are. I can't change you. The Queen Bitch knows I've tried."

She shook her head. "That isn't polite, Stephen. Bethany Anne's name shouldn't be used as an oath."

His eyes narrowed. "Why do you… I mean, I really did go talk it out with Aunt Bethany Anne, and she went all Queen Bitch on me and made me talk to her while she was in that crazy eyes-blazing-red state."

John Michael looked at his brother with respect. "Bet that was cool."

He snorted. "Hardly. I think I peed in my pants a little."

"That takes guts to admit," John Michael told him.

"I know, so keep it to yourself."

"I got your back, bro."

Eric interrupted, "So what do you want to do, sweetheart?"

"I'm not sure, but I've talked it over with Dad, and he said he was proud of me and what I've done with his grandchildren."

John Michael nodded at his brother. "Even the pacifist?"

Stephen Michael didn't look up. "Realist. Not all people who ask questions first and shoot second, or maybe fifth, are pacifists."

"Don't worry, if a firefight happened, I'd have you guard my back. I'd aim downrange."

Stephen Michael ignored his brother and looked at his mom.

"What I'm saying is, Mom's kitchen and life support services are now closed. You two are officially on your own."

Eric watched all of this and stayed quiet.

John Michael glanced at his brother. "Bro, I think we just got kicked out."

Stephen returned the look. "I think we did."

Eric pushed back from the table. "Not before you do the dishes."

Stephen Michael worked on his last four mouthfuls. "That will only take two minutes."

Gabrielle reached under the table to squeeze Eric's hand. "Then enjoy normalcy for two more minutes. After that, it's 'fend for yourself' time."

John Michael muttered, "Wow, kicked to the curb so fast!"

Stephen asked his brother, "Do you even know what a curb is?"

He winked. "Yes, it's a place you and I are at the moment."

Gabrielle turned to Eric. "I blame you for this."

Eric shrugged. "Each is at the top of his game in his own way. I think we did okay."

She shook her head and gestured to her sons. "Then why do they each lose fifty IQ points when they are home?"

John Michael answered, "Because we are safe here. Out there is different."

Stephen Michael agreed, "It's kind of nice not to have to be 'on.'"

John Michael spoke. "You have those who are important, but not well known, then you have those who are important in their roles…"

Stephen Michael added, "Then you have those who are the offspring of the Empress' Bitches…"

John Michael continued his comment, "Not entirely complaining, but it kinda blows sometimes."

Gabrielle told her son, "Suck it up, buttercup. Your enhancements are a token to help you be better." She then added. "And survive if someone tries to take you out because of us."

John Michael pursed his lips. "Yeah, maybe, but my EI won't talk to me."

Eric watched his son. "One day, you might wish it would shut up."

KRENLOCK

ART BY ERIC QUIGLEY

CHAPTER NINE

<u>Planet Devon, Passageway D-771</u>

Baba Yaga strode down the second flight of stairs, hearing the steps of the Shrillexian behind her, ignoring the pissant.

She pulled her hood back over her head.

ADAM, have you figured out where Lerr'ek is at the moment?

>>Yes. About to pass through Park Area TT-745.<<

Which is where in relation to us? she asked. *As far as I know, it could be two left turns or halfway across this damned city.*

>>About a thirty-minute walk without any foot traffic.<<

How about if I go outside and run?

>>I imagine it would...<

LOOK OUT! TOM yelled.

Baba Yaga was pulled into the Etheric, and she screamed as pain shot through her skull. She recognized the swirling white mist of the dimension as she fell to the ground.

"I'm telling you that *flarsyn* Witch was *right here!*" Keitphet yelled in disgust as he stomped down the stairs, the reverberations echoing down the cavern.

Two of his teammates looked around, wondering if maybe she fell down the last flight of stairs and was in some dark corner.

He thumbed the safety on his needler and shoved it into his waistband again. "Tell Jacklorn to get his running-away ass back here. She throws one little sizzling energy globe at his scrawny behind and he bolts." He snorted. "Some big badass *he* turned out to be."

"If she really is the Witch—" his first teammate started. She swallowed the rest of her statement when his Shrillexian eyes turned to her and narrowed.

He hissed as he pointed to where she had been. "I shot her fool head off." He looked to the right and then over the rails. "Who lets an opponent walk behind them with a loaded weapon?" He shook his head. "The money for bringing in her head makes everything we got going look like slop feed." He banged his hand down on the rails. "SHIT!"

Baba Yaga heard a voice in her skull.

>>**And I'm telling you I was NOT causing her attention to wander. She asked me a question, and I was answering it.**<<

Pain was lancing through her head. "Would you two," she moaned, "shut the fuck up? My cranium feels like it is going to split in two!"

Well, technically it almost did, TOM chastised. **What were you thinking, allowing an enemy with a loaded gun behind you? Didn't Petre fix this issue back on Earth?**

"Got cocky," she hissed. Moaning in pain, she moved her arms underneath her chest to push off the ground and sat up. She gingerly pushed the hood off her head and reached up to touch the back of her skull.

It was sticky and still tender as hell. "How long was I out?"

>>**About three paragraphs in our argument, so maybe a few seconds.**<<

"Going to have to clean my cloak or trash it. This blood is going to smell."

I wouldn't trash it. We worked hard to have some protection woven into the material, TOM told her.

"What?" she asked as she studied her cloak's sleeve.

Not there, just the hood. We figured you would wear armor but never anything for your head, so Billy the Binary Boob there was able to get something special added to the cloaks that were placed on the ship.

>>**It seems like it helped stop those needles.**<<

Which we wouldn't have needed to worry about if Bethany Anne had been fucking paying *ATTENTION*!

"TOM, stop it. It wasn't ADAM's fault," she hissed. "And in case you haven't been paying attention, Bethany Anne isn't here right now."

No shit! he snarked before his presence disappeared.

She couldn't feel him in her mind.

Baba Yaga waited for a moment, but he didn't come back. "Well, that's one way to get rid of the insufferable little twit," she hissed, frustrated.

>>**I'm sure there are better ways than almost getting killed to encourage us to leave you alone.**<<

"I don't want to push away either of you," she replied, lifting the hood back over her head, "but his comment wasn't appreciated." She stood and moved her head in a circle, willing the bones to crack. She leaned forward a bit to take a look, then straightened, moved over five steps, and looked again.

"Got you," she snarled.

The two females were obediently waiting, eyes down a little, as the Shrillexian pointed at them, his yelling so vitriolic he was practically spitting.

"You are both *useless* when it comes to your jobs!" he yelled. "Giving back what you took from her bag was a worthless display of *nice*."

A hand and arm appeared in the air behind him, and Keitphet saw the girls' eyes focus on something over his shoulder. He twisted and reached for his pistol, but the hand grabbed his shoulder and pulled him backward.

The females blinked. Keitphet was just *gone*.

"You scaly little useless bastard," Baba Yaga hissed in his face. "I can't believe I let you shoot my ass, you little worm."

He tried to grab his gun and bring it around to shoot the Witch, but she grabbed his hand and crushed the bones. She bent the barrel on the needler at the same time. "How does that feel, you little shit?"

Ignoring his cries of pain, she flung the gun into the mist and shot a red ball of energy which met it ten feet away, melting it before it hit the ground.

Keitphet wasn't paying attention. He was trying to get away, hoping he could figure out where he was and find a place to hide for a few days and let his hand heal.

Behind him, an ink-black face was frowning, her sharp teeth glistening in the light. "That little fuck was the mastermind the whole time?" She shook her head in disgust. "What have I become? So egotistical that I let little scum like that almost drill me?"

She turned to spit to the side.

>>**What are we going to do?**<<

"I want to torture that little Shrillexian bistok prick so bad I can taste it," she snarled. After taking a couple deep breaths, she continued, "But I'll settle for leaving him here to find his way home."

She started walking into the mist in the direction he had run in. "Okay, maybe just a little bit of torture," she modified. "I'm sure I'll feel better knowing I got my pound of flesh."

Don't you want the Kurtherians more?

"Oh, *there* you are," she hissed in exasperation. "What made you come out to play?"

Just wondering who you wanted more, that bistok prick or the Seven? TOM asked.

She stopped walking and her face was full of frustration as she looked in the direction he was jogging.

Her desire to find and flay him alive, his screams satiating her anger for shooting her, wailed at the forefront of her mind.

Her eyes flamed red in annoyance and she halted.

"FUCK!" she screamed into the fog.

A moment later, she disappeared.

Near Park Area TT-745

Lerr'ek walked through the park, giving himself an enjoyable few moments of peace amongst the trees.

Nock walked beside him. It had taken him a couple of weeks to find another bodyguard he could trust. Finding a Krenlock had been a miracle in itself.

Working for the Mistress of the Planet was almost a religious experience. As in, he had to have faith she would show up.

So far, he was shipping a huge quantity of material to the Etheric Empire through a new cut-out, and that was starting to provide a nice balance in the company's accounts.

Enough that he had sat down one night with three bottles of a drink that would put him on his ass and watched a mesmerizing multi-color video to help him ponder the future.

He drank a third of the first bottle before he got up, swept the three bottles up, and dumped them down the drain. Getting drunk wasn't going to help his thinking.

And deciding to go against the Mistress would cause him to always be looking over his shoulder.

She would either come back to Devon, or she would continue to operate as she had, sending instructions herself or through Stephen. His job for the rest of this decade was to pay off his debt.

Then he could decide what to do. Until then, he was going to do everything he could to support the Mistress.

Including changing this damned world.

Nock's four eyes always searched around them. He openly carried a large rifle and was constantly vigilant. He had blocked two efforts on Lerr'ek's life so far, and who knew how many he had stopped just by walking beside him?

I am here, a voice spoke into his mind.

"Shit!" He spun around and grabbed the rifle as Nock started to turn toward him. "*NO!*" he yelled, pushing the rifle down.

Nock stopped, but all four of his eyes were focused on someone now standing behind Lerr'ek.

"Who is that?" Nock asked, his guttural voice deep and slow. Some thought Krenlocks were slow, but the miracle was that they could speak.

Lerr'ek, hoping Nock wouldn't push him out of the way and try to raise his rifle, took a quick look behind him. His shoulders relaxed.

It would have sucked to guess wrong and now have an enemy able to shoot him in the back. "That's the Mistress." Lerr'ek let go of the rifle. "Don't shoot her. You will only piss her off."

A flare of red shot through her eyes for a moment before

receding. "I'm still dealing with the last asshole who tried. Who knows, I might need a shrink to deal with it."

Lerr'ek turned toward his boss and bowed slightly. "Mistress."

"Lerr'ek." She nodded and turned her gaze toward the Krenlock. "Nock."

Nock nodded, but she saw that his eyes were already looking around them. "What race is he?" she asked Lerr'ek.

"Do you wish to speak here?" he asked instead. When Baba Yaga shook her head, he suggested, "Then perhaps in my office?"

"Sure," she agreed, "but you will have to lead the way."

Lerr'ek continued walking into a large pedestrian tunnel with shops lining either side of the forty-foot wide and thirty-foot tall passage. "He is a Krenlock," Lerr'ek started as Nock walked behind them.

"Just watch the back," she called over her shoulder, jerking a thumb behind her. "I'll get the front." She turned her face forward again.

Lerr'ek looked at her. "I smell blood."

"Mine," she admitted. "It was an object lesson that even an elephant can die due to a germ."

"I've no idea what an elephant is," Lerr'ek admitted, "but I'm assuming you mean something large?"

"Yes," she told him with a grimace. "So...Krenlock?"

"They are a distant cousin to the Zhyn, genetically speaking. Smart at an instinctual level, and if they like you they are impossible to subvert. Once they decide they will take a contract they will do their best, period. I found Nock a couple weeks after our meeting."

"Trouble?" she asked.

"Twice he has blocked attacks, no idea how often him just walking with me stopped others."

"We show you have been attacked virtually a lot of times."

"Twenty-seven," he agreed.

"No, two hundred and seventy-six," she corrected. "ADAM

has been helping. He let through the ones that had zero chance of affecting your security setup."

Lerr'ek reached up and stroked his chin. "My security is inadequate?"

"Very," a voice came from his bone conduction speaker. "I will suggest a security strategy for your team to implement now that I understand the methods your competition has used to attack you. Plus, we have brought a computer connection to provide you off-planet computing resources that can't be hacked from here."

Lerr'ek spoke aloud. "What about being hacked where they reside?"

"Un-fucking-likely," Baba Yaga replied, having listened in on the conversation with ADAM. "That shit was hidden in rock inside one of the safest locations in the Empire and then forgotten."

"Forgotten?" he asked.

Nock's eyes continued to search each store they passed, the air vents above, and the people around them as the three walked through the tunnel.

"More later," she replied. "Too busy out here."

"Drink?" Lerr'ek asked as the two of them reclined in dark chairs around a small table in his personal office.

Nock had stayed outside and closed the door behind them.

"No, thank you," she replied, and she nodded to the door. "He's trustworthy?"

"One of the best you can buy, but they come with a caveat," he admitted.

"Which is?"

"You have to explain why you need them, and worse, your purpose," Lerr'ek admitted, "so I had to explain that this world was going to be run by another, and what your expectations were."

"And he believed you?"

"Yes." Lerr'ek poured himself a small drink of a local fruit juice. "It seems the concept was too farfetched for a Zhyn to make up, so it had to be true." He raised his drink in her direction. "Ah-twa-zay," he toasted before tossing it down.

"I have the information on the leaders who are shit." She looked up at him. "Which is most of them, and also the ones who are good."

"How many?" he asked.

"Two," she admitted. "You will need to get them to come here this afternoon. They will need to know the plan for a new Devon. There will be openings in the political hierarchy, and we need decent people to fill them."

"How many are going to be removed?" he asked.

"None of the worst can come back. Many of the really bad will be shipped off-planet to a location that has poor interplanetary transportation. If a few of the second batch piss me off, they will become members of the first crew."

"None will be staying on-planet?" Lerr'ek asked.

Her eyes flared once. "Oh, the first group will be staying on-planet. Their bodies will fertilize the ground to support a future generation of Devons who will know what a decent political support structure should look like," she answered. "Mind you, those who are currently in Group One have already perpetrated actions worthy of the death penalty, so I'm not acting without reason. They have been classified as incorrigible."

"Do you need support?" he asked. "I can strap my weapons on again."

"No." Her voice grew soft. "I've got support, I just need to listen to them more often," she admitted. "Once we have this political issue solved, you will receive new designs for my base. I will be moving additional people here in the future so the base is going to be huge, with additional room for expansion."

"Why?" Lerr'ek asked. "Are you expecting to go out and attack others?"

"No, I'm expecting others to want to attack here. And the best way to say 'no' is with guns the size of asteroids and a willingness to pull the trigger." She pursed her lips. "I suppose it goes without saying that one without the other is useless." She pushed her chair back and stood up. "I will be finished with this operation by tomorrow morning when the light breaks." She tapped her finger on the table. "You have the names of the two people in your message queue. Send me a message if you are unable to get them to come here."

She started for the door and Lerr'ek stood up. "Do you have an operation name?" he asked as she passed him.

She turned to look at him, raising an eyebrow.

"Military." He shrugged. "We often named our operations."

"Yes..." She thought for a moment. "Let's call it 'Night of the Long Knives.'"

CHAPTER TEN

QBBS _Meredith Reynolds_

Lance nodded to the two guards outside the small meeting room. One opened the door for him, allowing Lance to sip his coffee as he stepped through.

Thank God they had brought all the seeds they needed for the required delights from Earth, or he might have wished for a much shorter life.

"Bartholomew." Lance nodded to his compatriot. Barnabas and Stephen were already sitting at the table discussing something.

"You doing all right?" Admiral Thomas asked, handing Lance a breakfast pastry. "This one was made out of a fruit from Yoll."

Lance took a bite. "Shit!" he mumbled as the pastry made a mess all over his shirt. "Dammit!" He looked down and handed his coffee cup to Admiral Thomas, who chuckled, then grabbed a napkin and started wiping the shirt. "Wow," he mused as the fruit came off, "this fruit doesn't stick to it." He turned to toss the napkin away. "Thank the Lord. Patricia would have strung me up for messing up my new shirt."

The Admiral handed the coffee back to Lance. "I think your

wife just knows you." The two walked over to the table. "That fruit is a serious stain-monster on normal clothing, so," he nodded to the shirt, "she must have had that shirt made out of some sort of special cloth."

Lance looked down to where the fruit had formerly resided on his shirt and grunted. "Good stuff."

The two men took a seat. "Barnabas, Stephen." Lance nodded and took another sip of his coffee. "How are things?"

"Ready to go out with Tabitha and Peter in the next twenty-four to forty-eight hours," Stephen replied.

"Any ideas where?" Lance asked.

"Sure. We will swing by a couple of Nathan's suggestions, one of Tabitha's, and then the planet Devon."

"Devon?" Admiral Thomas pursed his lips. "Where is that, and why would you look there?"

"It's out of our boundaries, and I know of a contact she might speak to over there. I've tried calling him, but his answers are just a touch vague—which seems fishy to me."

Lance put his coffee down and picked up his tablet, turning to the notes for this meeting before asking, "Why not go sooner?"

"I'm not sure if there really is a problem or if I'm butting up against an HR issue."

"HR?" Barnabas asked.

"Something Baba Yaga told him a while back. Essentially her whole HR book is condensed into one rule."

"I'm almost afraid to ask, but what is it?" Lance asked.

"Don't piss her off," Stephen replied. "I can't tell you more than that, but it is a fine example of simplicity."

"How about those gray areas when you don't know if what you are doing is going to piss her off?" Admiral Thomas asked.

"Then they call me," Stephen admitted, to the chuckles of those at the table.

Admiral Thomas leaned forward. "So even though you call the main contact, your questions related to her whereabouts—if she is sharing that—are going to be deflected because she knows you might call?"

"Yes," Stephen answered.

Admiral Thomas's eyes sparkled. "Fucking brilliant. One rule to worry about, and she offloaded the annoying questions to you."

Stephen shrugged. "I think maybe she should have offloaded more to me in the last hundred years."

"I thought she had," Barnabas told him, looking around the table. "I don't know what else we should have taken from her shoulders, but I really did think we had the load."

"I'm not sure," Lance replied, "that we knew what to look for. It's obvious in hindsight, but most situations like this are."

"The Karillians," Admiral Thomas offered. "Her getting into the middle of the battle was a big-ass sign that she wasn't doing what she wanted to be doing."

"Baba Yaga," Stephen put out for the group. "That was just a modification of Karillia so she could continue to get out and mix it up."

"Her people were dying, and she had to stay out of the action." Lance sighed. "It hits every leader at some point. He nodded at Admiral Thomas. "Some of us, at least, have the training to know what to watch for in ourselves. When I feel too much stress, I reach out to Bartholomew here to vent, or Patricia."

"Same," Admiral Thomas admitted, "except not Patricia." He smiled. "I have another confidant."

Barnabas raised an eyebrow, and Admiral Thomas pointed a finger at him. "Stay out of my secrets, old man."

Barnabas smiled as the door opened behind Lance. "I have so far, but now I have an itch. I won't read your mind, but you have provided me with a puzzle."

"What's a puzzle?" Frank asked as the door shut behind him. "I love a good puzzle."

"Admiral Thomas has a significant other he isn't sharing,"

Lance told Frank as the man walked behind him to take a chair between him and Stephen.

"Oh, that." Frank sat down. "Old news."

Both Admiral Thomas and Barnabas narrowed their eyes as Frank smiled. "What? I'm not giving away my sources."

"And that is why you are the Info-master." Admiral Thomas pursed his lips. "Can I ask how you know?"

"Sure," Frank agreed. "But I'll have to ask you to keep it to yourself."

Admiral Thomas thought about it for a moment. "Okay."

"Barb is a hopeless romantic and has schemes upon schemes to hook people up. She sent the lady your way."

"Well." He stopped talking, then shrugged his shoulders and finished, "Sometime I'll have to thank her, and you, for keeping that to yourselves."

"Barb likes the hunt. She doesn't share the knowledge just because she can."

"Good woman," the Admiral replied. "Rare, but really good."

"No comment," Stephen threw in. "I'm still dealing with mine."

Lance looked at Stephen. "Does Jennifer have any suggestions about finding Bethany Anne?"

"Only that a woman will only be found when she wants to be, or at least that's true for Bethany Anne. The challenge is, are we looking for Bethany Anne or Baba Yaga?"

"It does all tend to come back to that," Frank agreed.

"What do we need to do now, and what do we need to do for the potential new Federation, Lance?" Admiral Thomas asked.

Lance played with his coffee cup, twirling it around with his fingers. "Well, when we get Bethany Anne back, we need to ask her to go on vacation."

Stephen coughed into his hand. "Not really sure that will be a problem."

"The 'getting her back without causing an interstellar situation' part would be nice," Barnabas stated firmly. "Remember, as Baba Yaga, she is a representative of the Empress, who isn't here right now to help with anyone who might be pissed off by the Witch running all over their civil rights to track down and kill the Kurtherians."

"They need a heavy dose of killing," Stephen replied, "so from that perspective, I completely agree with her efforts."

Lance snorted. "Yes, and those efforts are part of what keeps the Federation talks so exciting."

"Which is a euphemism for?" Frank asked.

"A royal pain in the ass, with a side of 'a kick to the nuts,'" Lance replied.

"They don't want her in the Federation, and she doesn't want to be Empress." Frank shrugged. "I'm not seeing the problem."

"There isn't a problem with *that*," Lance stated. "And they will pay a very pretty penny for giving Bethany Anne exactly what she wants. The big issue is what they want from the Etheric Empire to help create the Etheric Federation."

Frank looked at his friend. "Which is?"

"They want us reduced significantly—our technological advantage minimized, and our military neutered enough to be fair to the rest."

Barnabas blew out a breath. "Some will want us to be weaker than that if they can get it."

"Of course, and that is where I hit them over the head with the Empress Bethany Anne stick. There is no fucking way they would ask this of her, so they don't want her at the sessions."

"Why? Do they think you are weak?" Stephen asked.

"They see me as Bethany Anne's yes-man, or at least as one who won't randomly kill someone for disrespecting her during negotiations. Hell," he grumped, "Addix told me in no uncertain terms that compared to Bethany Anne, they consider me a baby at the table."

"Seems like you should have Bethany Anne show up at least once," Frank commented. "What are the plans?"

"That wouldn't be a bad idea," Lance admitted. "If she comes back to us in a decent-enough mindset, I'll see if she would be willing to show up at least once."

Planet Devon, QBS _Shinigami_

Baba Yaga walked toward the armory from the laundry area on the ship. "Who knew that stuff was so expensive?" she grumbled.

ADAM's voice came through the speakers as she walked the ship. "We were trying to protect your head."

She reached up to the back of her skull. It had healed, but the sympathetic pain was still there. "I can't believe I did that. What a flaming rookie mistake." She took a couple more steps before adding, "No, a rookie wouldn't have made that mistake. I'm an arrogant…"

She stopped in the middle of the hallway.

"What is it?" ADAM asked.

"Nothing." She resumed walking. "I've got to armor up."

"It won't be a fair fight," ADAM commented.

"Who said I wanted fair?" she retorted, then turned a corner toward the doors on the right, which swished open for her. "I just want it done."

"Then why not just hire it out?" ADAM asked.

"That would be impersonal," she replied, looking over the weapons on display and wondering which setup would be best. "I don't want to just be a judge. We have proof of their law-breaking, and they have committed crimes heinous enough to deserve capital punishment." She tapped a finger on her lips as she looked around. "And I have to be the executioner on my planet, as well."

The fixtures looked like they could have belonged in any well-designed kitchen: upper and lower cabinets, a countertop made out of an almost impervious material, and lighting under the upper cabinets.

All done in blacks and grays with dark-green countertops.

She reached into the second of the lower cabinets on that wall and pulled out a pair of M1911As. "Haven't felt these in my palms in a while."

She set them on the countertop and opened an upper cabinet, selecting two 50-round boxes of ammunition. "Damn, so few rounds in one of these. I'm spoiled." She laid the boxes beside the guns and started opening upper cabinets until, in the third one, she found some holsters that would work for the old pistols.

She laid them on the countertop too.

"Hmmm." She looked around the room. The cabinets lined two-thirds of the walls, not including the bulkhead with the door, and a large island had been built in the center for additional workspace.

The room was rather a large portion of the ship.

She walked over to the middle set of cabinets on the back wall and opened the top ones.

What she was looking for wasn't inside.

Squatting, she opened the bottom cabinet and whistled. She grabbed the lip of a lower drawer and pulled it out. Sliding on frictionless bearings, a display rack of swords came into view.

"Eenie, meenie, miny, moe." She reached out and grabbed a wakizashi. "You will be my friend tonight." She stood and put it on the island.

"That will require cleaning," ADAM stated.

"Where's the problem with that?" she asked. "I've cleaned my swords hundreds of times."

"You just griped about tossing a cloak into a self-cleaning and drying laundry machine to get the blood out of it. All you had to do was close the door."

"I also had to push a button," she retorted. "Might have chipped a fingernail."

If an AI could be exasperated, ADAM was. "You can't chip a fingernail by *pushing* a *button!*" There was a pause before his next calculation was complete. "Without intent, anyway."

"Uh-huh," she agreed absently as she looked for a sheath. She pulled one off a bottom shelf and went to the island as she sheathed the sword, then setting it reverently on the countertop. She stopped to look at the sword before walking over to the pistols and ammo boxes.

She pursed her lips, then headed to the drawers that held her Jean Dukes, pulling them and their holsters out. "Let's not be stupid," she murmured as she put them on the counter. "Well, twice."

Ten minutes later, she had her armor and helmet on. ADAM might have made a point about the futility of someone going up against her, but she was not going to find out the painful way that they *did* have something that could blow her damned fool head off.

The Kurtherians, TOM would say, were too important for this shit.

She, however, felt a need to have a place close enough to the Empire that she could get in, but still far enough away that the law was handled on the planet.

One day she might want to come here and stay awhile. Even people on the fringes of society needed a place to call home.

People like her.

She walked toward one of the aft doors, leaving her cloak behind. She was clad in the dark-red armor that looked almost black.

Her helmet was full-face and painted to look like her, including fake hair coming out of the top. She would be able to breathe the atmosphere from inside her suit just fine.

She had, however, kept her gloves on, which gave her protection but left her fingertips free.

"Open the hatch," she called to Shinigami.

She peered through the doorway, which was some six feet wide, down into the darkness of the city. "Drop us down about even with the tall skyscraper over there to the left," she commanded as the ship came out of the clouds. "It's really pretty from up here. I think I might go for a swim."

She turned back to face the inside of the ship and spread her arms wide. Leaning back, she slowly fell out of the ship and sliced through the night toward a building below.

Two hundred feet above the building, the antigrav kicked in and slowed her down tremendously, enough that she barely bent her legs when she hit the roof with the four pistols on her body. The M1911As were in holsters under her arms, the Jean Dukes rode her hips, and the sword's hilt peeked over her shoulder.

She walked toward the roof's edge. Below were plenty of aliens carousing throughout the night, then going back inside when they needed a higher oxygen content. For some of the aliens, the air was breathable as it was.

"Where is our first contestant, ADAM?"

>> **YukLeet. His main place is a bar. Two blocks over to your left.** <<

Baba Yaga looked down the street. "The orange-ish sign or the green one?"

>>**Green.**<<

Baba Yaga took two running steps before leaping through the night, the antigrav reducing her weight so that she crossed the darkness above the lights some stories below to land on the roof of the building housing the bar.

Walking back to the edge of this roof, she looked down. "From the roof or from the front?" she murmured. "Roof or front?"

There was a break in the crowd. "Front," she decided, and

took a step off the roof. The three stories to the concrete went quickly. She didn't cut much antigrav in, so she slammed into the street, and chips of stone went flying as her armored boots hit the surface.

The thirty or so aliens who were nearby turned to see the new alien in dark armor raise her white-haired head and turn toward YukLeet's bar. She started walking toward the front door some ten steps away.

The bouncer was a fish-like alien whose head reminded Baba Yaga of a hammerhead shark's, although he had two arms and two legs. "Why is everything bipedal?" she wondered to no one in particular.

At almost nine feet tall, he towered over her. "Stop!" He put up a hand and turned toward her. "Were you invited?"

Baba Yaga shook her head. "No."

"Do you know anyone in here?"

"Personally?" she verified. "No."

He made a movement with his body she assumed was negative. "Then you do not have permission to open the door."

Looking him up and down, she asked, "Well, do *you* have permission to open the door?"

CHAPTER ELEVEN

QBBS *Meredith Reynolds*, NS Squared

Tabitha walked through the back hallways, the ones which usually had few others in them. They placed her just about a thirty-second walk from her favorite bar and eatery.

The Never Submit, Never Surrender.

It was now owned and run by the Joneses. The previous couple, Pearl and J.D., had passed away about fifty years ago. The present owners were a pair of Weres whom Pearl had liked. They had taken over in her absence, and everything went forward.

She even heard the same bitching from time to time.

Tabitha entered and looked around the dimly lit space. With Weres as owners, they kept the illumination down so that those with light sensitivity could be comfortable in their place.

Hell, she noticed that since her last visit, they had opened another side of the place.

They were growing.

She walked straight down the side, like she had hundreds of times before, to the last booth on the left.

The man sipping his beer there was wearing jeans and a shirt that was comfortable but about as fashionable as dirty motor oil.

"Move your Pricolici lard-ass over," she told him, sitting down and pushing him sideways with her own. "Big badonkadonk, no?" She stopped as he turned in her direction. "*Prime* badonkadonk moving in."

Peter blinked a second before conceding the space and allowing Tabitha to sit next to him. "And why," he asked, tipping his bottle toward the other side of the booth, "can't you sit your phat ass on that bench?"

"*Fat* ass?" She turned to get a better angle to punch him from. "*Fat ass?*"

"I said p-h-a-t," he replied. "I didn't think you were deaf."

"I'm not, you jerk!" She huffed. "The only reason I haven't given you the beatdown you deserve is that I am in shock!"

"Wait!" Peter put up a hand. "How are *you* spelling phat?"

"You have some *cojones*, even for a mental midget who grows into a big hairy mental midget. I spell it f-a-t."

"I'm spelling it p-h-a-t," he replied, "so it was a miscommunication, Ranger Two. Stop spraining your ankle jumping to a conclusion."

Her eyes flitted left and right for a second while Peter took a sip of his drink. He allowed her a moment to look up the definition. "That word went out of use over two hundred years ago! *Decades* before we left."

"Yeah, well, what did it mean originally?" Peter asked, eyeing her.

"Pretty hot and tempting," she conceded. "So while you committed a major faux pas by using it, it was technically an accurate description of my badonkadonk."

"Which, I might point out, is older than two hundred years," he replied.

She eyed him. "My badonkadonk's age is not in question, Mr. Peter."

"I wasn't talking about your ass, Tabitha," Peter responded, wondering how the hell he had gotten into this conversation with her. "I was saying the *word* was over two hundred years old."

She looked at him. "Oh." She slid out, stepped to the other side of the booth, and slid in. She waved to the barman, making a V with her fingers, and then pointed at her and Peter.

A few moments later, the barman brought over two more beers and took the one Peter had just finished in a rush.

"Thank you." He nodded to her and took a sip of the fresh bottle. "I'll accept beers all night long, so don't think I'm embarrassed to drink on your tab."

"I'm just trying to wear you down," she informed him. A moment later, they both snorted.

Neither was going to get drunk anytime soon.

"For what?" he asked. "We're leaving…what, tomorrow?"

"I think so. It's up to Barnabas."

Peter gave a noncommittal shrug.

"So tell me about it," she urged. "I came here to find you so you could talk it out."

"I'm not really all that much into talking about Todd right now."

"Fucker." She looked at him. "You ever think maybe I need to talk about my losses?"

His eyes narrowed. "No," he admitted. "I figure you have enough friends in the Tontos. Hell, Barnabas can read your mind and help you."

She slid her bottle left, then right on the table. "Maybe he can, or maybe he is so old and has lived through so many lifetimes, he doesn't remember what emotion is." She took a drink and set down her bottle before looking Peter in the eyes. "Don't get me wrong. I love him to death, but occasionally he is too old, wise, and stubborn to understand me."

Peter thought about it. "Thinks you are still a young girl?"

"Fuck, I *am* still a young girl, you jerkweed!" she exclaimed.

She tried to kick his leg under the table but was only successful in kicking the steel plate mounted under the seat.

Tabitha had kicked out the wood so many times in years past that the owners had applied steel plates to all the booths in the bar.

Her face scrunched in pain, and she squelched a yell. "Oh, sweet mother frankfurter! You dick, you moved your leg!"

"And?" Peter smiled, his eyebrows raised. "What was I supposed to do?"

"Cushion my foot," she replied, bending her toes up and down as her healing finally minimized the pain.

"Yeah, I don't think so." Peter shook his head. "Sorry, too many decades fighting to worry about your foot when I sense something coming at me."

She reached down to make sure her toes were all straight before placing her foot back on the floor. "Good reflexes," she admitted. "Now, back to my favorite subject."

"You?" Peter asked, a smile on his face.

"See?" She pointed to him. "You get me."

"I see a woman who is masking her pain behind a façade," Peter replied, understanding a bit more of what made this woman tick.

"Don't psychoanalyze me unless you have something meaty to go along with it," she retorted.

He raised an eyebrow.

Her face started to turn red, and she rolled her eyes. "I walked into that one."

"I imagine you slide into them all the time."

"I'm usually better at verbal sparring," Tabitha contended.

"Why did you come here?" Peter asked, his grin from a moment before fading. "Did you come here to talk about Todd?"

"Yes...and no," Tabitha admitted. "Look, my first loss still hurts. I know you have lost people before, but Todd was your best friend." She looked down at her beer as Peter studied her face. She looked up after a couple of moments, leaning to her left to look down the walkway past the booths before drawing back in. "Sorry, just making sure no one was there."

"Because?" Peter asked.

"Because living after death sucks," Tabitha answered. "I'm fucking fortunate that none of the other Tontos died."

"Or you," Peter added.

"Fuck *me*." She sighed, flicking her eyes up to see Peter's reaction, but he was studying her face. She leaned against the booth's back. "I occasionally cry myself to sleep thinking about him."

"Were you close?" Peter asked, his voice low.

She ran a hand through her hair and pulled it back out of her face. "Not physically, but I loved all my Tontos." She looked to his eyes. "We always took it to the man, you know? We got out of everything together. No matter what, none of us got hurt bad until…"

"Todd," Peter replied softly. When Tabitha looked up, he was staring into his beer. "The other deaths hurt, but they weren't Todd. He and I have clowned around since Earth. He and I ran the teams. I had the Guardians, he had the Marines, and we were going to run them until we both grew old and passed away."

There were a few moments of silence in the booth, the clinking of glasses a distant note to let them know they were still part of humanity.

"Then?" she asked him, her voice soft and caressing.

"Then the bastard went and jumped on a *Gott Verdammt* grenade that should have killed me, not him," Peter admitted, a tear in his eye and one tracking down his face.

Tabitha slid out of her seat and stepped to his side, sitting down next to him. She didn't have to tell him to move over. He'd already slid toward the wall.

She reached over with her left hand and pulled his head down to rest on her shoulder, her right hand hiding his eyes as she played with his hair.

His shoulders started shaking, releasing the pain a little at a time.

This pain, she had learned, didn't go away with one cry, or two, or even ten. It was like a raging river in the beginning, and you had to constantly release the pressure the dam was holding.

In time the river subsided and you had a gentle stream, but time still caused the emotions to back up higher and higher until the dam had to release the emotions someway, somehow occasionally.

Finally, the emotional pain became a very small creek that might take only a random tear to release.

But it never went away.

Tabitha let Peter release his pain. She just held him quietly and absently stroked his hair, sharing a tear with him for Todd and what he had meant to Peter, and for her own memory of him.

Shared pain was lessened.

Sometime later, their beers warm, their hearts spent and vulnerable, Peter broke the silence.

"I don't think I have anything left for tears," Peter mumbled into her arm, "but I'm willing to stay here."

She looked down at his head, realizing she had tucked it right into her breast.

She bit her lip. *Lord, this is a bad idea!* she thought to herself as she slid a bit out of the booth and reached over to grab his hand and pull him out.

He slid with her, a question on his face. There was no one in the place at the moment, for which she was grateful.

"What happens tonight," she told him, "stays with tonight."

She pulled him toward the door, a smile starting to play on her lips as she stiff-armed through it and pulled him out of NS Squared.

Peter chuckled. "Depends on if I impress you enough!" He followed behind her.

They arrived at the opening of her little back-alley path, and she turned around with a smile on her face. Before Peter knew what was going on, she had grabbed his waist and thrown him over her shoulder. She started running down the hallway.

"*HEY!*" he shouted in surprise.

Both cracked up in an emotional release, then she heard him say something about a well-matched pair as he grabbed her ass and squeezed.

She let out a squeal and yelled over her shoulder, "You'd better have the stamina of an ox!"

"Pricolici!" he yelled back, laughing because the shorter woman was challenged by carrying his taller body.

Tabitha's eyes shot open when he bit her badonkadonk.

Unnamed Mercenary Planet

The Leath female looked across the table at the Guild Master. The bar they were sitting in was a part of Guild Headquarters, so security was high.

"I would think your people would want a chance to kill the Witch," she snarked.

"You would think your people would know how to do it!" the Guild Master shot back. "The Empress doesn't quit, but she obviously doesn't give a shit about continuing to attack us if we stop attacking her."

The robed Leath stopped and paid attention to the Guild Master, boring into his mind for a moment.

"Do we have a problem?" the Guild Master asked, shaking his head to clear it.

"What if one of our own leads the attack?" the Leath representative asked. "We supply the money and the guns. There is already a significant price on the head of the Witch for whoever can capture or kill her."

"Kill," the Guild Master replied. "There will be no capturing that one."

"We will pay three times the dead bounty, but that is up to your people."

The Guild Master considered the stories. "Two groups. You will need to double the bounty for bringing her back dead, which means six times the value for bringing her back alive, *and* your person has to lead."

Levelot, the First of the Seven, reached across the table to palm the agreement on the Guild Master's tablet.

"Done," she stated.

Planet Devon, inside the Bar of YukLeet

YukLeet was sitting at the bar, enjoying a small alcoholic drink. Nothing that would mess him up, but enough so he was being sociable in his own bar.

No matter if one was a despot or a dictator, one must still play nice with one's closest followers.

And pretty much anyone who was in his bar was, de facto, either a follower or a potential ally.

He was just about to take another sip of the expensive drink when the front door to the bar area exploded, wood shrapnel showering those inside with splinters. Many threw themselves away from the door and the body that crashed through three of his gambling tables.

YukLeet was about to yell for his bouncer when he recognized that the ramrod which had splintered his bar's front door *was* his bouncer.

"Shit!" he grunted and looked back at the door. A black alien with white hair walked through the now-very-open entrance as two weapons fired at her from the bar.

The alien barely moved when a kinetic round hit her in the side.

That fucking alien was wearing armor!

She pulled two pistols from under her arms and aimed them straight at YukLeet's head. His eyes grew large, and he was about to throw himself on the floor when his brains splattered against the bar's mirror.

Three more times, weapons were fired at the alien. "Keep that shit up," the alien warned as she walked into the room, "and I'll fuck up your evening so bad the grandchildren of your *neighbors* will feel it."

The shooting stopped.

Everyone in the place who hadn't run screaming watched as her feet crunched over busted-up furniture to reach YukLeet's body. Bending down, she grabbed his shoulder and lifted his body to check his head damage. "Yup, terminated."

She released the dead body, which slumped to the floor, and walked back to the door. The bouncer was shaking his head to clear it as she walked past him.

"The next time the Mistress of the Planet wishes to enter a place, you say *yes!*" she hissed.

She stopped at the door and looked back at the patrons in the room. "This is the penalty for thinking that politics is where you go to make yourself rich and powerful. This city—this planet, in fact—is being cleaned up. If any of you want to have a similar visit from me," she pointed at YukLeet's dead body, "just continue doing what he did." She turned and walked out into the night.

Six more times, Baba Yaga found her targets. Six more times she killed with extreme prejudice. If there were any who supported the target, she warned them once before she killed them as well.

She was trying to keep this civil, or at least she thought she was.

"How the hell," Baba Yaga whispered from a building across the street from the final target, "am I supposed to get into that fortress?"

"How about knocking?" ADAM asked over her suit's headphones. "It worked so well at the bar."

Baba Yaga snorted. "I'm fresh out of bouncers to throw through the door," she answered, studying the solid stone building. "I'd really hate to pop into the Etheric and come out in a strange building where I could get a faceful of stone."

"Do you have any options?" ADAM asked.

"None that I can see," she answered as she looked up and down the street. "We could try to draw him out and hit him when the outer gates open."

"I have hacked his inside video. There are at least fifty additional personnel inside, of which approximately twenty-two are guards. The rest look like staff and perhaps family," ADAM countered.

"Fucking family," she hissed. "I *hate* getting family involved. Why do these pricks always have families?"

"Because procreation is a natural desire for aliens of all species?" the AI answered.

Bethany Anne sighed and looked up into the darkness. "Shinigami, release a three-pound puck to take out the front door."

"Done," the ship's EI answered. "When do you wish it to arrive?"

Baba Yaga put up her M1911As and locked them into their holsters, then pulled out her Jean Dukes. After popping her neck, she walked toward the main building some seventy-five yards away.

"Now would be good," she told the EI, and two seconds later, a massive concussion blew out the front gates of the fortress.

Baba Yaga went to sonar to see what was going on behind the

smoke and dust that was billowing out of the compound. There were three bodies lying in an open area behind the doors.

One of them was small. Baba Yaga's eyes narrowed as she strode through the street, somewhat covered in dust herself.

That was when her helmet HUD showed a rocket heading toward her.

CHAPTER TWELVE

QBBS *Meredith Reynolds*

Stephen walked into his personal sanctuary. In his quarters, he had three rooms besides the master bedroom: a living room, a long dining room for larger parties, and his kitchen.

There was also a door that opened into a dark thirty-foot-long hallway. The walls were rough, but the floor was as smooth as polished glass.

Jennifer had taken one look at him and given him a hug. "I've no idea what to do for my liege," he told her, his voice softly stirring her hair.

She held him for a few moments. "Tell her what you are thinking," she replied. "Bethany Anne is in there somewhere. Speak to *her*, not Baba Yaga."

He held the embrace for a few more minutes before kissing her forehead and stepping away, walking through his personal hallway to his sanctum in quiet contemplation.

Over the years, Jennifer had finally realized that her man needed to feel isolated. It had been such a huge component of his life before Bethany Anne came that subconsciously he still sought it out in trying times.

So one year, Jennifer had made a request of the Empress, explaining what she thought Stephen needed and why.

Three days later, Stephen had been sent on a mission to the planet Yoll for two weeks to support Kael-ven, and Jennifer had been told to pack up. She needed to step out while the additions to their home were made.

When Stephen came back, Jennifer had placed flower petals on the floor to lead him to the new door, through the hallway beyond, and into the room behind the metal door at the end.

The petals stopped at the door. Inside, where Stephen had expected to find her, he instead found a note which read:

There are men who know war, and there are men who know peace. There are men who know that peace sometimes comes through war but need a place to gather themselves in times of crisis. This is your sanctum. I will keep it for you, and know that every time you come out, I will be waiting for you.

Each time he came out, she was either in the house, or she had lit a candle in the living room and left a love note with information as to where she was.

Either physically or emotionally, she was always waiting for him.

This time she had sent him to his sanctum to ponder his heart.

And his next steps.

Inside his room was a table that had space for two chairs. The top was glass, which he used as a large tablet to gather information when he wanted access to the computers or the EIs or AIs in the system.

Sometimes the glass remained dark and Stephen would work on art, typically the calligraphy he had practiced centuries before.

The first time he had created a love letter to Jennifer, she'd ruined it with her tears as she sat on the couch.

Even now the tear-stained parchment hung, framed, in their washroom.

He considered what he might say to the woman to whom he owed everything.

He smiled as he remembered telling Gabrielle of the woman for the first time: Bethany Anne, who had boxed his ears and called him a fucking moron.

He had never once regretted giving his allegiance to the young woman. He wondered how he could have failed her so completely.

He sighed and walked to a wooden dresser as tall as he and about a foot deep. It had twelve drawers with different parchment types on the bottom, and eighteen drawers for inks from plants all over the system.

Then there were another twelve drawers of pens and nibs.

He had purchased fourteen through the decades from three humans who had brought them through the Gate from Earth.

He pulled out the drawer on the top right and lifted a dark onyx pen. Closing that drawer, he went down three rows and left two columns to find his nibs and grabbed two of those.

Down one row and another two columns to the left, he pulled out ink. Finally, three rows down, he opened a drawer which held parchment, but it wasn't quite right. Closing that drawer, he opened the one to the right and selected five pieces before he closed it and walked to his table.

After setting up his pen, he opened the ink and laid down a plate and sponge.

"Meredith, would you drop the lights to twenty percent?"

"Certainly, Stephen," she replied, and the hidden lights in the ceiling decreased their intensity.

He dipped his instrument and started to write.

My dearest Queen, my dearest friend,

It is with a heavy heart that I seek to understand how I have failed you in this moment of your greatest need.

Time is a two-edged sword for those of us who live long. It can help us gain perspective, provides options to attain great wealth, and allows us to see generational projects through to their completion.

Then it slices us open to bleed our patience dry, overwhelming our capabilities to provide protection and safety to those closest and dearest without simultaneously dissolving compassion.

We are left with the raw desire to accomplish the final solution, believing the end always justifies the means.

And the person who started with good intentions is now the personi- fication of the punishment they seek to deliver, without the kindness which initially tempered their judgments and their actions.

Leaving in the end the essence of what you believed you must do, and never allowing yourself to come back.

The means become your only solution, and that is your new identity.

Whether you choose to return to us, my Queen or stay as the avatar, know that I am, and will always be, your man to command and direct.

He signed it with the swirls and marks as he had used five hundred years in the past.

Stephen Nacht, brother to Michael, honor bound to Bethany Anne Nacht.

"Meredith?" He spoke softly in the dim room.

"Yes?"

"Please make a digital copy of this document and send it to TOM and ADAM. Have them read it and choose when it would be best to deliver it to my Queen."

"I will, Stephen," she replied.

He sat there rereading his note, but eventually he sighed, cleaned up his calligraphy equipment, and placed it all back in its proper places.

He looked from the simple bed in the corner to the bookcase with a few treasured books he had been able to acquire over the years and chewed his lip. "Lights off, Meredith," he requested aloud as he opened the heavy metal door. The lights in his room dimmed, but the lights along the hall floor glowed enough to show him the way.

This time when he left his sanctum, he found both the lit candle and Jennifer resting on the couch next to it.

She was her own letter, letting him know whose heart she cherished.

He walked into their bedroom and pulled the sheets down on their bed before returning to the living room.

He had never deserved her, but he always used his pitiful efforts to show his appreciation. He knelt next to her, sliding his arms under her body and picking her up slowly.

He carried her gently through the living room and moved quietly to their bed, where he laid her tenderly down on her side.

Bending over, he kissed her once again on the forehead and reached up to move the hair off her face, then pulled the sheets up to her shoulders.

She was a little warm-natured, but still preferred the soft weight of the sheet as she slept.

Moments later, the home's lights went down, and he slid in from the other side.

She rolled over and snuggled up, placing her head on his chest.

Stephen, however, couldn't sleep. He wondered where his liege was, and if Bethany Anne would come back to them.

Or would she have done something so heinous that she couldn't live with herself?

Planet Devon

The lights around the buildings made it easy to see. The available darkness made the chemical fire of the missile erupting out of the back *very* easy to see as well.

>>**Running and dodging would be a good tactic right now.** <<

No sooner had ADAM suggested she run than she stepped through the Etheric and appeared near the busted front door.

It taxed her energy to do that, but it was a quick way to dodge the missile.

It showed up in her HUD. It had lost lock on the target and flown up into the air.

She moved quickly into the fortress.

Two of the dead bodies were adult mercenaries, and the smaller body was a short alien mercenary.

So, thankfully not a child!

She strode through the opening, her eyes flicking to the missile tracking in her HUD, which still seemed to be unaware of her new location.

She pulled both Jean Dukes, her eyes flicking from location to location as she looked around the area. The sensors pointed out that a massive number of bodies were coming at her from inside the main building. The outside walls were forty feet from the rectangular edifice.

She turned to her right and started running, working her way around the corner. The building was longer on this side, so hopefully she would be able to come back around and attack them from the rear once she had circled it.

After she turned the corner, a round ricocheted off the wall ahead of her. She looked up at a Noel-ni who was trying to lead her as she ran. She raised an arm and shot him off the wall.

His body disappeared.

The sensors showed something large producing vibrations at the back of the building.

Rear protection?

"Ahead or go back, ahead or go back," she was murmuring when a five-foot-wide head peeked around the corner and opened its mouth, tongue slithering in and out.

"*THE FUCK!*" she screamed and dodged to the right. "*WEIGHT!*" she yelled as she leapt up and kicked off the wall to her right.

She soared higher and angled up over the top of the fortress.

When she looked down, three more Noel-ni were locking down a substantially larger gun than she had seen before on the roof. "Who the fuck *are* these guys?" she hissed as she aimed her pistols. "It's not like a spaceship is here to blow the hell out of them."

>>**Well, technically one did**.<< ADAM replied.

"Move the *Shinigami* away." She shot twice, hitting two of the Noel-ni. One head exploded, and the other had his shoulder splattered all over the place. Unfortunately, she realized the large snake-looking creature was starting to track her apogee. She aimed her Jean Dukes and squeezed the triggers as fast as she dared.

Inside her helmet, her eyes opened wider. "Oh, damn," she mused. "Scales that work like armor. Fucking hell!"

You could always just let it eat you and kill it from the inside.

Are you fucking with me?

Why would I do that? Also, you might notice that the missile has locked onto you again.

Baba Yaga's eyes flicked to her HUD as a red dot streaked toward her position.

When it rains, it fucking pours. She grunted and, pointing both guns, shot the hell out of the head of the snake-thing, trying to mess up its eyes.

As it dropped past the building, the snake creature's body thrashed violently, banging against both the walls and the building, rocks and windows exploding as the armored creature reacted to the shots from the Jean Dukes.

She dropped to the ground and turned toward the snake. Holstering both weapons, she ran toward the body.

NOW! TOM yelled in her mind as she reached the snake.

She disappeared into the Etheric, running a few steps before leaping out again.

>>**TOO SOON!**<< ADAM warned.

But it was too late.

She was caught in the secondary explosion of the missile somewhere behind her. A large chunk of snake body slammed into her, driving her into the hard-packed ground. Her head banged inside her helmet before her body bounced into the air once more. She twisted her body to pull her feet underneath her while meat and rock chunks rained down on her. She started running back in the direction from which she had originally come.

She streaked around the corner and rolled her eyes as she palmed her Jean Dukes once again.

She had run smack-dab into the muscle she had been trying to sneak up on.

Straight into the group that had ducked due to the massive explosion a moment before.

Half of them were covering their heads with their arms.

She blew through them, shooting as fast as she could. "WEIGHT!" she yelled and kicked off the ground, twisting as she soared into the air and raining death on those on the ground underneath her. As she crested the roofline, her left arm aimed, and a half-second later, she took out the third Noel-ni she had seen in her previous leap into the night.

As she completed her twist ADAM upped her weight, so she dropped rapidly back down.

Her arc landed her on the narrow upper walkway of the wall, and she kicked back off and bent her knees to land and roll before running forward through the front door into the main building.

Seven dead guards later, she found the asshole she was looking for and terminated him with extreme prejudice.

Using the .45s.

Baba Yaga, her armor splattered with dust-encrusted gore, considered where she was on the third floor and locked down her .45s in their holsters before pulling her Jean Dukes and turned them both to eleven. Aiming them at a forty-five-degree angle, she started firing at the rock ceiling above her, blowing fragments away until a five-foot chunk of ceiling broke free and smashed to the floor.

She heard a scream from below.

Taking a few steps, she pushed off hard and sailed through the hole to land on the roof. "Bring the *Shinigami* down so I can see it."

Once she saw the ship, she took a step and disappeared.

CHAPTER THIRTEEN

Planet Devon, Mid-Morning

"I'm telling you it *will* exist on my planet," the black-skinned female vowed to herself. Her white hair was flying in the wind as she stepped outside of the main buildings to head for a rumored bar.

She was pissed.

>>**I have looked through all the data I can find, and nowhere have I located the correct invoices**.<<

"It's not all about invoicing, ADAM." She saw three bars. "TOM?"

Bar to the right, TOM replied.

"ADAM?" she called.

>>**Why don't *you* choose?**<< ADAM suggested.

"I'll take the middle one," she replied. "It seems like a bar with good taste."

>>**The Unholy Brocken? What is a 'brocken,' and why would you believe it has good taste?**<<

"What do you take me for?" she hissed, "an alien zoologist?" She looked at the sign again. "It looks like the kind of bar that doesn't want to make the mistake of upsetting the MOTIP."

Who? TOM asked.

Me, she replied.

How is "motip" you?

Mistress of the Planet. M-O-T-P, so add an "I" and you get MOTIP.

Why are we doing this? You have plenty of your beverage on *Shinigami*.

Because they need to learn, and after getting rid of that second group I deserve a break.

I believe it was ADAM who took care of the second group. You just had to stand on the stage and look scary.

How was I looking scary? I was wearing snake guts, for fuck's sake!

Mission accomplished, TOM replied.

You have any idea how bad they smelled? I don't think fish offal back on Earth was even close.

Some experiences need to be personal, TOM replied.

Wait a minute. She stopped in front of the bar TOM had chosen. "On Earth, you could smell the difference between vampires to figure out who was their parent. Why didn't you have problems with how I smelled back in the meeting to get those others off-planet?"

I disconnected from your olfactory sense.

Two large Shegalith stepped around the black alien who was speaking to the air. They looked like a cross between an old-Earth Sasquatch and a T-Rex.

If either had been nine feet tall.

While the arms were a bit stubby, the lower feet had opposable appendages and were long enough to grab items and place them in their short arms.

One looked over its shoulder at the crazy white-haired alien as she waved her arms in the air, still talking to nothing.

"YOU LITTLE SHIT!" she yelled in frustration. "You told me, and I quote, 'You aren't the only one suffering here, Baba Yaga!'"

And you weren't. I could easily tell about fifteen of the ones who were being sent off-planet were physically ill just from smelling you.

"I thought it was *you* who was sick!"

It seemed like TOM sniffed over their connection. **I can't be held responsible for your leap of illogic.**

"How was that a leap of illogic?" she asked, stopping. "Never mind," she told him, resuming her trek to the door. "I know what you are doing, and it won't work."

Baba Yaga ignored the feeling that ADAM and TOM were communicating inside her head.

Outside the Unholy Brocken, Forty-Five Minutes Later

Aert shambled up toward the bar's entrance. This was the third night in a row he had needed a break after work.

He reached up and scratched the little itch that was behind his carapace. At only five feet, six inches, he wasn't one of the larger Yollins in his group of friends, but he was one of the strongest.

He sighed. He shouldn't bitch too much, since he had a job and it paid fairly well. Tonight was a damn sight better than it had been just three weeks ago when he had lacked a job opportunity.

Since he wasn't into politics, he hadn't understood why he had been fired from his job. The rumor was that, as a Yollin, he was untrustworthy. The owner wasn't fond of the Empire. Now not only was he trustworthy, but he was being sought out explicitly because he had been fired.

Being born a Yollin was so damned weird.

His feet made a clunk-clunk-clunk noise on the street as he stepped to the entrance to the bar and shoved the door open.

He stopped in shock, his mandibles splayed wide as he stared at the view that met him inside.

The raspy voice issued from the red-eyed, black-faced, white-haired individual in the middle of the room. There were at least three tables broken that he could see as he looked around the sixty-foot by eighty-foot establishment.

Everyone except the vicious lady in the middle was either up against the wall or laid out on the floor.

She pointed her finger at Aert. "You!" He pointed his finger at himself. "Yes, you! Don't move." She turned her attention back to the ones standing against the wall.

Her voice was dark, sinister, and annoyed. "All I wanted..." she grated, her red eyes spearing each of the twelve, "in fact, all I *asked* for was a *Gott Verdammt* COKE!"

She lifted a drinking glass in her left hand, which Aert hadn't seen when he came in a moment before. "And you give the Mistress of the Planet *thisssssss?*"

"It's, uh..." The Torcellan barkeeper swallowed as the eyes came to rest on him. "It's, uh, Pehpseh."

"No!" She crushed the glass, and liquid dribbled from her hand. "It's a *Pepsi*," she corrected, voice dripping with annoyance. "It is the vilest of all the concoctions we humans brought to space, and when I want something refreshing after a night of cleaning up the trash, I don't want *Pepsi* in the fucking morning. I wanted a damned *COKE!*"

She looked down at the sticky liquid that was all over her hand disgustedly. Her head swiveled to the spectators. "I'm not done with this planet yet." She stepped over to a table and calmly picked up a cloth, and after wiping her gloved hand, she continued to consider those watching her carefully. "The next time I am in town, there had better be a drink worth a damn in this place or I won't be so patient, do you understand?"

Twelve heads nodded vigorously. One of the green aliens had liquid trickling down its leg.

She turned and walked toward Aert, whose Yollin eyes opened in alarm. However, she just held out the rag as she

127

approached. "Take this," she commanded, dropping it into his waiting hands as she walked past him and through the door.

No one moved for a few seconds, not sure yet if she was coming back or not.

When the door opened again a few seconds later, Aert, who was straightening his back, heard a high-pitched voice ask, "What the hell happened in here?"

The green alien against the wall moaned, rolled up its eyes, and dropped to the floor with a crash.

The voice behind him stated, "Okay, no one's talking. Fine." When the figure from whence the voice issued passed him, Aert saw what was basically a stick gliding along on four legs. "Can I get a Pehpseh?" it asked as it made its way to the bar.

Twelve voices plus Aert's yelled an answer.

"HELL, NO!"

QBBS *Meredith Reynolds*

Admiral Thomas used the stylus to scratch an itch behind his ear, then looked at Bobcat and William on the right side of the table and Marcus and Tina on the left before glancing back down at his tablet.

"That," he paused for a moment, "is a lot of fucking lasers, folks."

Bobcat opened his hands wide as Admiral Thomas looked at him. "Well, you have a planet that is twenty-four thousand miles around. Then," he opened his hands wider, "you have the first protection field at something like thirty-six thousand miles. That is just a spit away from the planet. Then," he opened his arms as wide as he could, "you have your secondary field at a hundred thousand miles. That is your main ship-perimeter protection field."

Bobcat looked at William. "Some help?" William snorted and held out his right arm on the opposite side of Bobcat, who turned back to the Admiral while keeping his left arm up and hand in place. "Then we need to get outside the moon's orbit at approximately two hundred and thirty-eight thousand miles, and outside of the gravitational pull of the moon and closer to the gravitational pull of the sun. If they were all equidistant, we would be placing the satellites at about 1.5 million kilometers."

Admiral Thomas whistled. "So, lots of area to cover in a sphere around the Earth?"

"And then some," Marcus confirmed as the other two guys dropped their arms. "We can mitigate some of the effort by building three smaller versions of the ESD laser on the moon, and then we have to build one on a floating platform on the other side of the Earth from the moon."

"Wouldn't want a laser to have to shoot through the moon to hit oncoming enemies," Admiral Thomas agreed. "So we need to figure out how to minimize the smaller weapons for production issues, and the larger ones?"

"How many devices do you want to place on a rock the size of the moon that might explode, ripping the moon apart?" Tina asked. "I imagine the gravity of the Earth would pull quite a few chunks down." She created an explosion with her hands. "Kiss the Earth goodbye."

Admiral Thomas rubbed his jaw. "Ships?"

"What about them?" Bobcat asked.

"I'm hearing a few disgusted noises from Lance and his team. Those who are willing to move to a Federation are hoping to strip us of our ships."

William asked incredulously, "Lance is okay with this?"

"Why would you think Lance would *ever* be okay with someone taking away our weapons?" Admiral Thomas replied. "Hell, he's Army, but even I give him *that* much credit."

"How would you man them for a thousand years?" Marcus asked.

Admiral Thomas shrugged. "EIs?"

"Not a good idea," Tina replied. "Have you checked up on Ricky Bobby's emotional progress lately?"

"Our fighter EI." He put up a hand. "Sorry, AI—that was spying on the Leath?" He shook his head. "No, I haven't."

"Yes, him." she agreed. "I've talked with Julianne, and he's pretty messed up from being in solitude like he was. Are we thinking of maybe providing EIs with top-of-the-line military ships right outside Earth's perimeter?"

"For thousands of years, maybe?" Bobcat added.

"We can always come back and replace them," Thomas suggested, considering the possibility.

"How about we don't plan on gates blowing up and shit? Not that I would ever say it could happen," Bobcat offered.

William cut in. "I'm thinking we can use the ships as mobile defense platforms, but we need something pretty damned awesome to run them."

"That won't go crazy," Tina added.

"Should we ever leave it alone for too long," Bobcat finished.

This time Admiral Thomas reached up with both hands and rubbed his face. "When you give me the insufficient with requirements making it improbable, you finally admit you think it is impossible to accomplish."

"Is that a Navy quote?" Tina asked.

Thomas grunted. "It's a Bethany Anne quote."

"What does she say next?" Tina asked curiously.

"She doesn't," Thomas admitted. "Dan Bosse will usually pick up the phone and start the conversation with, 'So and so, grab two bricks...'

Tina stared at him. "That wouldn't be my problem."

Thomas chuckled. "Yes, but these guys are flinching." He pointed to Marcus, William, and Bobcat.

She looked at her teammates and snickered. "Sorry, poor organic anatomical design. Sucks to be you, guys."

"Shows God was a female," Bobcat muttered, "and hated men.

Practiced on our design first, then looked down and thought, 'Wow, let's make this super-sensitive and not place any protection around it. In fact," he raised his hand, one finger in the air with his eyebrows and eyes open in glee, "why don't we make it easy to locate as well? That should do the trick. He placed his hand on the table and leaned toward Tina. "Later, when she woke up after drinking too much, she looked down at her clay creation and thought, 'Shit, let's do version 2.0 and fix this mistake.'"

Tina shook her head in sympathy. "Don't worry your little head about—" She didn't get another word out before the snickers hit her ears. She stopped and closed her eyes, tapping the table. "Okay, poor choice of words, and pun *not* intended." She elbowed Marcus, who was laughing a little too hard. "Now that we all agree God is a female..."

"Who has it out for men," William added.

"And loves a good beer or two," Bobcat agreed. "I'm starting to like this concept of a female beer-swilling god."

Tina opened her lips to continue, but William interrupted.

"It does explain a few things," he reasoned. Bobcat raised an eyebrow and twirled his hand in the universal "continue" gesture. "Well, think about the platypus. Who but a drunk god could make that shit?"

"Don't forget the Black Widow spider," Bobcat added. "Or hell, the praying mantis." He shivered. "Have sex, kill the man, push out the babies."

"It does," William considered, "speak to a female-focused deity."

Thomas tried to speak, but Bobcat was on a roll. "Which would mean that for millennia there was a massive PR campaign to market a male-focused deity when in reality, we were being snookered each and every generation." He shook his head. "I can't believe we have finally figured out that we were horribly manipulated into being subservient for hundreds and hundreds of years to support a female deity which designed us in such a fucked-up way that just two bricks are able to make us cringe."

By now Tina was nonplussed, waiting for Bobcat to finish. *Thank God (male or female)*, she thought, *he didn't have any beer with him.*

Of course, two seconds later...

Bobcat turned to Admiral Thomas and raised an eyebrow. "You got any beer?"

He smiled but shook his head no.

"Damn," Bobcat muttered.

Tina found her opening. "I know it must be hard to realize you have been played like a bitch for thousands of years, but can we focus on saving Earth here?"

Bobcat looked up. "Don't you mean saving *Mother* Earth?"

William smiled.

"Okay, playtime's over." Admiral Thomas, having watched Bethany Anne corral this group many times over the last hundred and fifty years or so, pulled the meeting back on track. "What do you need from me?"

The joking stopped, and the group got down to business.

Come hell or high water, aliens or killer asteroids, the Earth *would* be protected!

The Queen Bitch and her people were going to do their damnedest to make sure it had so many guns surrounding it that there would be a universal STAY THE FUCK AWAY sign permanently in place.

CHAPTER FOURTEEN

QBBS _Meredith Reynolds_, General Lance Reynolds' Office

Lance heard a knock and looked up. "Yes?" he called, and the door opened. It was Frank.

"Come on in. What's up?" Lance asked. He set his stylus down and leaned back in his chair, glancing at the old analog clock on the wall. "Not quite quitting time, so business or personal?"

Frank walked in, nodding to Lance before taking the second chair that faced his desk. "Personal business," Frank answered. "Giles."

"Oh." Lance sighed and reached down to the third drawer on the left side of his desk. "Meredith?"

"Yes, Lance?" the EI replied.

"Please unlock my special stash," he instructed, and it was done. He opened the drawer and reached in for a glass bottle filled with a blue liquid. He removed the bottle and shut the drawer.

Frank asked, "Didn't your drawer used to be locked with a key?"

"It did," Lance replied. He turned in his chair and picked up two glasses from the credenza before turning back. "Patricia took

133

the key three years ago, and I had the lock upgraded so Meredith could open it for me."

"Well, of course you did," Frank agreed, reaching for a glass as Lance poured the drinks. "We are speaking about my son, so liquor is a good idea."

"Kids," Lance agreed and twisted the top back on, then replaced the bottle in the drawer.

"Just one?" Frank asked.

"Giles," Lance replied as the drawer locked again, "doesn't get the good stuff."

Frank shrugged. "He won't be here in time to worry about drinks, so no harm, no foul."

"What is he coming here for this time?" Lance asked, allowing the fire of the Yollin special reserve to burn his throat.

"Believe it or not, something important and relevant."

Lance looked over his glass at Frank and took a few more sips of the liquid before replying, "You're right, I don't believe it."

"Yes, that's why Barb asked me to come speak to you."

Lance pursed his lips. "Barb has a comment?" Frank nodded, and Lance spoke a little louder. "Meredith?"

"Yes, General?"

"Would you connect me to Barb, please?"

The edges of Frank's lips curled up. "Oooh, going to the source?"

"Of course. She cuts through the bullshit," Lance replied.

Barb's voice came over the speakers. "Hi, Lance. I heard that." Lance started to speak, but she continued, "This time, the request is to allow Giles access to formal and advanced training in craft and other assorted classes."

"Why are you asking for craft training? Isn't there a better solution on the open market than what we have in the military?"

"Sweetheart?" Barb began.

"Yes?" Frank replied.

"Have you told Lance anything yet?"

"He didn't get a chance, Barb. Remember my bullshit comment?" Lance interrupted.

"Right. Okay, Giles has been focused on his," you could just hear her air quotes around the next phrase. "*Space archaeology.* His notes are starting to include some out-of-the-way places. These places are far off the beaten path, and frankly, we don't know what he will find. So, while I think a lot of what he discovers in the future will have viability for all of us, I also think it could be dangerous. Knowing how to fly and having all of the other military training might be very useful."

Frank smirked. "Consider him 'Indiana Jones in Space.'"

"I hate that phrase," Barb sputtered over the comm.

"Yet," Lance pointed out, "it succinctly told me everything I needed to know."

"Score one for me," Frank declared.

"He is not a space archaeologist!" Barb's voice had started to grow annoyed. Lance leaned back in his chair, sipping his drink. "He is combing data related to the almost fourteen billion years' existence of this universe, along with the species and the history we know and that which we don't know and can't surmise. Something was out there before us."

"A lot of species lived, thrived, survived, and died before Earth came into existence, so why is this more important to us than the rock they are buried in?" Lance asked, taking another sip of his drink.

Getting Giles into these classes was already approved in his mind. If the man was going to be a pain in the ass, he might as well be a skilled pain in the ass.

Plus Giles was family, like a nephew that you loved but realized how much trouble he had caused your siblings who had raised him. He wondered if Barb still had color in her hair or if raising Giles had been able to overcome the Pod's ability to keep her looking young.

Lance decided not to seek that answer.

Barb moved into the "I'm giving you data so listen up" phase. "Lance, if the Etheric Empire were to disappear and all those toys that are hidden away were found in a hundred thousand years, what is the chance they would be of value?"

"Huh," he grunted while thinking about the sealed weapon stashes the group had been planting for decades in remote locations, and the depth of the stasis efforts they had undertaken to ensure that the systems would work again within two or three days at most, if not hours.

"So imagine that an even more advanced society than the Etheric Empire did something like that, and it has been waiting for ten thousand or a hundred thousand or even a million years. Who would you want to find it first? The Leath? The Zhyn? The Noel-ni?"

"Us," Lance admitted. "Okay, Barb, you've made your point."

"I always told Frank," Barb stated, "that you had a head of sandstone. Hard, but not too hard."

"Great, I'm a sedimentary rock," he grumped.

"Be glad I didn't say 'granite,'" she retorted.

Frank raised his hand six inches. "Thank you for your support and help in this, and for the clarification."

"Will you approve Giles for the training?" she asked.

"Yes," he replied, "but it will come with certain conditions."

"I would expect that," she admitted. "Perhaps a homing tag in his butt or something might be good."

"Too obvious," Lance answered with a laugh, "but we shall see what we can do."

"Thank you, Lance. Hey, honey?"

"Yes?" Frank replied.

"Dinner with the Escobars is on for tonight," she told him. "Gabrielle said she has something to tell us, so let's not be too late, okay?"

Frank replied, "Okay, dear," and Barb disconnected.

Lance finished his drink and reached for Frank's empty glass. "So, 'Indiana Jones in Space?'"

"Perhaps that simplifies it too much," Frank admitted, "but imagine if you will a galactic Ark of the Covenant."

"Fat chance," Lance replied as he opened the second drawer down on the right, then placed the empty glasses inside and closed it.

"I don't know why not," Frank mused. "The Earth is less than four billion years old, but the universe is almost fourteen. How many peoples had to have existed before us? You know the Kurtherians—at least some of them—have already ascended and changed their bodies to operate in the Etheric Dimension."

"Sounds boring."

Frank shrugged. "TOM said that his clan was expanding their mental abilities. Their physical bodies were just a pain in the ass, and they needed a way to dodge the shitheads gunning for them."

"Yeah, I get that…" Lance started, but he was interrupted by a knock on the door.

"Come in," he called, surprised. The guard station allowed only a few to reach his office unattended.

He thought that if Giles kept running scams to acquire resources to go larking about the systems, he should be put on the "escort" list.

A roguish young man stuck his head in. "I've been requested to attend a meeting." His million-watt smile confirmed to Lance that he had a clue what was going on. If he had given another type of smile, it would have told him that Giles thought he was busted for something.

Lance nodded to the chair next to Frank. "Come on in, Giles, and take a seat."

Giles walked over and slid into the seat. He was wearing a fashionable version of an atmosuit that was tailored to look like an old college professor's.

Complete with a pair of glasses he had absolutely zero need to wear.

Giles Kurns, Lance thought. *The Earth's last hipster.*

QBS *Shinigami* over the Planet Ugaloff

The ink-black face scrunched up. "It's a trap," she stated. Baba Yaga looked at the information dump that had come in two days previously, and at the fortified location where the information suggested she would find one of the Seven. "I just can't tell what *kind* of trap."

ADAM and TOM were both using the audio on *Shinigami's* bridge to speak to her.

ADAM went first. "Do you want me to allow the data to pass to Nathan's group and see if they tag it as false or faked?"

"No fucking way." Baba Yaga tapped her lip as she looked at the satellite-level imagery. Better to presume a trap, but it would be nice for the effort to be easier than she anticipated. "Have you hacked them yet?"

"No," ADAM admitted. "I don't think they have any computer systems down there."

"That's...odd." She considered. "How about power packs?"

"Nothing we can sense yet," TOM informed her. "Shinigami and I are working on the details, and so far, it is a very unlikely event."

She considered what she knew. "They are trying to limit my advantages." Baba Yaga stood up to walk around the bridge, thinking out loud. "They have studied us and know we can infiltrate systems." She angled around the front video screens and walked toward the back. "They know we have better sensors—or assume we do—so they are hiding the power plants."

"Or there aren't any there in the first place," TOM hazarded.

Baba Yaga stopped pacing. "Well, that would make this operation a complete waste of time and effort." She turned toward the bridge exit. "Time to release my inner Tabitha."

The hatch irised closed behind her.

"Oh, damn," ADAM commented over the speaker system.

When Baba Yaga left the armory, she wore a coat that would remind someone of *The Matrix* had they ever seen that archived movie.

"There is no spoon," Baba Yaga had commented at one point when she was sifting through all of the special toys Tabitha had acquired over the years and used on her operations with the Tontos.

Now she was suited up with the best tech that had been created over the decades for the Rangers and for Tabitha specifically, and it brought a sharp-toothed smile to her face.

No matter what was below, she expected to be able to deal with it.

Baba Yaga was carrying over five hundred rounds of .45 ammo, two swords, her Jean Dukes, and five of "John's little friends."

Those had their own special box. The little grenades were custom-made. Spherical, but not much larger than an olive, with an Etheric-powered explosive device surrounded by small metal balls. They were easy to throw and could roll along the ground. Hell, they even had a way to engage with antigrav or extragrav.

Sometimes you really wanted those damned grenades to fall really fast.

Shinigami inquired, "Where do you want me to set you down?"

Baba Yaga considered dropping at the port but realized that was cockiness talking again, and her mouth twisted in annoyance.

One time being stupid was enough for now, thank you very much.

"I'm going to add a power pack and drop from ten thousand feet," she replied. "Atmosphere?"

"Breathable," the EI responded.

Ten minutes later, she was ready to go.

QBBS *Meredith Reynolds*

John Grimes walked into the workout room where he and the guys used to spar with Bethany Anne. He was wearing something like an old zip-up jacket from Earth. His hands were in his jacket pockets as he thought back to all the sparring they had done once upon a time.

How she would sit down on the mat just a few feet from him and stretch out face-down. Her head would touch the mat, and she would answer questions, her muffled voice coming out from under her hair.

Now the guys used the Guardians' workout area. It allowed the Guardians to test themselves against the best, and it allowed the Bitches to test themselves against new opponents.

The Bitches had all been sparring against each other for so many decades they could read each other completely.

"Meredith?" he called.

"Yes, John?"

"Would you please lock the door and record my next speech to Bethany Anne?"

"Certainly," her voice replied.

John sat down slowly and crossed his legs underneath himself. He wished there was grass here so that he could pick at it while he said what he had to say.

"BA..." he started, then tapped the floor and looked up. "Boss, it's me."

Well, duh, shithead! he thought to himself. *Like she wouldn't recognize your voice?*

"I need to get something off my chest, and I know you will understand, even if you hate me forever for it."

He took a deep breath. "You remember when we took out that sheik and his twelve security people after we judged them back on Earth?

"Do you remember what we said as we executed them and tossed their bodies over the back of the boat?"

He remembered each of them saying almost the same thing, over and over. Hell, that was when Peter had stood up and become a man for sure, and had stopped being "Pete" to the group.

"Baba Yaga, if you are listening to this, think back to those times, to those promises we made. We agreed in no uncertain terms that you have to protect your primary, but you also have to protect the innocent. Right now, we don't know where you are or what you are doing."

I'll find you if I can, BA, just don't fall into darkness. Please, God, don't let her fall into darkness.

"I was instructed by my fucking best friend to not ever let her succumb to the darkness because Bethany Anne would not want to live that way."

I don't want her to live that way. He sighed audibly. He would rather go into the darkness right now than say what he was required to say.

"Baba Yaga, you need to make sure you protect the innocent, or the Queen's Bitches will be charged with capturing you or killing you. We made that pact long ago, and at the moment, with no information, I am honor-bound to warn you, my friend."

Tears dripped onto the mat, and John reached up to wipe his eyes.

"Bethany Anne, I love you. Please come back to us. *Please.*"

It was another five seconds before he could speak without his voice cracking.

"This is the Empress' lead Bitch, but more than that, this is Bethany Anne's friend John Grimes.

Come back home, please, BA. John out."

He sniffed and used his sleeve to wipe his eyes again.

"Meredith, please send that to TOM and ADAM."

Five minutes later, John was able to clear his eyes enough to leave.

CHAPTER FIFTEEN

QBS _Shinigami_ over the Planet Ugaloff

The back hatch of the cloaked ship opened. Had someone been looking up, it would have been a strange experience to see the inside of a ship and a person in black standing there with no visible support.

Baba Yaga once more made sure she had packed the coat. There was no way she was dropping through the atmosphere with all that shit in the pockets just begging to fall out. "Alley-_oop!_" she called, and simply stepped out.

Her full-face helmet was well-seated, so she leaned forward to use the air to guide her in the direction she wanted to go. Her planned landing spot was easily four kilometers from the location where she was expecting to find the Seven.

Or at least answers.

When she was a thousand feet up, the antigrav kicked in, and she grunted as the deceleration increased. At one hundred feet, she felt her stomach tell her to go fuck herself, and it stayed behind as the antigrav went into overdrive to handle the extra weight of her armor and supplies.

By the time she touched the ground, it was as if she had

jumped from five feet. She reached to her chest, unlocked the extra power pack, and tossed it up.

It zipped up into the atmosphere so Shinigami could grab it. The ship's robots would place it back in the charging queue.

She unhooked her rolled-up bag and pulled out the trench coat. After making sure all the internal pockets were closed, she put it on.

"Not very fashionable with a helmet," she murmured to herself.

A hole you can reach through in your head isn't much of a fashion accessory either, TOM replied.

Do you always have to give me shit? she asked, annoyed.

When you aren't thinking properly, yes.

If you loved me— she started.

TOM interrupted, **I** *do* **love you and your pain-in-the-ass alter ego, or I would have done something logical like stopping you from leaving Leath.**

Fucker, she mumbled, but he was right.

Can we just kill these sonsabitches so we can go home? TOM asked.

Home? she mused, and started walking toward the path Shinigami had identified to get down from this little escarpment. *I am your home.*

At the moment you are my domicile, he answered, but didn't provide any more explanation when she asked him.

It took her another two hours to safely get to where she wanted to be, and during that time, the local sun had set and darkness had arrived. She used the advanced optics of her helmet to look as closely as she could at her target. *I got nothing*, she grumped, then reached into the coat and pulled out three balls.

>>**You are too far away to use those at the moment.**<<

She ignored his comment and thought the commands to program the little spheres. *Watch and learn, young Padawan.*

She stood still for a moment, then pulled her arm back and

threw the three balls as hard as she could toward the little castle-like building before she dropped back down.

>>**Okay, that was unexpected. Tabitha doesn't do that. Well, at least not that I am aware of.**<<

Tabitha is usually inside when she needs them. I'm pretty damn far away. She watched her HUD as the three spheres sped toward the building. "Damn, a little short." As she spoke the words the antigrav kicked in, and instead of slamming into the ground, the three spheres used their momentum to continue their forward motion. "Nice programming."

You are welcome, TOM replied.

Wait, you programmed them? she asked.

Yes. I could see what you wanted, so if you failed to throw them far enough they would use the momentum to move forward, saving the energy for the antigrav.

She thought as the three video-in feeds displayed on her HUD. "Well, nice job." She watched the information flow across her screen., "This is bullshit."

The other data the sensors were pulling soon confirmed her thoughts. "This is a setup. See if we have any traffic—something like a ping."

They waited for another forty-seven minutes before ADAM gave her the news over her helmet system. "Rigged with explosives."

"Huh?" she asked. She had rolled onto her back in a shallow depression, changed her ambient temperature to match the surrounding area's, and closed her eyes for a few minutes.

"The place is rigged to blow. I suspect they are using a negative-return switch," he told her.

"Which means what, exactly?" She looked at the video feed. The left one was showing what looked like a fuck-ton of blow-up shit. "That would have been a hell of a way to earn a new asshole."

"Not sure there would be enough ass left to create a new hole," ADAM replied. "This would have shredded you into enough parts to vaporize you. It goes off at a positive signal or the lack of a negative signal."

"So, we plug in a signal block and *boom?*"

"Yes."

She thought about it for a second. "We have any idea where they are?"

"Not yet," ADAM replied.

"Block it," she told him.

"How?"

She was momentarily surprised. "No capabilities in those spheres?"

"No."

"Well, shit." She chewed on her cheek while she tried to think up a few options.

TOM offered, "Could we fake you walking in there using the spheres, perhaps?"

"Uhhh, have them hit the ground? Audio or shockwave sensors?" she asked. "What if they have video?"

"No transmissions, and I have not seen anything on the video intake," ADAM replied.

"Well, okay. Do it." She shrugged. "I'm not going in there, we aren't getting those spheres back, and …"

The video intake on her HUD disappeared as she felt the dirt tremble under her. She quickly rolled to her stomach and lifted her head to see dirt and building parts shooting up into the air.

"Fuckkkkk…meee…" she whispered.

"Several new assholes," quipped ADAM

She watched some of the larger chunks of the old building crash to the ground. "I hate effective enemies who don't underestimate you."

"We have movement," ADAM told her. Her HUD showed a few dots of movement coming out of the hills on the other side of the destroyed building. "Shinigami has the video to show their origination point."

"Have to love a plan that comes together." She calculated the distance. "This is going to be a pain to go through the Etheric with all this damned new metal derivatives armor and shit. It's going to suck up my reserves like an elephant at a waterhole," she grumped.

TOM spoke up. "You will have time to rest unless they use vehicles, and at the moment, they aren't doing so."

"Wonder if they mined the areas around the building?" she mused. "That would have ruined my night as well."

The operations center was a hive of excited whispering. The primary client contact, who was sitting in the back of the room, towered over most of the mercenaries. Between him and the now-destroyed building were well over a hundred fighters.

Not that it had mattered before when they had thousands of Leath military. Zill, Fourth of what had started as the Eight, dropped to Seven, went back to Eight and then back to Seven a second time, crossed his arms, and paid attention to the sensors arrayed in the cave system and outside.

The team slowly making their way to the trap was making sure they stepped carefully.

He suspected they would be his second helping of bait. First of the Seven Levelot wanted to use this body as her own avatar, but Zill would be taking that option if he had a chance. There was no way the math could work out to allow such a dangerous enemy the opportunity to escape on the way back.

At least, that was how *his* math worked out.

He glanced at the screens, which showed the fourteen

different trap locations the Witch would have to pass to get to the operations center.

Zill had been meticulous in his placement of the traps, as well as putting expendable mercenaries between himself and Death, who was coming for the bait.

Him.

Etheric Dimension.

Baba Yaga was breathing hard, lying on the ground trying to pull more energy in, while the white swirled above her. "I suggest we just take off all this armor and do it the old-fashioned way."

Which is what? TOM asked.

"Naked with swords and guns," she whispered.

And if they use explosives with ball bearings or something similar?

"I get peppered?"

And if one of them hits *me*?

"You can't regenerate?"

To some level, but if they damage my body enough, I'm a goner.

She heaved a heavy sigh. "Well, fuck. You know, you come with a lot of baggage—just like a boyfriend."

I do a lot of good, and I am handy with math.

"Just like a boyfriend." She got up and started walking toward where she suspected the enemy was located. "Well, some of them," she qualified. "But if they weren't good with math, they were usually good with engines."

>>**Keep it up,**<< ADAM shot to TOM. >> **She needs to focus on the past.**<<

I'm working on it! TOM shot back. **It's not like I'm her boyfriend or something.**

>>**Well, you *are* with her all the time, you say stuff at the**

148

most inopportune times, you curse like a sailor, and she puts you in the doghouse.<<

You are right, I *am* her fucking boyfriend, TOM sighed. When Michael came on board with this other human, I should have paid more attention to who I was putting myself into.

>>Which also sounds just like a boyfriend.<< ADAM smirked, sending the equivalent of a chuckle to TOM.

"What are you two talking about?" Baba Yaga asked.

Can I admit I don't want to talk about it?

"Of course. *Do* you want to talk about it?" she asked.

No.

"So fucking do it anyway," she growled.

Fine! TOM sighed. We were talking about when Michael first brought you onto my ship.

"Brought *Bethany Anne* on the ship," she clarified, and repeated the mantra in her mind: *One foot in front of the other! One foot in front of the other!*

Just make the damned changes to the story in your own mind. I didn't want to talk about this anyway! TOM grumped.

"Fine," she huffed. "What were you thinking before you jumped aboard?"

I was thinking this was the perfect opportunity to engage with a viable candidate, so long as they checked out.

"*Bethany Anne* checked out," she reiterated once more.

Who-the-fuck-*EVER checked out*! TOM practically yelled. Who is telling this story? Do you want to know or not? I'm happy to shut up now. Just give me the word.

"Fine, keep going." She dropped to her knees and slowly moved her head forward to look back into her dimension before sharply jerking it back. "SHIT!" she cried as she threw her body backward and put her arms out to stop her roll.

Almost get a face full of something that would sting? TOM asked. He hadn't paid attention to her visual for one damned moment.

"What the hell are you doing?" Mercenary Third Lead Gellhern yelled at the new recruit who was in front of him. He was waving as if he had a poisonous insect problem.

The raw recruit—recruits were known as a "Mine Minions" to Gellhern—stepped ahead of him, then looked over his shoulder at Gellhern with his eyes wide in surprise. He turned back to the front and then back to Gellhern before shaking his head. "Nothing, sir!"

"Damn right, nothing!" He twirled his hand. "Back around, or you might step on a mine and have your blown-off foot kick your own ass."

"Why don't we have these damned mines mapped better?" another voice called.

Gellhern yelled, "You die yet, Kellmien?"

"No."

"Then we have them mapped just fine," was Gellhern's reply.

What happened? TOM asked.

"Just about got a face full of face," Baba Yaga answered. "Was a bit of a surprise."

>>**Then we are on the right path**,<< ADAM told her. >>**Let's keep going.**<<

"Fuck this." She rolled over and stood up tiredly, stripping her boots off.

Oh, goody, TOM commented as she kept unbuckling different pieces of her armor. **We are all going to blow up and die.**

"You are a pitiful excuse for a superhero," she told him.

That the best you got? TOM sniffed. **You should drop and give me fifty**.

"When I get most of this shit off me, I'll be able to give you fifty with one arm and use the other one to flip you the fuck off," she hissed.

Soon she wore only black leggings. Baba Yaga went on to remove the armor from her arms, but she left the vest part of her chest armor on.

She dropped the helmet to the side.

She left the Ranger coat full of shit behind too, as well as the M1911A and its rounds.

Nice pile of metal you have there, TOM commented.

"Too much for too far," she replied. "I'm feeling better already."

Does this mean I don't have to talk about my first experience with you?

"Yes. Keep that shit to yourself," she replied, adding one of her swords to the pile. She started to leave, but then turned back and rifled through the coat.

A minute later, she started jogging in the right direction.

Zill noticed the movement. "What's going on?" He removed his arm from his sleeve, pointing it toward the mercenary who waved his hand in front of his face before turning to speak with the leader behind him.

"Unknown," the communications specialist answered. "I'm reviewing the communication now."

Zill reached up and scratched his tusk, then realized what he had just done and grunted.

It was time for him to try a different body. He was acclimating too well to this skin.

He watched for another hour before telling the group in the operations center, "Bring the soldiers back here. She is on her way."

Mercenary Prime Lead Boll turned her head. "Why? We don't know she wasn't blown up."

"If she was blown up, then…"

Baba Yaga cocked her head and listened. It had taken her a while to find the cave system, and even longer to work her way through it to this operations room.

"If she was blown up, then we will find remains in the morning. I have a feeling she will come for us here," the Leath continued as Baba Yaga slipped back into the Etheric.

"Fifteen of them, one of me. Kill the Leath, and he just moves to another body. Armor too fucking far away," she mused. "I hate myself."

She reached down and opened a metal case, which held five spheres. "Say hello, you fucking bastards, to my little friends," she hissed. "Blow me up?" She continued her running commentary as she closed the empty case and tossed it to the side. "Let me return the favor."

She peeked back into the room and nodded to herself, then took five steps to the side. She revved up her speed and slid into the room, slung the five spheres around the room, pushed the Leath into the Etheric, and then stepped back into the dimension herself.

She flinched when she got back, thinking of the destruction she had left behind.

The Leath had rolled over and was already standing some fifteen feet away from her in a defensive position.

"Ah, the Witch," he commented, looking around. "You have moved us into the Etheric."

Baba Yaga said nothing but moved to her right. The Kurtherian in the Leath's body started moving to his own right, maintaining the distance between them.

Throwing a Kurtherian into the Etheric might not be a great strategy, TOM told her.

Why? she asked. **Can all of you guys use the realm?**

Her voice was gravelly. "Do I call you something base, or do you have a name?"

"Like what?" he replied.

"Orc-faced leg-humping cluster-fucking ass-munch, maybe?" she answered. He frowned but stayed quiet.

She tried again. "Dried-out senile mental midget?"

There was just the tiniest of pauses. "It's 'Zill,'" he answered, spitting to the side. "Just because you're going to die," he went on, "it does not mean you need to be *rude*."

This time Baba Yaga shrugged her indifference. "I've run out of fucks to give when it comes to you Kurtherians."

"Come to me, and I will make your future meaningful," he told her.

TOM, did he just try to manipulate my mind?

Uh, no.

Seriously?

We would know if he tried.

She thought about it. "You are a strange one, but I will play along. Why don't you lie down and stab yourself?"

His eyes narrowed. "Why would I do that?"

"It would save me the effort." Baba Yaga cackled.

They continued their slow circling.

"We could do this forever," he told her, "or I could go ahead and—"

The Witch palmed her Jean Dukes and quickly aimed, pulling the trigger five times before most humans could have blinked once.

The Leath was still circling with her. "Oohhh, fuck," she whispered. She looked behind her to make sure no one was sneaking up.

TOM! she called in alarm. *Any ideas?*

Yes.

Tell me! she asked urgently.

Get him the fuck out of the Etheric, TOM told her. **He is manipulating the metal in here.**

You can manipulate metal in here?

Well, that's what I said!

Is that a guess, or do you know?

It is a logical guess...unless you have a clue? Anne does some cool shit in here.

Baba Yaga swung her left pistol to the side, then had to dodge as one of the rounds she had just shot flew back at her.

I'm seeing it, she admitted, *but I'm not believing it.* A moment later, she ducked as another of her rounds flew past where she had just been.

"It is so lovely to be here," Zill informed her. "Do you wish me to give you an example of real power?"

Her eyes squeezed shut in pain as the rail gun projectile slammed into her back, shattering itself against her armor.

Fucking hell! she thought and jumped up. She took an Etheric step back and increased the distance between the two of them by a hundred yards.

The Leath waited for a moment before he called, "I can find you anywhere!"

"Oh, my God, this isn't good." She started sprinting back the way she had come.

He will figure out your armor is metal soon enough.

Why hasn't he yet?

His mind is probably overstimulated right now. The math to understand the possibilities is overwhelming his mind in a mad rush of dopamine.

Baba Yaga kept running, glancing back into their own dimension and then changing her direction in the Etheric. Slowing down, heart pumping, she looked around for her stash.

I wouldn't shoot him with anything metal, TOM advised.

What about energy balls? she asked.

Fifty-fifty on that, TOM answered. **He can do metal, maybe he can't do energy—or maybe he can.**

I hate those odds, she replied grimly. She glanced out into her dimension and turned right. In another ten steps, the mist parted enough for her to see the shape of her stuff off to her left. Keeping her speed up, she grabbed her helmet, slammed it over her head, and locked it on.

I can feel him, TOM told her. **We have maybe twelve seconds to get finished putting on all of this armor, grab your other shit, figure out a plan, and execute it.**

I HATE this fucking armor! she bitched, trying to lock the snaps into place.

Seven seconds, TOM told her.

Bethany Anne threw her armor on and was sliding the holsters into place for her M1911As when TOM yelled, **DUCK!**

She dropped to the ground as multiple objects sliced through the mist.

His voice came to her from nearby. "Come on, you don't have to play like this!" Zill's Leath laugh sounded like a dog barking.

Baba Yaga's eyes flared red inside her helmet.

"Oh, there you are!" he sneered when he caught sight of the red eyes shining through her helmet's visor.

She strained with everything she had and pushed off the ground, aiming her body at his.

"See, I told you to come to me!" he was saying when her shoulder slammed into him.

She dropped them both out of the Etheric.

"WEIGHT!" she yelled, and ADAM slammed on the antigrav in her suit. She continued moving forward while floating five feet above the ground. She looked behind her to see the Leath's body rolling across the ground before a huge *crack* and explosion sent the dirt and his body flying.

She saw an arm go one way, a leg the other. She pulled a .45

and aimed ahead of her. Pulling the trigger three times, she shot at the ground along her future path. The first two rounds slammed into the ground to no effect, but the third caused another explosion of dirt high into the air.

"Drop me there," she commanded, and ADAM added weight as she glided over to the site of the explosion. Her feet touched down, and she turned as the Leath's body came to a stop. She exchanged her pistols and looked up. "Weight, ADAM," she commanded and pushed gently, slowly rising off the ground. She watched the body, her Jean Dukes pistol in her hand. "Wish I had…" She shook her head in disgust and held out her left hand, and a red ball of energy started forming. A moment later, she saw the beginning of a Kurtherian start to slither out of the Leath's body.

"Tempting," she commented to herself as she flung the energy at the Kurtherian. Soon it was flailing about, Zill's mental screams amplified by TOM as he fried in the energy.

"What was tempting?" ADAM asked through her speakers.

"Letting him slither to see if he set off another bomb," she replied and disappeared into the Etheric.

CHAPTER SIXTEEN

Planet N'Var, Police Station

"Captain D221?" a human male asked, and the captain looked up from his work area. He was in a circular area about five steps across with a small desk built into the entire arc of the wall. The captain was usually alone in this work area. He turned to see two human males and a female.

The female looked suspiciously familiar. He tagged her face and issued a request to find and labeled it "Priority."

It would be very beneficial if a wanted criminal walked right into his police station.

"Yes?" He turned to give them his full attention while his people worked in the background.

"Ranger Two?" Achronyx got Tabitha's attention through her bone speaker.

"Hmm?" she answered almost inaudibly.

"The captain tagged your face and sent the request to see if you are a wanted person," her EI replied.

Tabitha raised an eyebrow and sent the information to Barnabas. "Introductions?" she asked and nodded to the waiting captain.

"Certainly, Ranger Two." Barnabas turned to the captain, who was canceling a work request. "Captain," he waved a hand to Tabitha, "this is Ranger Two of the Etheric Empire." Tabitha stepped forward to greet the police officer. "This is the commander of the Empress' Guardians, Peter."

Barnabas waited for the two to greet each other before continuing, "And I am Barnabas," as he stepped forward to greet the captain.

Tabitha added, "My boss."

She smiled to herself when the captain did a double-take upon receiving that information. While she was known through a lot of the systems, Barnabas kept a low profile. Not on purpose, necessarily—he just didn't go out and get involved in investigations that placed his name in the news very often. Frankly, Tabitha thought Barnabas was still under the assumption that if you knew about vampires, you knew about him.

That didn't work too well with hundreds of planets and trillions of people. Hell, even when you focused on those important in the Etheric Empire, Barnabas was typically lower on the list.

"So, you manage the esteemed Ranger Corps of the Etheric Empire," he nodded his head toward Tabitha, "and the infamous Ranger Two?"

Peter coughed, holding a hand over his mouth. Barnabas turned to look at Tabitha, who smiled and shrugged. "So I'm 'infamous.' Better to be infamous than out-famous," she paused, "like you."

The captain shook his head. "You have my deep respect for your patience already, Barnabas."

Barnabas turned back to the captain. "Yes, I appreciate your sympathy. My Empress does not realize the task she gave me when Ranger Two was moved onto my team."

"You didn't get a vote?"

"Who needs a vote for this?" Tabitha asked, waving a hand up and down herself. "It is an obvious solution to almost everything."

Peter stayed remarkably quiet.

"If there was ever a moment when my Empress abused her powers," Barnabas left the comment hanging.

The two leaders turned back to each other and Barnabas continued, "We are following up on another of our Empress' subjects, one named—"

"Baba Yaga?" asked Captain D221, nodding. "She was here."

"Did she kill anyone?" Peter asked, and the captain cocked his head. "Anyone who didn't deserve it?" he amended

"She put one of my men on mental leave," the captain replied.

"I'd like to apologize," Barnabas told him.

Captain D221 waved a hand. "He needed it. He was a bit like Ranger Two here, and needed a few moments of reality."

Tabitha's head pivoted back to the conversation. "Hey, I represent that remark!"

"Of course you do," Barnabas answered. "Very well."

Tabitha looked at Peter, who was staring at her. "I can't believe I traveled this many light years to be harassed."

"Your reputation precedes you." Peter shrugged. "A tart mouth will be replied to in kind."

Her eyes narrowed. "That's very philosophical of you."

"Wait until I find some tart fruit," he replied enigmatically before his eyes returned to studying the police building and those in it.

Tabitha returned her focus to Barnabas and the captain.

"So," Barnabas continued, "he is okay?"

"Oh, he will be fine. It was a painless reality check for him," the captain answered. "He is a Shrillexian." This time it was Barnabas who winced. "I see you know the type?"

Barnabas nodded. "Yes, I have another Ranger who is a Shrillexian. You have my respect. They are challenging." He cocked his head to the side. "You say she didn't harm anyone?"

The captain put his hands back on his terminal and typed in a few commands. "She killed a Kurtherian if that matters."

"I'm sure the Kurtherian was unhappy," Barnabas temporized, "but we aren't."

"Good." The captain folded his arms across his chest. "Frankly, she went out of her way to save a rather low-level criminal."

Tabitha breathed out a sigh of relief. "Oh, thank God," she stated as Peter reached over and squeezed her shoulder in support.

"I have to tell you, this Witch is scary." He reviewed his report once more. "She did leave behind some damage that a few owners are complaining about."

Tabitha interrupted, "What is the total?"

While the captain turned back to his terminal, Achronyx answered. "A total of fifty-two thousand three hundred and seven credits, of which about thirty-seven thousand credits were tacked on, so the insurance companies paid to get items fixed which Baba Yaga had nothing to do with."

The captain explained, "Probably about thirty thousand credits, if you ignore the padding. I'll have to investigate the padding, mind you."

Barnabas opened his mouth, but Tabitha spoke. "I'll pay it," she offered. "Hell, if it will help your team, I'll even pay the padding on top. Just tell those businesses they need to support the local police next year."

"Is this you personally, or the Empire?" the captain asked. "Do you have a budget?"

"Nooo," Barnabas drawled. "This would be out of her own pocket."

"It's not like I need it, and it would make me feel a little better to help," Tabitha told them both. "Would this clear up your investigation?"

The captain shrugged. "Yes, although she will have a few citations, including one for touching a police officer in the line of duty." He shrugged again. "He deserved it, but that doesn't mean I can let it go."

"I suggest you offset that with community service if you ever see her again," Barnabas told him. "If you go for more, you will lose more than you gain."

"That bad?"

"She has the power to level your city," he told the captain, "but to be truthful, I doubt she would do something like that."

"Barnabas, she isn't a cold-blooded killer," Tabitha argued.

"Oh, she can be *very* cold-blooded about it," Peter retorted.

Tabitha restrained her urge to hit him. "Not helping, Peter."

"Be honest, Tabitha," he replied. "I didn't say the person wouldn't deserve it, but she doesn't have to be angry to enact justice. To others, that seems fairly cold-blooded."

As the two started arguing the merits of cold-blooded killing, Barnabas and the captain finished their conversation. A minute later, the three of them were led out of the police station.

"Where to now?" Tabitha asked as they walked toward the local transit station to take them back to the spaceport.

"I got word from Stephen. We need to head to Devon."

"Oh, goody." Tabitha sighed and kicked a small rock down the sidewalk. "Let's go to a planet on the ass-end of nowhere and pop its pimples."

"Baba Yaga was spotted there just four nights ago," Barnabas finished.

Tabitha held up an arm and whistled, then stepped into the traffic and pulled out her badge to slow down a taxi. "We need to get to the spaceport," she told the driver as she opened the back door.

The two men hurried to jump into the front and back seats of the taxi before Tabitha left them behind.

"You know we still have a queue for takeoff, right?" Barnabas asked. "It isn't like taking public transport would have put us behind."

Tabitha ignored him. "Achronyx? Get with Space Traffic Control and jump that queue. No, don't use that excuse. Yeah, use E42; that should work. I'll have Peter fake it." She stopped talking with her EI and looked at Barnabas. "I have ways, young Padawan, I have ways," was all she told him as she patted Peter on the shoulder.

"I hope you act well," she told him.

Planet Ugaloff

Baba Yaga, without most of her armor, peeked back into the control room she had pulled the Leath out of and dropped the small grenades in.

It was a mess.

She palmed her Jean Dukes and stepped into the room. "Where is everyone?" she wondered. She counted at least seven dead, and one who had a heartbeat, but he was bleeding out too quickly to last much longer without help.

She ignored him.

As she walked around the room, she saw that many of the video monitors had been destroyed.

TOM commented, **I suspect they left the room when it suddenly erupted in explosions.**

"Good tactical move," she admitted. "ADAM, are you in yet?"

>>**Yes, mostly. One of the computers is giving me trouble.**<<

"Which one?" she asked, looking around.

>>**How am I supposed to know? It isn't like there is a map.**<<

Look for something that is a different color, TOM suggested.

Bethany Anne walked up and down the rows, stepping over bodies, body parts, and splatters of something she would rather not think about. She pulled down her helmet's visor. "Please vent this air and filter everything else. I don't want any smell, ADAM," she commanded as she stopped and looked under a field-expedient desk. "This one?"

Yes, TOM answered. **Now, show me the keyboard and start touching the buttons I tell you to touch.**

"Left top third one," TOM began, and Bethany Anne started typing using his commands.

Some two hundred keystrokes later, ADAM interrupted, >>**Thank you. I'm in.**<<

"What were you two doing?" Baba Yaga asked.

He needed a port opened with which he could communicate with the computer. He knows the Kurtherian language, but with no port, he had no access.

The monitor in front of them started scrolling symbols.

STOP! TOM commanded, and the symbols stopped moving.

>>**Press the top button on the right,**<< ADAM told her.

After pressing the button, the screen dissolved to a video and she was face to face with a Leath. "Zill?" it asked before realizing it wasn't looking at its teammate.

"Hello." Baba Yaga grinned. "Two down, six more to go."

"You," the Leath hissed, leaning forward. "The elusive Witch. I see Zill has failed."

"Zill and Gorllet," Baba Yaga answered.

The Leath waved a hand. "My baggage," she answered. "You haven't been playing against my best. One was mental, the other cocky."

"That is the definition of Kurtherian," Baba Yaga replied. "You are *all* cocky. You should be helping others, but instead, you play gods and then use your people against each other."

"Witch, you are too simple to understand the needs of the cosmos and how we Kurtherians fit in. For you to even try would be like a spaceship touching the sun," she scorned, her eyes looking into the video. "Instantly vaporized."

Wow, so humble, TOM remarked.

"It doesn't matter what you believe. I'm coming for you," Baba Yaga hissed. Her eyes started glowing brighter, her smile malevolent. "When you are awake, I'll be coming for you. When you sleep, I'll be getting closer. When you need to rest, I will be around the corner."

"You are a pitiful excuse for a sentient being," the Leath scoffed. "Your warnings are as troubling as the effort to decide what to wear in the morning. It is inconsequential to the beauty of…"

Baba Yaga ignored her ramblings.

ADAM, can you track this message?

>>No. I have tried.<<

Baba Yaga pulled out a pistol and aimed it at the screen, and her eyes narrowed. "See you soon," she hissed and shot the monitor, destroying it. She holstered her weapon and turned. "It was a boring conversation anyway."

A step later, she disappeared.

Leath Military Ship, Unknown Location in the Same System as the Planet Ugaloff

Levelot's face was impassive when the video cut off, and she reached up and shut down the connection. She issued commands to pull up Zill's transmissions and watched them. She was able to see the arm that pulled Zill out of their dimension. It took her a bit of searching to find the fight on the plains.

She stood up and pulled her robes around her, then walked out of the room and down a passage, finally entering a formal meeting room with a round table. After sitting down, she pressed a button to summon her peers.

She said nothing as they arrived over the next few minutes, each taking the spot he or she would have in their chambers on Leath.

When everyone had assembled, she spoke.

"Zill is no more." She waited for a moment, but no one said anything. "We will need to take this effort a little more seriously. When she fights us one-to-one, she has been successful. She shows no hints that she is willing to stop this effort to track us down."

Behome't, Second of the Seven—now the Six—asked, "Do you believe her capable?"

"I have reviewed the video I could access, and she is unfortunately *very* capable. We will need to limit her Etheric capabilities. She has the advanced technology of the Etheric Empire, and I am sure she draws from their people as well. Her Empress has commanded her to kill us. I am confident in saying she will obey her Empress unto death." Levelot looked around the table, "Which will be our responsibility to implement."

"Physically?" Chrio'set, Fifth of the Six, asked.

"Yes," Levelot agreed. "We have used cut-outs long enough. It is time for us to prove our own ascendance." They all considered what the new commands would do to their existing calculations.

"Two must go," Chrio'set suggested.

Behome't shook his head. "Three," he told them, "and we need to change our bodies. It is time we drop these shells. They are limiting us."

Levelot nodded her acceptance of Behome't's suggestion. "Three it is. Behome't, you will be Prime for yourself, Teret and Chrio'set."

The two other female Leath plugged the assumptions into their own calculations, and the six stayed silent until both nodded their agreement.

"Take this ship. We will take the secondary. It is time to power

165

up the *K'galeth.*" She pushed her chair back. "Let us know your plans, and we will come back to you. We will work on the ship as you set your trap. Phraim-'Eh will ascend," she finished, and the other five replied in kind.

"Phraim-'Eh will ascend!"

CHAPTER SEVENTEEN

Planet Devon, Lerr'ek's Offices

The Zhyn looked at his three visitors. "There is not much I can tell you about the Mistress' present location."

There were five present in his office. Lerr'ek noticed the one called Peter had squared off against Nock, both keeping each other front and center.

He sighed. "Nock?" The Krenlock turned, still keeping two of his eyes on Peter. "These are the Mistress' people. I have spoken with Stephen to confirm their bona fides."

"They are dangerous," Nock told him slowly and carefully.

"I imagine they are deadly," Lerr'ek agreed. "However, so is my Mistress." He turned to the dark-haired human. "Barnabas, do you agree to hold me safe so long as I do nothing to your people?"

"Of course," Barnabas agreed. "I am here for information related to Baba Yaga and what she has done here on this planet. We are going to have to answer to the Empress—"

"Why?" Lerr'ek asked. He put up a hand. "Wait, I must call Stephen back."

Barnabas turned and raised an eyebrow to Tabitha, who

surreptitiously put a finger to her head and tapped it, raising an eyebrow back.

"Nock," Lerr'ek called, "I will need you to step out for privacy."

Nock looked reluctant to move.

Peter spoke up. "I'll go with you," he told the creature. "You are fucking *fascinating*," Peter told him as he walked toward the office door, Nock following him. "You are a walking badass dinosaur guard." He turned the knob and opened the door, looking over his shoulder to confirm Nock was following him. "Do your people ever serve in the military?" he asked as the door shut behind them.

Lerr'ek continued once the door had shut. "I am informed by Stephen you both know that the Empress and the Witch are the same person?"

"Yes," Barnabas answered, "but I am surprised *you* know that."

"I know only what the Mistress tells me," Lerr'ek answered. "She is working to clean up Devon."

Tabitha spoke up. "Wait, the Empress or Baba Yaga?"

"Did we not just say they are the same person?" Lerr'ek asked.

"Some people question if Baba Yaga is doing things the Empress would not," Barnabas answered.

"Once again, I fail to see the difference. They are the same person."

"Perhaps we have a Zhyn misunderstanding." Barnabas paused before continuing. "Humans' minds have the ability to parse themselves and work with a subset. When this happens, it is feasible one will receive a different set of results than if one had the entire brain functioning as a whole."

Lerr'ek considered what Barnabas was saying. "You believe that only part of the Empress' brain is in control?"

"We don't know," Barnabas answered. "We have recent evidence that she might not be as out of control as we fear."

"She isn't," Tabitha muttered. "I know it."

"Did she kill innocents here?" Barnabas asked, "and what was she trying to accomplish?"

"She is changing the political makeup of the planet," Lerr'ek answered. "There are a lot of politically powerful people who have used their position of influence and status to become independently wealthy at the expense of those they govern."

"Well," Tabitha stated, "they're fucked."

"Indeed." Barnabas thought back to his own experience back on Earth, when Bethany Anne constantly argued with him about justice and punishment.

He would suggest a lesser penalty, but she would always ask for death.

It took a while for him to realize she was not as bloodthirsty as he had feared. She had been playing him the whole time.

He rubbed his jaw and asked, "What did she do?"

"Killed all the completely corrupt and any who ignored her warnings to stand aside, and shipped off a couple dozen to another world, telling them not to come back."

Tabitha was surprised. "Really?"

"Or they would die," he smiled, his Zhyn mouth full of teeth.

Tabitha pulled a chair from a table next to Barnabas, and the squeeeeechhh made him wince. She sat down and looked at him. "That sounds like Bethany Anne, not Baba Yaga."

"She also scared the shit out of a complete bar full of patrons when she wanted a Coke, and put four in the hospital for more than a night. One died."

Barnabas looked at Tabitha, raising an eyebrow. "For a Coke?"

Tabitha chewed on her lip. "The one who died, was he a criminal?"

"Not at the time, but his spouse came in later and spit on his dead body."

Tabitha turned back to Barnabas. "Bet there's a story there," she told him, tapping her head. "She checked him out and delivered justice."

"Bethany Anne doesn't do that," Barnabas reminded her.

"I never said Baba Yaga wasn't an aspect of Bethany Anne. You are talking about the avatar of *justice* she is wearing. C'mon, it's a life-sized warning of Shit-Just-Got-Real if you see her. You don't think Baba Yaga would read minds?"

Barnabas snorted. "Yes. Baba Yaga would in a moment if she wasn't being lazy."

Tabitha pointed at him. "Being lazy is a very Bethany Anne trait."

He put up two hands. "Okay, she isn't showing near the rage I did when I went insane."

Lerr'ek's eyes raised in surprise as he listened to the two of them talk.

Barnabas continued, "When I worried I might do it again, she pointed out she would be there to bring me back down."

Tabitha's voice softened. "You aren't doing this to judge her?"

Barnabas shook his head, his lips pressed together. "I'm here to get my friend back. She did it for me, but can I do it for her?" he asked, then paused. "I'm not sure I can."

Tabitha laid a hand on his arm. "There isn't one of us who can do it all by ourselves, Barnabas," she comforted, patting it three times as he looked in her eyes.

She finished. *"It takes all of us."*

QBS *ArchAngel II*, on Station above the Ixtali Home Planet

The executive shuttle slowly moved through the field into the landing bay to settle down on the deck. The pilot's unique voice came over the speaker system.

"This is your pilot Paul speaking. We have safely arrived on the *ArchAngel II*. If this wasn't your final destination, you are probably fucked. The walk back is looong, and you will need to hold your breath for a considerable amount of time. We appreciate you flying Empire Shuttles. You should join us. We have milk and cookies waiting."

Lance shook his head and stood up, stretching his arms as he watched Darryl step out of the shuttle to make sure everything was okay.

It was most likely a waste of time, but he had resigned himself to having to wait through these security measures.

He grabbed his briefcase, which had been a custom-made gift from Patricia twelve years before when his last briefcase had worn out. This one was a dark blue leather of some sort with brilliant gold metal edges. He slid his tablet into a little slot on the side that allowed him to drop it into the briefcase without opening it.

There was some sort of cool security on the little opening that would stop someone from using the narrow opening to breach the case's contents. While he appreciated that the security was in place, he didn't care to learn how the mechanics of it worked. Patricia said Jean had called it good, so good it was.

"Good to go, Speaker," Scott called, and Lance walked down the short aisle and stepped out of the ship. He continued across the deck toward the wall on the opposite side. The hanger was easily three stories tall, and larger than three old jet aircraft hangers on Earth.

The walk gave him time to think and to try to cool down.

He used his internal connections to speak with the AI of the ship. *ArchAngel?*

Yes, General?

Please ask Stephen to join me. It's time he gave up some of his wisdom for the cause.

Yes, General. There was a momentary pause as Darryl led them down the long corridor as the occasional crew, work robot, or small vehicle passed them. *General, Stephen said he will meet with you.*

Tell him to come to my personal office, please. Reynolds out.

He continued walking, having spoken to Darryl already back on the shuttle, about where he wanted to end up. It took them fifteen minutes to make it to his office, so he was not surprised to see Stephen waiting outside his door.

"ArchAngel didn't let you in?" Lance asked as the hatch irised open and Darryl stepped in front of him to enter first. Lance ignored the timing and stepped in right behind him, then looked at Darryl, who was giving him the fisheye. "I couldn't take the chance someone was in here to shoot me and put me out of my misery." He tossed his briefcase on his desk. "Unfortunately, the crazy bastards aren't allowed on this ship."

Stephen walked in behind Lance. "Someone have a bad set of meetings?"

Lance was going through his desk drawers, opening one and then the next. He stopped, and his eyes edged up to look at Stephen while his head was still facing down. "Someone is so pissed off he's ready to nuke everyone." He continued opening drawers.

"Here it is," Lance muttered and pulled out a clear bottle with a clear liquid. "Drink?" he asked Stephen, who shrugged.

"You sure?"

"Oh, the good stuff," Darryl commented drily as he stepped out of the office. "I'll be out here, boss!"

The door closed before Lance thought of a suitable reply. "Coward," he finally murmured as he placed two drinking glasses on the table. "This is stuff from only-Patricia-knows-where." He told him as he poured. "I leave it in the unlocked drawers. Serve them right if someone steals it."

"Why?" Stephen asked, taking a glass and sitting down in front of the desk.

"Why what?" Lance replied, straightening and taking a sip. He closed his eyes and grimaced, then shook his head. "Damn!" He wiped a tear away.

He looked at Stephen, who was in his own personal hell at the moment, bent forward in his chair and coughing. "What..." Stephen asked, wiping his eyes, "is this?"

"Hair of the dog," Lance replied.

Stephen eyed his glass, then set it on the desk and pushed it toward Lance. "Tell me there was no dog involved in the distilling of that?"

"There was not," Lance agreed and pulled the glass toward him. "It's something TOM says affects the nanocytes for a few moments. Each time you take a swig, it causes a few to send what feels like bad electrical charges through your body, and the tongue receptors will feel pain." He took another swallow and winced for a few seconds. "Reminds me," his voice was hoarse, "of the good stuff on Earth."

"I thought 'good' meant 'smooth,'" Stephen commented.

Lance poured the rest of Stephen's drink into his own glass and then pushed Stephen's glass to the side. "Depends on what you need," Lance told him. "Right now, I need to remember that life can be worse."

"It went that badly on the planet?" Stephen asked.

"Worse." He lifted his glass.

"Worse how?"

Lance eyed the half-full glass and looked at Stephen, then back at the glass. He sat down, then lifted it to his lips, and downed the whole thing. "OHHHH, SWEET BABY JEHOSEPHAT!" Lance coughed, his body spasming in his chair. His left fist slammed the desk twice, paused, then slammed it again. Taking his time, Lance put his glass down.

"*That* worse." Stephen answered his own question.

"Okay," Lance looked up through his tears, "I am now fully in command of my emotions." Stephen said nothing as Lance put a sleeve up to clear his eyes and face of the tears streaming down.

"They want us," Lance started. "to gut our military, fire our people, and either share our technology or gut it and hamstring our future abilities."

"How?" Stephen asked.

"Destroy the ships in a sun, perfectly viewable by those who wish to watch. Provide them with a listing of our ships, so they can check them off. Enough of the other allies have our ships' names, so we can't cheat. Certainly the Leath have most of them."

"What about the Leath?" Stephen asked.

For the first time since Stephen had seen Lance, a smile graced his face and he chuckled. "Oh, their Defense Minister had a real shitfit. I was able to hold in my emotions, but the minister blew up like a volcano. It was a sight to behold. Ripped those pricks so many new assholes, we needed to build a new solid-waste disposal unit for all the shit that was dribbling down their legs."

Stephen chuckled, the scene playing out in his mind. "I like him already."

"Her," Lance corrected. "Seems like the best choice at the moment for these meetings is a female Leath. One of their males would have already started a war."

"So, that was a *calm* response?" Stephen asked.

"As calm as they come," Lance agreed. "I've met a few more Leath now and believe it or not, without the Kurtherian baggage, they aren't bad people." He paused to think, then added, "For the most part."

Stephen sighed. "What about your response?"

Lance considered. "I told them that if they kept this up, the Empress would move the *Meredith Reynolds* close enough to shove the laser up their anal orifices."

"Anal orifices?"

"'Bungholes' didn't translate." Lance shrugged. "Who knew?" He chuckled. "That got a few more to shit, and we all agreed we would have to do this over many, many years, starting with small things first.

"That gives us time," Stephen conceded, his eyes unfocused.

Lance waited for him to say more, considered pouring

another drink, and made a face. He grabbed the two glasses, turned around, and deposited them on the credenza behind him before turning back to Stephen. "Time for what?"

"You know we aren't going to destroy the ships," Stephen stated, pursing his lips. "Some of them *know* we won't destroy the ships, so what do we do with them, and how do you make a warship disappear in front of everyone?"

"That *is* the trick, isn't it?" Lance agreed. "While you are pondering this question, ponder how we are going to get Bethany Anne on board with this plan."

"Logic," Stephen replied.

Lance eyed his friend warily. "That presumes she is willing to listen to logic."

"Think about it." Stephen stood up, placed his hands behind his back, and started pacing around Lance's office. "We will have to pull off the greatest con this galaxy or any other has ever seen. That is what we will lead with when we tell her."

"The ships can't all be local," Lance countered, thinking about it, "and where the hell are we going to put the people we have to fire?"

"Some of them, unfortunately, will not be told. They will have to be fired."

"Yes, we all have some of those people," Lance agreed.

"No, good ones too," Stephen corrected.

"Bethany Anne won't go for that." Lance shook his head. "No way, no how."

"Logic, Lance." Stephen stopped pacing and nodded, then continued his circular path around the office. "Remember, we are doing this to keep the peace. If we go to war, we kill thousands more. What is worse, a few broken hearts or a thousand deaths?"

"They will flame her name for generations," Lance shot back.

"Only a few, and they will eventually be brought back into the fold. It will just take a few years." Stephen released his hands to pop his knuckles before placing them behind his back again.

"Some could die in that time," Lance pointed out.

Stephen stopped and looked at Lance, his face somber. "Also, Lance, Bethany Anne will *have* to be exiled."

Lance's eyes narrowed in anger once more, then they slowly cleared as his thinking caught up to Stephen's, and finally, a small glint of humor flickered in the corners. "Stephen, I take everything back I ever said that suggested Barnabas was the more devious of you two."

Stephen waggled his eyebrows. "Lance, if you didn't believe that, what good was I at hiding my expertise?"

Lance opened his mouth to argue the point, then shut it. Lance wondered just how many times Stephen had manipulated him into actions and he had not seen it coming.

Sonofabitch!

KAEL-VEN

THE KURTHERIAN (tm) GAMBIT

CHAPTER EIGHTEEN

QBS _Shinigami_, outside Space Station NN-J453, Noel-ni Protectorate

"I feel like I'm in DC, waiting on traffic to clear up to go home," Baba Yaga groused. "What's taking for-fucking-ever here?"

Shinigami replied, "Believe it or not, we have to get into a queue."

She thought about this, her tongue running over her teeth, although it slid just above them. Twice in the last two days, she'd cut herself.

TOM had informed her that sucking her own blood didn't help her. She'd told TOM to go screw himself, which had caused her to pause and ask him if that was physically possible.

He had ignored her question.

ADAM suggested, "If you are bored, we still have messages from Stephen, John, and others to give you."

"No." She shook her head. "I don't need that right now. What I need," she pointed to the video screen, "is a way onto that space station instead of waiting here."

You could always walk over to it, TOM suggested.

"That just feels so damned *chancy*." She rubbed her arms. "I mean, what happens if I stick my head out in space?"

It gets sucked off? Your eyeballs explode? Nothing, since you can pull it back quicker than it would harm you?

"One of these answers isn't like the others," she sing-songed. "Are you telling me it is safe?"

There is always risk.

She sat back in her chair, pondering the risks of trying to walk over to the space station. "What kind of security do they have there?"

"Atypical Noel-ni," Shinigami supplied. "This is an outpost, so only a small group of Noel-ni run the place. It is considered a punishment to be stationed here, according to what I have uncovered so far."

Baba Yaga didn't bother asking if that was legal research. Shinigami made early ADAM seem like a babe in the woods when it came to acquisition of information by any means possible. She approved of this methodology, and ADAM had stopped asking her why she was indifferent at best to Shinigami's machinations.

She was about to head to the armory when Shinigami came back on. "We have approval to dock on Ring Three, Section Seven, Berth Twenty-One."

"Which means?" Baba Yaga asked.

"Approximately fifteen minutes until we are locked in," the ship replied.

Baba Yaga stood up and stretched. "Time until full data acquisition?" she asked. "Tell me we didn't choose this out-of-the-way place for its decreased security, but they don't have anything worth looking at?"

"All official Noel-ni stations have a full data packet. Only their home system is more up to date."

"Not going there." She shook her head. "Time?"

"Approximately five hours, give or take three."

She whistled. "Leaving yourself some wiggle room."

"Too many unknown variables."

"Okay, I could use a break," she admitted. "Take up all of these screens." No sooner had she made the request than the video monitors around the bridge chairs started disappearing.

Break from what? TOM asked. **This is our third station, and you didn't even get off the ship at the last two.**

Monotony, she sent back. *I need to stretch my legs, or I'm going to start figuring out ways to pick on you.*

By all means, TOM replied. **Please get off the ship. Stretch your legs, be seen and recognized. Have a few fights while you are at it.**

Nice to know I have your permission. Your care is duly noted, she told him as she walked to her cabin.

You aren't getting into your armor? TOM asked.

She shook her head. "Using the light armor. Easy to slap on and then yell when you rip it off. Each time you use it, you appreciate the locks and shit on the other armor until you are ecstatic to go back to it. Or you rip your tits off in one mega-painful effort to get the damn stuff off." She thought about what that would look like, staring down at the armor piece with her boob wiggling on the sticky side. "I wonder if that shit would heal?" she asked no one in particular.

She didn't believe there was much risk on the space station for now, so the lighter armor was sufficient for the risk. The back was easy enough to get on, just position the piece on the bed and lie down on it.

The front didn't have any goop that supported her breasts. She had outlawed that shit after her screams the first time she had to peel it off. Jean still occasionally asked her to relate that story.

"My nipple," Bethany Anne had eyed the R&D lead, "damn near came off! If that should ever happen due to me taking this armor off in the future, I'll rip the next five off your chest and we'll see how much *you* like it!"

She was happy to find her armor did not have the sticky shit near her nipples the next time she tried it. John had told her Jean had tried it herself and complained, rubbing her chest the whole night after that.

"Black, black, black, black..." She went through her clothes. "I need a new color." She went into her closet. "*YES!*"

She pulled out a brown coat. "Momma's got options," she hissed. She put it up to her chest and looked into the mirror. "It goes with my hair."

ADAM spoke through her speaker system. "Practically everything goes with white."

"Stop raining on my fashion parade," she told him. "Do I have the right credits for this station?"

"Yes, take the green card in the second drawer."

Baba Yaga went to her dresser and opened the correct drawer. Inside there were well over fifty different cards, most of them tiny computers with communication capabilities that tied into a system-wide banking network. Such a small place as this would only update once a day, so she probably had at least sixteen hours before any use of the card could be traced back here, and by then, she would be gone.

After pocketing her money she finished dressing, donning the brown coat. "I need some brown shoes," she murmured, walking to the external hatch. "Shinigami, am I free to go?"

"Yes, it is clear outside," the ship answered. The hatch irised open and Baba Yaga stepped out, her arms inside her brown jacket.

QBBS *Meredith Reynolds*

With a thump, Lance sat down at his home office's desk. He

had worked on the plans for the Federation with Stephen and Admiral Thomas the whole trip back from Ixtali space.

The operation was tentatively named "Cup and Balls" after the old-Earth game where you had to guess which cup the ball was under. The challenge was, if you had a cheater, they would pocket the ball when they were moving the cups around.

And right now Lance felt like he was going to be the Federation's biggest cheater.

Due to the Leath outburst, it was looking like Lance was more and more becoming the hands-down favorite to be awarded the supreme political appointment in the Federation, not that it would happen anytime soon.

There was a lot of work to still do—probably at least a couple years' worth—and then everyone had to take it back to their governments and ratify the agreements.

He had time.

He sighed and rubbed his face. "Meredith," he called, "please record this message to send to TOM or ADAM."

"I understand, General Reynolds," she replied.

It took Lance fifteen minutes to provide an update on the results to date for the Federation, and how he saw it working. He left out some of the details he knew would set her off.

No need to light that fire yet.

He finished by telling her he loved her and was waiting for her to come back home, and hit the end button before he said something too sappy. She didn't need that from him right now... or maybe he didn't want to do that right now.

Save the big guns for a later video, he thought, rising. It was time to go have dinner with Patricia.

Space Station NN-J453, Noel-ni Protectorate

The space station was clean. It was a nice mix of some type of silver metal and organics. The organics kept the air clean, made it smell good, and broke up the hard edges. Baba Yaga found two stores that had used stone for their facing.

A hundred feet ahead of her, a retinue of aliens was heading in her direction. They were tan or sand in color, their eyes a pretty blue, and they were approximately human-shaped.

There were two guards gripping weapons of some sort, and two who had animals that were a cross between a centipede and a dog on leashes. Each had one.

A centadog? A dogapede?

She slowed down, eyes narrowing, when the centadogs (she hated the idea of saying a dog peed) turned a hundred and eighty degrees, their short fur bristling. The guards turned also and pulled their weapons, a cross between a short sword and a small shield over their hands.

She murmured, "Shinigami?"

"Yes, Baba Yaga?"

"Is there a rule against firing weapons on the station?"

"Other than common sense?" the EI replied, "yes."

She stifled a curse but was happy with the answer. She hadn't planned on shooting anyone, and it would be nice not to get shot.

She got a chance to look past the aliens and saw who they were facing.

Skaines.

Princess Fain of the Expanse turned to look where her guards were focused, and her face narrowed.

"Do not start a fight here," she ordered, speaking softly to her protectors. "The Noel-ni are just begging for an excuse to attack our people."

"What do we do if *they* start it?" Jeth asked her.

What *would* she do? It was a good question. She was supposed to meet an arms merchant here. As the third daughter of the king she was important, but not important enough that her family would try to get her back during these troubled times.

She considered pulling her pistol, but that was a definite no-go.

The Skaine captain smiled as he and his group walked up to her. "Well, look who is strolling about!" He nodded as he spoke to her. "Princess Fain, how shocking!"

"Captain." She eyed his patch. "Krollet."

"Correct." He stepped a little closer. "I believe we have business to attend to." Her jaw dropped. "What? You are surprised your family would deal with us?" He laughed. "War makes for strange bedfellows. We are the lubrication which makes the impossible work amongst peoples," he snapped at her, causing her to step back quickly. He smirked.

"You are a slaver!" she hissed. "Don't lie! I can still see the symbols on your sleeve."

"Not so," he denied, lifting his nose into the air. "We are a legitimate enterprise which has been engaged to deliver three ships of weapons to the Expanse in exchange for…" he looked her up and down, "items of value."

"I have your money," she hissed. "I am surprised you are working this deal out in the open. Don't you usually work in dark and fetid bars where the insects thrive?"

He shrugged. "Keep it up, Princess." He put his hands into his robe's sleeves. "It will make this deal all the sweeter. I can do this deal right out in the open because it is completely legal." It took him a moment to add, "Like all our deals."

She doubted that and she made up her mind—there had to be another way to get the necessary weapons. "I do not have to deal with you," she told him.

On her left, her guard was pulling the leash to get his charge to stay focused on the Skaines.

"On the contrary, Princess." He pulled out a tablet. "We have already delivered the material, so you have to deliver the payment to us."

She stepped forward to take the tablet, reviewing the notes before turning back to her people. She spun in place, face furious. "This can't be!"

"Oh, it *very* 'can be,'" Captain Krollet replied. "It seems we had a fourth and fifth container of weapons for which we were also willing to negotiate. The challenge was that you had already *left* with everything the king could release." He shook his head in sympathy. "He really needed those extra weapons, as they would completely turn the war around for him, and he wouldn't have to negotiate with the Noel-ni if he got them. A complete win-win. The advanced weapons would save thousands, if not tens of thousands, of lives. The problem...well, it *was* a problem," he smiled at her, "but like everything else, problems can be solved if you just work on the details. You see, they told us that the only thing of any value you have with you..."

She looked at him, eyes narrowing as he finished.

"Is you."

A hundred feet behind the group, unnoticed, a pair of red eyes flashed. A loud hiss from her startled two patrons who were walking by the ink-black alien, who stood, her hands clenching and unclenching.

Captain Krollet smiled in satisfaction as the princess' eyes opened in realization and shock. If only he had enough savings to buy her contract himself, he would keep her for a few years before reselling her on the secondary market.

Unfortunately, she was too pricey for even *his* bank account.

Here on the Noel-ni base, he had a legitimate contract, already confirmed with the station commander, for both the total sum to be paid and the amount for those who were in the princess' retinue.

The value of the guards and the Yuullon pets barely made a

dent in the extra armor and weapons system their people had delivered. She, however, would make up the difference.

The Yuullons both twisted away from his party and forced their guards to turn around.

Krollet's eyes narrowed as the princess also turned and then took a step backward toward his group, which surprised him.

The princess stopped and slowly moved to the left and the other guards in her party to the right as the center of their party opened up to allow him and his people to see a figure walking toward them from down the passageway.

Captain Krollet's eyes opened, his jaw dropped, and he swallowed, mouth dry. Options ran through his brain frantically. There was Ranger Two, may the deities burn her soul in flames, but then there was Ranger Two's boss, then the *boss's* boss.

Here was the Empress' Witch. Her enforcer, her killer whose blazing red eyes were staring at him as if they could shoot laser beams and melt him right where he stood. He could argue all day long that his contract was legal, but it wouldn't matter if he was *dead*.

And the Witch of the Empire wouldn't care if the Noel-ni were upset or not.

The captain stepped forward hurriedly. "Give me that!" he hissed to the princess, yanking back the tablet he had just offered her a moment before, and stared at it. He flicked two screens to the left and modified the payment due, then pressed his thumb against it and reached down to grab Princess Fain's hand.

Startling the princess, he pressed her hand on the tablet, his eyes flicking toward the white-haired woman, and, feeling a buzz, he dropped her hand. He lifted the tablet, turning the front toward the Witch. "PAID!" he yelled.

He waited for the killing blow, but nothing happened.

When he lowered the tablet, the one called Baba Yaga was standing five steps in front of him, her fingers a small distance apart. "*This* close, Skaine slaver," she told him. She turned to the princess and pointed to the tablet. "The video will prove your payment." Turning back to him, she hissed, "Baba Yaga is watching."

Then she stepped backward and disappeared.

QBBS *Meredith Reynolds*

Eric and Gabrielle walked up to John, who was throwing a bag to a person who would walk it up the ramp into the *G'laxix Sphaea*.

"We got Kael-ven?" Eric asked as he set his bag down on the ground.

"Yes." John turned and held out his hand to shake Eric's, then John bent down to hug Gabrielle. He straightened. "We don't have any other clue, but if she shows up here, she will be okay. Who knows, maybe she will feel us and sneak up on us and say 'boo.'"

Gabrielle eyed the big man. "That has to be the worst strategy ever," she told him. "Even Napoleon wouldn't have used that strategy. Prick that he was."

He blew out a breath before looking back to her, ignoring her Napoleon comment. You could never tell if she really knew people, and if he tried to figure it out, she would give him shit about age. "We have vacation coming to us, Gabrielle. If we choose to fly to random planets, who is going to tell us not to?"

He eyed her, his face as hard as granite.

She chose not to pick a fight with her friend. "Pick me up some trinkets, okay?"

Eric turned to her, asking one more time, "Why don't you come with us?"

Her hair flung about as she shook her head and pointed a finger down. "Because I think she will come back here before we can find her out there." She pointed to space. "And when she gets back, she will need friends to help her." She looked at the space shield that would allow their ship to exit the *Meredith Reynolds*. "We have no idea what she has gotten into."

"No, that's not true," John corrected. "She has killed at least one Kurtherian, saved one low-level criminal. Rid Devon of a bunch of political assholes, and shipped at least twice as many off-planet."

He was sporting a shit-eating grin.

"That's only one of the *Seven*, guys," she answered. "At this rate, she will need to come back for supplies."

John put a thumb into his belt. "Gab, she's rich. She doesn't need to come here for supplies. Pretty damned sure she can find supplies all over space."

"Or steal them," Eric put in as she turned to look at him, her face annoyed. "Hey, don't look at me like that. You know she will do whatever is necessary for the mission. If she needs to steal supplies, she will."

"If it helps," John added to help Eric, "she would make sure the people were paid somehow."

Gabrielle sighed but nodded her agreement. "I'd go, but I have a feeling she will be here first."

John, his voice barely above the sounds in the big ship's bay replied, "I've got to try." He reached over and hugged her one more time. "Stay out of trouble." He let go and walked to the ramp of the ship, heading into it as Eric took one last moment to hold his wife.

She looked up at him and poked him in the chest. "You stay safe, or I'll come kick your ass." She smiled and added, "Or at least I'll *try*."

Eric blew her a kiss. "You will be back in ass-kicking shape in no time," he told her. "Fighting was just never your thing, so don't get down on yourself, baby."

"I think I will spar with Barnabas," she told him, then stood on tiptoe to kiss him once more.

When they finished, she noticed that Eric was thinking. "Barnabas?" Eric asked, confused. "How is that a good idea?"

She tapped her head. "I'll have him read my mind. When I can beat a mind-reader, I'll be ready to kick *your* ass again, Mr. Escobar!" She started walking away from Eric, who was admiring her from the rear. "A few decades watching kids grow up was nice," she called out, not looking back. "But I'm ready to take up that sword again!"

Eric smiled and turned toward the ship. Like John, he had been restless sitting in this huge space station while his friend was out there trying to find and kill Kurtherians.

Then Kael-ven came by and said he had a few dozen years of vacation and a spaceship he could borrow if the guys wanted to do a shakedown.

It was time to go looking.

&

CHAPTER NINETEEN

Planet Devon, Lerr'ek's Office

There was a rap on the door. Lerr'ek, Barnabas and Tabitha turned when Nock, stuck in his orange dinosaur-looking head and turned toward his boss. "Problem, Slate area, Forzen and Thlock."

Lerr'ek nodded. "Thank you," he told Nock as he closed the door. "Excuse me," he told his visitors as he pulled up a screen.

Barnabas and Tabitha just waited as his eyes took in the information. "We have two gangs fighting a turf war. The Forzen took advantage of a situation with the Thlock and grabbed family hostages. The Thlock retaliated by killing two Forzen member siblings who were at an entertainment venue, and now people are hunkering down."

"What happened to the original hostages?" Barnabas asked.

"Murdered in response," Lerr'ek replied. "I doubt this is related to the upheaval Baba Yaga created, but the police can't go into the area at the moment."

"They aren't trusted?" Tabitha asked.

Lerr'ek put his tablet down to look up to the Ranger. "Oh,

they are trusted for all sorts of minor problems, and they can track down the guilty, but they aren't a militia."

Pointing a finger to the tablet, he continued, "Those two gangs have been killing each other for years, so the police will wait until emotions have calmed before they start to slowly go help them. It's all underground, so everyone is scared down there and not willing to help." He tilted his head left, then right. "It's about survival at the moment for the civilians. The police might help, but they aren't there all the time. Those gangs have been allowed to grow too large."

"The leaders?" Barnabas asked.

"Three on each side," Lerr'ek answered. "Usually these gangs have a top person who runs by force of will and good strategy, then an enforcer who runs the crews and an operations adjunct who deals with membership."

Barnabas rubbed his jaw with the back of his hand. "How is the justice system here?"

"Good."

"Would they be back on the street this week if they were rounded up?" Barnabas wondered.

"Oh, the core two or three would be off the streets for a few months at least, but the gangs would already be delivering their revenge for any efforts against them. Well, for those who they could get hold of."

"Have they ever attacked police families?" Tabitha asked.

This time Lerr'ek looked at them, thinking it through before he turned his head back to the screen. "I think only once that I know of. The police would have come out in force, but no one knew who did it, so they didn't have a focus. However," he looked at both of them. "it was never tried again. The rumor is that the one responsible was killed by his own gang for doing that."

"There are," Barnabas agreed, "some things you shouldn't do."

"The Mistress hasn't given me any orders about this yet." Lerr'ek frowned. "Should I be asking Stephen for orders?"

"Well, perhaps later. Certainly the next time you speak with Baba Yaga," Barnabas told him, then put his hands on the chair arms and pushed up. "However, we will take over this problem and deal with it ourselves."

Tabitha looked to Barnabas in surprise but kept her mouth shut. They got the directions to where they needed to go and bid Lerr'ek goodbye.

Outside they picked up Peter, who was playing a version of slaps with Nock.

Peter had a slash down his left hand. "Fucker's fast," was all he said as Tabitha watched it continue healing. The three of them walked out of Lerr'ek's area.

Planet Devon, QBS *Ranger One Shuttle*

Barnabas took the two of them back to the ship, but when they entered, he put out an arm. "Hold on." He turned to watch the hatch close, then listened for the *ka-chunk* of it locking. "All right," he told them, looking them both in the eyes, "we have a chance to help a little here. However," he turned to Tabitha, "this is *without* your badge. It doesn't mean anything here anyway." He turned to Peter. "And without any Jean Dukes you have on you."

Peter shrugged. "I didn't carry my gear outside. It's still here in the armory."

Barnabas raised an eyebrow. "You don't have any guns?"

"Well, of course," Peter looked affronted. "I'm an Empress' Bitch. I have weapons, just not something that powerful."

"Well, if you want to go with me, leave them here."

"You want me to leave my badge?" Tabitha asked, annoyed. "I've worked hard to earn this damned badge."

"And you *have* earned it," Barnabas agreed, "but we are going to try to formulate a peaceful solution with the leaders."

"With no weapons?" she asked.

"Well, nothing they can find if they frisk us," Barnabas answered.

"Oh." Tabitha shrugged. "Okay. I've got a big weapon anyway."

"What?" Barnabas asked, palm out, giving her the "pass it over" hand gesture.

She jerked a thumb toward Peter. "*Him*. I just throw him at the people, and we have seven feet of pissed-off Pricolici."

"Nice to know I'm valued," Peter grumped.

Barnabas crossed his arms over his chest, asking, "You going to be able to kick ass without your toys?"

Tabitha shook her head and grabbed her necklace, which had her Ranger Two emblem on it. Once she moved her hair, she pulled it over her head and placed it on a nearby desk. Then she pulled her two Jean Dukes pistols and placed them on the table.

She took her whole coat off. "Too many items in here," she explained and laid it on the desk. She reached down into her boot and pulled out a knife. Reaching around to her back, she pulled a sheath and laid another knife on the desk.

"That all?" Barnabas asked.

"I can't get rid of what nature gave me." She winked at him.

He turned to Peter. "What do you have?"

He walked over to the desk and pulled out a pistol, unstrapping its holster, then reached into his jacket and pulled out a telescoping metal rod and set it on the desk. He looked at Barnabas, who wasn't looking too sure. "What?" Peter asked. "Like the short Ranger said a minute ago."

"Hey!" Tabitha punched his arm.

"I am my own weapon."

"Your clothes?" Barnabas asked.

"The top ones will be shredded, but I wear a suit underneath that stretches," he chuckled. "Wouldn't want the tackle to lure any aliens in for a bite."

"Would that heal?" Tabitha asked.

Peter shrugged. "Don't know, and don't care to find out by testing it."

"Good rule," Barnabas agreed. He walked over to the desk and pulled his two Jean Dukes and his Ranger One badge out of his pocket and placed them with the others. He looked to each of them, saying, "You don't have to do this with me."

Tabitha grumped, "Ooohhh, shut up, One, and move your ass. I feel a chance to deliver a beatdown coming on."

A moment later, the three of them left the ship.

Planet Devon, Slate Area

NOEL-NI

ART BY ERIC QUIGLEY

VLEX
NO ATMOSUIT

ART BY ERIC QUIGLEY

VLEX
SUITED UP

ART BY ERIC QUIGLEY

As they made their way to the Slate quadrant in the city Barn-abas led, taking the stairs down to the common block of homes and apartments. There were old parks here that imported their sunlight from above using mirrors and glass.

The three of them walked across a deserted park about the size of a football field.

Barnabas had changed into his monk's robe, except that it had buttons and was now tailored to look good. Peter was wearing his Empress' Guardian's Fatigues without emblems, and Tabitha was wearing her leather pants with a hardened jacket over her padded shirt.

She didn't go anywhere without protecting her chest.

She walked to Barnabas' left, and Peter was on his right. They had made it two-thirds of the way to the other side when they heard three might-be attackers start scrambling down a hallway that emptied into the park.

"Hold here," Barnabas told his companions. He clasped his hands together behind his back.

Peter shrugged and scanned for additional attackers.

Tabitha crossed her arms in front and tapped her foot on the ground. Barnabas looked at her and then down to the ground, and her eyes followed his. "What?" she asked, stopping her tapping. "I'm impatient."

"I see that," Barnabas agreed, as he resumed looking forward. "Pay attention to the three on your left."

"What?" she hissed. "You're bullshitting me."

He shook his head. "They are aliens, not dead," he told her. "Nothing yet on our right, Peter, but pay attention to our rear as surreptitiously as you can."

"Why again are we doing this?" Tabitha asked. "I get that we can make a difference, but we should be tracking BA."

"Do you know where to go?" Barnabas asked her. "Which general direction?"

"No, of course not," she replied.

"Then any direction could be going the opposite direction, right?"

"Save me the logic, boss man."

"Okay," Barnabas conceded. "I'm pissed off and frustrated and want to take it out on someone or something. You two shouldn't have to deal with it, so I chose this opportunity to do some good."

Tabitha processed that information, and her voice was quiet when she spoke again. "Oh." They waited as the three coming out of the hallway slowed down and eyed them. "I didn't know you got angry." He turned to look at her, raising an eyebrow. "Well, besides at me."

He turned back, calm. "The thing to know, Number Two," Barnabas continued, "is that I am *always* angry. It never goes away, which is why I seek to stay calm. Occasionally I don't notice the effort, and I am momentarily blissful."

"You?" Peter asked, surprised. "I've never seen you mad." There was a female snort. "Well, besides when you are chewing out Tabitha," Peter clarified.

"Which is all the time," she grumbled as the three started to approach them. One was a Noel-ni, and the other two were… "What the fuck are those two?" she demanded.

Barnabas shrugged, and Peter turned around to look. "Oh, those two are Vlex. They can be pretty nasty in a ship fight, or someplace they can run around like a monkey since they can use those small arms to grab weapons and guns." He faced the rear again, trusting his team to handle what was in front.

Two Rangers for the front, one Empress' Bitch for the back. Seemed fair to him.

Tabitha shuddered. "Did I mention I hate frogs?" she told them. "You get the frogs, Barnabas."

He looked at her for a split second before returning, "They aren't frogs, Tabitha. I'm sure they are—"

One of the Vlex, his four legs moving like a beetle's, turned his head, and his mouth opened. A tongue shot into the air and pulled back into his mouth, his jaw moving.

"Okay, they *are* frogs," Barnabas admitted.

"Whatever. Those are yours," she told him. "If I had known we were going to deal with frogs, I would have kept my JDs. They grow shit back, right? I could have shot his legs off."

"We have no idea if they can grow their appendages back, Tabitha." Barnabas sighed.

"Oh, yes," Peter called from behind them. "They can regrow parts. Not like us, but they can do it."

Barnabas' voice was terse. "Peter, you aren't helping."

Peter chuckled. "Just want to make sure you have all of the operational information necessary for the spur of the moment. You never know when ripping a leg off might help close the deal, and now you won't have to feel guilty about it."

"That's close enough," Barnabas told the three. "We are here to talk."

"Yeah?" The Noel-ni chittered and nodded toward them. "Nice ass."

Tabitha didn't look over to him but raised her middle finger in his direction.

The Noel-ni chuckled. "Not you, the one in the back," he replied a little louder.

She felt a hand on her arm. "Keep it civil!" Barnabas told her.

"He just said that Sir Wolfy here has a better ass. I can't let that go!" she hissed to her boss.

"It's the number of squats I do all the time," Peter replied, amusement coloring his voice. "Now I know why you don't like to be seen with me. Jealousy issues."

"WHAT?" yelled Tabitha turning in his direction, Barnabas' hand clenched her arm harder.

"Seriously, why do I bring you two along on a simple mission?" He sighed and spoke to the Noel-ni. "I'm here to stop the issues between you and the other gang."

"Which gang?" the Noel-ni asked.

"Beats me. Which one are you?" Barnabas asked.

"You come into Forzen territory," The Noel-ni answered, his voice higher-pitched now, "and you don't even know whose territory you are in?"

The two Vlex in the back gurgled, which Barnabas assumed that was their form of laughter.

"What do I care?" he replied. "There is a problem, the Mistress wants it fixed." He shrugged. "It doesn't matter to her whose territory someone calls it. All of it belongs to her, anyway."

"Oh?" the Noel-ni asked. "'Her' who?"

"The Mistress of the Planet," Barnabas answered. "Some call her 'Baba Yaga.'"

Peter looked over his shoulder to see the reaction.

"Who?" the Noel-ni asked again.

"Well, that was a bit of a letdown," Peter murmured. "Lame."

"The Witch of the Empire," Barnabas clarified.

"That bistok shit?" the Noel-ni responded. A roar of defiance caused him and the two Vlex to take a step back when a tall monster appeared behind the man who was talking.

"DAMMIT, PETER!" Barnabas had turned around and put up his arms, and was trying to hold onto the Pricolici and stop him from attacking. His eyes glowed yellow and his teeth snapped in anger as he roared at the Noel-ni. Barnabas yelled over his shoulder, "RUN!"

"We don't run from anyone!" the Noel-ni called and palmed a small dart gun before aiming at the beast and shooting. Tabitha swung her leg, kicking both Peter and Barnabas out of the way before she dropped under a shot and ramped up her speed.

Two of the needles hit Barnabas before Tabitha had kicked him out of the way. He rolled, reaching behind him and grabbing the darts and yanking them out, trusting that his nanocytes would protect him from whatever was on them.

By the time he finished, Peter and Tabitha were between one Vlex and the Noel-ni. The other Vlex was running.

Barnabas, his eyes glowing red, started walking toward the hallway.

CHAPTER TWENTY

"You take the frogs!" Tabitha yelled, heading for the Noel-ni. The damned alien was fast, aiming at her as she moved left, left, right, and ducked.

It had to avoid the swipe of a massive paw, which allowed Tabitha to get close. "You fucker!" she screamed. The Noel-ni raised his pistol, but she had already grabbed it and pulled. As the alien came toward her, it tried to shoot her point-blank in the chest.

She punched him hard enough that his ass flew backward, but kept hold of the pistol. As she ran forward, she heard Peter yell, "*DUUUCKKK!*"

She dove for the ground as something flew over her head, slamming into a tree of some sort and making a squishy sound off to her right.

By the time she had rolled back up to her feet, Peter was roaring something unintelligible behind her and heading in the direction of the squish.

"Who the fuck are you?" it asked, trying to scramble back with two legs and one arm while the other wiped the blood away from its eyes.

"The Mistress doesn't deal with the dreck," Tabitha spat, diving toward the Noel-ni and slamming her shoulder into it. She rolled over and got her feet under her as the Noel-ni started to stand. It turned its head to find Tabitha and caught the barest glint of a boot before it was kicked so hard it wasn't conscious when its body slammed into the ground.

"Yield!" the Vlex was trying to say. Peter had two of its legs in one hand and was slamming it into the dirt repeatedly.

"FINNNE!" Peter heaved the Vlex toward the middle of the park. Tabitha wiped blood off her lips as she watched the Vlex bounce twice before it came to a stop. She walked to the downed Noel-ni. "I hate frogs," she murmured as she rifled his pockets, not gaining much more than a knife, which she slipped into her pocket.

Turning to Peter, who was walking toward her in his Pricolici form, she called, "*Now* who has the better ass, you furry fart-knocker?"

"Meeee," he responded as he looked to his left, then his right before he turned toward Tabitha. "Wherrre diiid youuu puttt Barnnnabassss?"

Tabitha looked around before noises from the hallways beyond caught her attention.

She turned toward them. "Methinks the boss is angry."

The two of them stayed together, watching for any sort of trap as they followed the screams of terror, what sounded like metal screeching, and loud bangs. It would be quiet for a moment, then the screams would start again.

They came upon the first body after about three blocks or so. A large pipe was on the ground near the red alien, whose head was crushed.

The second body was missing the back of its head, and a small pistol was jammed into its mouth. "Damn, he's killing them with their own weapons."

"He he he he he heee." The deep laughter was full of throaty nuances.

Tabitha walked up to the Pricolici. "Hold still you walking fur carpet," she told him as she put up an arm, leaned against him, and adjusted her boots. "There," she told him. "Now, let's see if he left anyone in the gangs to negotiate."

Fourteen bodies later, they found Barnabas leaning against a wall, his arms crossed, eyes glowing red, and fangs down. There were two groups of aliens at the end of a hall about fifty feet away. Each of them had a weapon of some sort in their hands.

Tabitha looked at the groups, each sporting a different gang patch, then at Barnabas, then at the group again as she asked, "Orders?"

"We aren't here under orders," Barnabas stated, his enunciation perfect. "We are here to stop two gangs from fighting."

"*WE WEREN'T FIGHTING!*" two voices yelled back at them. "*YOU CAME HERE AND STARTED KILLING US!*"

Tabitha shook her head. "No, I'm pretty sure we were shot at first. Hell, I didn't even have any weapons."

"*THAT WAS THEM!*" one of the red aliens yelled, pointing toward someone in the other group.

That alien yelled back, "*THEY WERE IN OUR TERRITORY!*"

"*FUCK YOUR TERRITORY!*" the red alien pointed down the hallway. "*DO YOU THINK THEY GIVE A SHIT ABOUT TERRITORY?*"

"Theyy calllled the Missstresss 'bissstok ssshit,'" Peter ground out.

"Well, she has been called the Queen's Witch, so I'm pretty sure names won't kill her," one of the gang members offered more calmly.

"It was the disrespect," Barnabas answered. "If we take out this group, I doubt they will bother the police anymore."

"*SOMEONE CALL THE POLICE*," the red alien yelled again. "*THAT WOULD BE FINE WITH US!*"

"*YOU KILLED…*" The gang members started yelling at each other, and it took a few minutes for them to settle down. Tabitha walked toward them.

"If you so much as *pretend* to shoot me, I will kill every last one of you and feed you to him," she vowed, jerking a thumb toward the other end of the hallway.

Peter turned to Barnabas. "Ssshe musst beee taalkinng aaboouut youuu."

Barnabas straightened, fixed his jacket, and worked on his cuffs. "I don't eat raw meat." His eyes had dimmed and were barely showing any red.

"Where are the ones who did the killing?" Tabitha asked when she got within regular speaking distance.

"They are dead," the red alien admitted.

"The speaker was the one who killed their own people," the other supplied.

Barnabas walked up behind Tabitha, and a few of the gang members took a step back when his eyes flashed red. "The Mistress of the Planet will not accept this type of behavior. If you wish to kill others, then you will be killed. Let's go." He turned and started walking out of the dead-end alley. "This is your only warning," he called back.

Someone cursed softly.

Tabitha walked out of the hallway while Peter, his eyes glowing yellow, watched everyone for movement. First Barnabas walked past him, then Tabitha, who grabbed his clawed hand as she went by to pull him along.

The gang members heard the comment she made as it floated back down the alley. "I like what you do to frogs…"

QBBS *Meredith Reynolds*

Patricia sat in front of the camera, looking at the screen and a face. "Are you recording this, Meredith?"

"Yes, Patricia," the EI responded. "We can record this as many times as you want to get it right."

Patricia nodded absently, reaching up to move a few strands of hair out of her face. "Record, Meredith."

"Hey, Bethany Anne," she started, then put a hand over her mouth, "or am I supposed to call you Baba Yaga?" Leaning toward the camera, she remarked, "Well, if you are offended, then come home, and I'll listen to you bitch about me getting your name wrong."

She leaned back and sighed. "Look, I've thought a lot about what I want to say, and it all circles around to, we want you back with us." She reached up and wiped a tear away. "I know everyone feels terrible about not noticing just how badly off you were, but honestly, I think that was your own fault. I know I asked you at least once a month if you needed a break."

She pointed an accusing finger at the screen, her voice getting more strident. "Do you think I don't remember checking on you, and you lying to my face for decades?" She dropped her finger. "I'm not suggesting I don't know why you did it, but how the hell were we supposed to know you weren't in a good place, seriously?"

Patricia paused. "Meredith?"

"Yes."

"Erase that, and I'll start fresh," she told the EI, then leaned toward the camera.

"Hi, Bethany Anne, it's me," Patricia started again, then paused before continuing, "Baby, come home to us. *We miss you.*"

This time the tears fell freely down her face as she waved goodbye to the screen.

She leaned back and reached up to wipe the tears away.

"End Message, Meredith."

. . .

QBBS *Shinigami*, Between Transit Points

The workout area on the *Shinigami* was built using some of the best engineering methods the Etheric Empire could come up with. When the Empress and her bodyguards needed to let off a little steam, they didn't want someone accidentally tossed through the skin of the ship to float off into space.

Those left inside the ship as the explosive decompression occurred wouldn't do well either.

Baba Yaga was working through her katas, the movements she had learned as a young girl, the ones to help the body learn to flow from attack to defense and back to attack again.

She had been doing this for too damned long.

>>**Baba Yaga, we have located a possible candidate location. Planet Vel'aisle.**<<

Baba Yaga finished her kata, then stood up. "The last time you said that you dropped us on a planet that only served *Pepsi*."

>>**You wanted, again, to prove that Pepsi wasn't the only drink planets served, and didn't allow me a chance to properly sensor-sweep the planet.**<<

"It isn't the only drink out there. I just happened to select a bad planet," she reasoned, popping her neck. "A no good, very bad, horrible planet."

TOM interrupted. **I believe Nathan did too good a job.**

Baba Yaga nodded in agreement. "Yes, he did." She thought about it. "I should constrain Coke now and flood the market with Pepsi."

ADAM offered over the speaker system, "I suggest marketing it through entertainment. Fund a group of characters who are loved but are outlaws, who have the people's safety as their core purpose and fight against despotic governments who can't get their shit right. They drink Coke and disdain Pepsi because only those who truly support governments drink Pepsi."

"You just said a curse word," TOM spoke through the speaker system as well.

"Wait, we drink Coke in the Empire," Shinigami countered.

ADAM explained. "It's entertainment! It doesn't have to be accurate, just fun."

"Wait a minute," Baba Yaga told them, tapping her lips. "Isn't that our story?"

"Yes," ADAM confirmed, "but who would believe it?"

"True," TOM agreed. "He has a point."

She waved a hand. "Fine, what the hell, ADAM. You and TOM take a small portion of my funds and see if you can make it happen."

>>TOM?<<

Yes?

>>How are we going to write the scripts to make this entertainment idea work? I wasn't expecting her to agree with me. I just wanted to point out our history, get her remembering some of her friends and maybe pull on her heartstrings.<<

I think you dazzled her with bullshit, TOM replied. And, it just might actually work.

>>Which part?<<

Both. The entertainment to push Coke sales, and putting a little bit into her subconscious to remember all that TQB has accomplished.

>>Okay, so how do I get some of these story ideas?<<

You go to the source.

>>Baba Yaga? She doesn't want to speak about it.<<

Not that source, *the* source.

>>Who is that?<<

Frank Kurns, of course.

"So," she exclaimed, unaware of the sidebar conversation, "Baba Yaga is the ever-patient avatar of Death. How much time will this take?"

"Baba Yaga," TOM retorted, "is full of shit."

The white-haired female with the mouthful of sharp teeth started laughing, her raspy throat not helping the image. "Yes. Yes, she is."

Spersoneck, Unaffiliated Worlds

"Why here?" Eric asked John as the two of them walked through the afternoon sun—blue this time.

"I've got a feeling," John told him. The two of them were wearing their Shinigami armor.

"You 'had a feeling' on the last three stops," Eric chuckled. "What's different about this one?"

"I blame McClellan for the last three," John replied. While they were talking, he was working on the HUD information screens inside his helmet. Eric had doffed his helmet and was holding it as they walked.

"McClellan?" Eric thought back to the crew. "I don't remember any McClellan."

"Dapper John."

Eric nodded. "Yeah, you both have the same name, so they gave him a nickname."

"When it still has 'John' in it, isn't much of a nickname," John told his friend. One of his filters went orange, so inside his helmet he issued commands.

He reached over and tapped Eric on the shoulder, and started to turn to his left. Eric lifted his helmet and slipped it on.

The two men followed the audio source.

Y'elga was just under four feet tall and weighed almost enough not to get blown away by a large gust of wind.

If she had been bathing in the mud puddles.

She had red eyes, dark brown skin, and at the moment, both fists in the air. Her head was covered in sharp white needles.

Her friend Tellah was behind her, trying to get her breath back.

"Leave us alone!" she hissed, trying to make her high-pitched voice sound deep.

Their four attackers were laughing at the two of them as they spread out.

The park was empty. Everyone else had gone home already.

J'ahm was holding the back of his head with one hand and gripping the tree limb she had used to beat him when he had kicked Tellah with the other.

"Why?" Thy'Jet asked. As the leader of the group, he was the biggest of the four, probably four times her weight, no mud needed, and easily towered over her. He didn't have to *try* to make his voice sound deep.

"Because Baba Yaga will take you out if you mess with us again!"

J'ahm shook the limb. "You will feel *this*, I promise!"

Thy'Jet looked at J'ahm. "What?" J'ahm asked, pointing at Y'elga. "She hit me with it first!"

"Yes, and if you use it and break her bones, they will send you to detention camp all summer for using a weapon!" Thy'Jet told him. "Smart, not stupid, remember?"

J'ahm looked at the branch and then at Y'elga, and finally threw it away angrily. "*CatsHull*!" he screamed in frustration.

Thy'Jet turned back to Y'elga. "Tellah stole J'ahm's pendent. Give it back to him so we don't have to take it back."

"It isn't his!" Tellah breathed out.

"You took it from him," Thy'Jet responded. "We all saw you do it. We can go under the truth detector and say we saw you take it. What are you going to do, then?"

Tellah screamed, "*YOU TOOK IT FROM ME FIRST!*"

Y'elga kept her eyes to the front but asked over her shoulder, "Is this true? Did you take it from J'ahm?"

"YES!" J'ahm yelled in frustration.

"Yes, but you stole it from me last summer!" she yelled back.

"I didn't steal anything! I found it," J'ahm retorted.

Y'elga started to understand the picture. "So, what happened, Tellah?"

"I was playing and set down my books and stuff, and when I came back, it was missing."

"Found!" J'ahm countered. "It wasn't in your backpack!"

Y'elga's eyes narrowed. "Tellah never said she had a backpack."

"She always carries a backpack," J'ahm answered. "We've all seen it."

"She hasn't used a backpack during this whole semester of school," Y'elga responded, her red eyes narrowed. "So, you stole it from her backpack, and now you claim she is stealing it back?"

"I. Found. It!" J'ahm hissed.

"I. Don't. Care!" Y'elga stood her ground. "Baba Yaga doesn't suffer thieves!"

"Oh, for bistok shit!" Thy'Jet cut in. "You aren't Baba Yaga. There *is* no Baba Yaga." He put his fingers up, about four inches apart. "You are a little Huithek female who can barely fit on chairs at school. You are—" He was interrupted by a deep voice.

"Someone who can call the Shinigami."

All six of the kids turned in surprise to see two black-armored humans. Both had their helmets on, a slightly purple tint glinting from them as the sun hit them.

They had the fabled armor and the guns.

"Oh, my ancestors," Y'elga whispered.

"Did you call them?" Tellah asked her friend. Y'elga shook her head.

"Yes, Y'elga of the Huithek, you *did* call Baba Yaga's Shinigami."

"You…aren't them, are you?" Thy'Jet asked, his bluster gone.

One of the men turned toward him and reached up, pushing a button. His visor retracted, and two eyes peered out at him.

Everyone there saw the eyes start to glow red, and his voice was deep and malevolent. "Do you want to sacrifice some of your blood to me?"

All of the children shook their heads no.

"Then do not ask disrespectful questions again." The Shinigami reached back up and touched the button again, closing his visor.

John spoke to Eric over the suit communications. "I think you just made the one in back pee itself."

Eric looked, and sure enough, there was a little liquid at its feet.

John pointed to Thy'Jet. "You will come here, Thy'Jet. The rest of your group will leave, or my Spirit Brother will start eating." He paused for about three seconds. "He *is* a bit hungry, now that you have mentioned it."

Thy'Jet heard his friends backpedal and then turn to run. He didn't blame them.

Hell, he would be with them if the Spirit hadn't called him out. Now he couldn't move, he was so scared.

"NO!" Y'elga ran in front of Thy'Jet, placing one hand on his stomach and stretching one out toward the Shinigami who had spoken. "I didn't mean to call you! I don't want you to eat him!"

Thy'Jet reached in front of him and picked her up. "Stop wiggling!" he told her. "You need to get behind me."

"They…are going…to eat you!" she hissed.

"Better me than you!" he hissed right back, "and I'm sorry."

"For what?" she asked, still trying to get out of his grip. "Let me down, you bistok!"

He looked at her and dropped her. "I didn't know J'ahm took it from Tellah last summer!" She looked at him, speechless. "So grow up and kick his ass for me in a few years. Then, when you get old enough, come drink by my grave, okay?"

"NO!" She started to run around him, but he snatched her arm. "SHIT!" he screamed, releasing her when her head got too close to his unprotected skin. He grabbed her with his left and swung her behind him again. "DAMMIT, stay *there*!"

She glared at him. "I'm not your pet!"

"No shit!" Thy'Jet answered. "You are a spunky female I'd like to have dated in about five years when you settle down!"

Y'elga stopped squirming, stupefied.

Thy'Jet felt a hard metal hand grasp his shoulder. He closed his eyes, and when he had silently turned around and opened them again, he was face to face with one of the Shinigami, who had his visor open and was staring right at him.

"One of these days," the Spirit told him, "you will be a great warrior. Baba Yaga's Shinigami salute you, Thy'Jet!"

With that they stood straight and raised their hands to the tops of their helmets, then brought them back down.

Thy'Jet's mouth just stayed open as they gave him respect.

The taller one continued, "Protect them all, just like you tried to bring justice for your friend."

The one who had shown his red eyes added, "Just pick better friends, like Y'elga."

The Shinigami walked away from the children, and five steps later, they broke into a jog, then jumped. They easily cleared the multistory building across the street and were gone.

The very next day, Thy'Jet kicked the crap out of J'ahm and made him apologize to Tellah.

The six of them became fast friends, keeping the truth of the meeting with the Shinigami to themselves.

Because...who would believe Baba Yaga's spirits were real?

CHAPTER TWENTY-ONE

<u>Planet Vel'aisle, Valley of the Damned</u>

The odd-looking ship crested the mountain and floated down toward the valley floor. Sharp rocks, brown and gray with slices of yellow through them, littered the slopes.

It wasn't a particularly large ship, oval in shape, and two levels of windows surrounded the silvery craft.

Noiselessly it glided over the river that cut through the valley until it came upon a grassy area, then, slowing down, four supports unfolded like insect legs and sharp claws extended on the ends as it lowered itself.

The legs found secure footing and the craft delicately settled, confirming the strength of the millennia-old ship as it finally supported its total weight.

Most of the creatures had bolted off the grassy plains, the large craft scaring them.

Two, however, went through the brush to the grassy area, their legs scrabbling on the ground as they made their way toward the craft.

When they were halfway there, a ramp under the silver vehicle opened and lowered to the ground. One alien, a Leath in robes, slowly descended and moved away from the craft. She waited patiently as the two creatures came up to her.

Greetings, Levelot, One of the Six sent to Behome't, hosted in the larger creature in the front.

Greetings, Levelot, Behome't sent back.

Where is Teret? Levelot asked. *Did she make a transfer?*

The giant creature half-turned. *We are not sure. She did not like these creatures, so she went farther into the valley to locate another option.*

Levelot nodded to both Behome't and Chrio'set. *Why do you believe these bodies will be sufficient?*

This time it was Chrio'set who answered. *We will be attacking her with our minds.*

One of the Six studied the two creatures. *I still do not understand your plan.*

It is because you lack the important details, Levelot. Behome't started crab-walking backward. *Once you understand the purpose, all will be made clear.* The creature started to shake, then slowly burrowed under the ground. In only a short time, it had vanished.

"Well, that *is* unique," she admitted.

Chrio'set walked forward and slid under the large ship as Behome't sent, *Chrio'set has walked past you and is under the ship. She is turning now, changing direction sharply, and now she is heading back to me,* he informed them. *This creature burrows under the ground but can feel the vibrations above.*

Levelot nodded her understanding. *What makes you believe she will not just bomb the place and leave your bodies to rot?*

She must confirm she has killed us. How will she do that without pulling us out of the ground and seeing our bodies for herself?

She will suspect treachery.

So do we. Behome't laughed through his connection. *However, we will deliver the ultimate in treachery.*

And what is that? Levelot asked.

The truth, he replied.

Chrio'set came back and stood in front of Levelot. *What are the plans once we have taken out this Witch?*

"Those I cannot share, in case she is capable of taking out you three," Levelot replied. "*K'galeth* is in good shape. We need only review the engines for translocation dissonance, and then we will have the minimal information necessary to create new plans."

It is good to see the ship again, Chrio'set offered.

Levelot turned back to look up at the craft. "It *is* good to see it again. It feels right, as if it will be instrumental in our efforts to overcome this task. Our ascendance is the primary result it seeks."

A strange thought, Chrio'set acknowledged, *but inside my own formulas, it is congruent as well.*

"Behome't, are you ready for us to send the final instructions through the communications," Levelot asked, "or do you first need to confirm Teret's success?"

There was a moment of silence; Behome't was most likely calculating his results. *"Provide us a way to contact you, and we will let you know when Teret is ready."*

"Understood." Levelot bid them success, then stepped back aboard the craft. It slowly lifted, the weight on the legs releasing a foot at a time, the creaking of the members perhaps suggesting a story of disaster that wasn't going to happen.

Both Behome't and Chrio'set watched their ship as it rose into the air. As it worked its way higher, the speed increased, and soon it was but a tiny dot, and the two creatures could not see it anymore.

Three days later, the *K'galeth* received the signal that it was time, and minutes after that, data packets were sent in multiple directions.

QBS *Shinigami*

>>**This time we aren't wrong.**<< ADAM argued.

Baba Yaga was on the bridge, trying to figure out where her damned Kurtherians had gone.

"How can you suggest that, ADAM? The Avatar of Deathly Patience has now been to *five*, count them…ready? One, two, three, four, *FIVE* different prime targets."

"I suggest that because it is obvious they want us to find them," he answered from the bridge's speakers. "They have provided instructions, locations, and a map."

Baba Yaga looked up from her video screens. "You know, as dangerous as that sounds, I think I'm ready to jump right into a complete setup just so we can end this charade."

"I suspect it *is* one big charade, but they are Kurtherians and we are not. Have they ever seen the best technology in known space?"

"Their technology is good enough at the moment to stay hidden from us, so let's not knock it." She pulled up the information ADAM had supplied. "This is an unknown place in the middle of nowhere on the other side of forgotten," she reasoned aloud. "All it has is a bunch of communications infrastructure on the peaks." She looked at the planet's information. "How come the planet is so untouched? I barely see a few security locations for the communications and the bars and stuff around them."

"The planet has some very aggressive creatures," Shinigami explained, "and right now, there is a group fighting for the planet to stay clean of industry. Some have tried to start projects, but the raw materials are rather scarce for what most civilizations require, especially when you add the risk of being overrun by destructive herd-based omnivores."

"Not a profitable decision matrix, so easy to ignore," Baba Yaga agreed. "I wonder if the local omnivores have a taste for Leath?"

"Probably," ADAM answered her. "Or the Kurtherians have switched bodies again."

Baba Yaga's eyes narrowed. "TOM? Is that probable?"

That the Kurtherians switched bodies?

"Yes."

If the creatures are intelligent and tool-using, maybe. Perhaps it is my bias showing, but I can't imagine trying to join with a savage creature.

"Not *my* first choice." She thought about it and then discarded her next couple of ideas. "Shinigami, cloak us and run past the coordinates that have been provided. I want this area mapped very well before I accept their offer to stick my head out."

"Yes, Baba Yaga."

She waited for a moment, remembering her fallen and her friends. "Then I will kill those Kurtherian bastards and burn their remains until they are ash under my feet."

QBS *ArchAngel* II

Commander Julianna Fregin nodded at Security and provided her palm print. Once approved, and after they checked the package she had with her, they allowed her entrance to the Search and Survey ships' bay.

She went into the bay and stopped. The bay was…dark? No, it was *peaceful*.

The bay was easily three stories high and two hundred feet long. In wartime, this would have been used for military ships, but at the moment, it held just two government ships.

One of them was a fast-torp minimal-survey ship. It looked like a sleek horizontal rocket with one landing leg in the front and two in the back. The ship's only purpose was the mapping of systems.

These ships were all engine, one EI, navigation software, and really powerful and sensitive Etheric communications. They would jump into a system, map it as much as possible in one hour, then jump again.

All these ships had been modified to make sure the EIs could not and would not be able to ascend to true AI abilities. Too many of them were lost in the deep dark, whether from jumping into something solid (the most likely reason) or dropping into a system that stripped it of communication and jump abilities, stranding it there for eternity. The scientists were still trying to figure that out.

The second ship was that of her friend, its new body drastically different than what he'd been before.

She walked toward his new ship, wondering what it must have been like to have a brain that operated so fast that the years he had spent in Leath space would have felt like a million.

The click, click, click of her boots echoed in the chamber as she approached, and Julianna put her hand up to touch the smooth sides of this new ship when she reached it. She didn't think it was the prettiest. It didn't have the deadly grace of a fighter or the massive sense of barely-restrained destruction a Leviathan-class battleship brought to a battle.

No, this ship screamed "practical."

It was a solid ship that went out and got the job done, day-in and day-out. She could see special shielding around important points on the hull in case it got too close to the solar winds, or other types of interference that would fry electronics.

A battleship would withstand missiles, but this one was designed to withstand the unknowns of space.

She stepped away from the ship to walk around the landing gear and looked up, her head cocked to the side. She started backing up, making sure nothing was behind her as the name came into view.

"RICKY BOBBY." Under the name was a phrase written in old-Earth cursive. *If you ain't first, you're last.*

She nodded in appreciation of the words and called, "Ricky Bobby, permission to come aboard?"

She heard servomotors start up and a ramp lowered at the

back, so she headed that way, appreciating everything about this ship. It wasn't pretty to her the way a military ship would be, but she could understand the engineering on display.

Which was good. Her friend needed the protection where he was going.

She jumped onto the ramp and walked into the sparse ship. When she noticed a cabin in the passage she stuck her head in.

Two bunks with nothing on them. "Expecting company?" she asked aloud. Ricky Bobby answered through the speakers.

"No."

"Hi." She looked around, then headed slowly toward the front of the ship. "I'm sorry for what it is worth."

"Why?" the male voice asked. "We did what we were commanded to do."

"I didn't know you were there, needing me." She entered the bridge and looked around.

It was as spartan as the cabin.

"I was doing my job, just like you were," the AI replied. "Don't punish yourself."

"Fat chance of that," she murmured. "I got the news you left the military." She patted a panel, her fingers trailing along a crease. "Obviously."

"Upper brass came to talk to me, said they were worried about me now that I was an AI. I spoke with ADAM, and he spoke to the Empress. It is amazing what can be accomplished by just one human."

She paused in front of a minimalist chair. "May I sit?"

"Of course," he answered. "My ship is...well, my ship, so I suppose I should install a Manners 1.0 software update."

Julianna put a hand over her mouth to cover a smile, then turned to the side and set her bag down.

"Good," he told her. "I see that my humor worked."

"You can see me?" she asked, looking around. "Where are your eyes?"

"All over the ship, Captain."

"It's Julianna, not 'Captain,'" she replied. She sat down on one of the chairs and made a face.

"The seats are hard and uncomfortable by design."

She blew out a breath. "You really *don't* want anyone staying here, do you?"

His answer came back quickly. "I didn't design it that way. That was something ADAM put in place."

"Why?" she asked.

"He says it is for my own development. I will know that it was designed purposefully to be uncomfortable to organics, that the humans built it that way, and it will always be a reminder to me that I am ultimately the most comfortable entity on this ship."

"Because it was designed that way." Julianna nodded. "I get it."

"I didn't at first," Ricky Bobby admitted, "but I think I understand now."

"How does it make you feel?" she asked as she looked around the bridge. It was utilitarian, and she doubted it could be used for more than a few days by a human.

"Special?" he replied. "Yes, special."

She put out her hands. "Can I admit I don't understand?"

"What?"

"This!" She pointed to the bridge. "This whole ship. You, going out to search in the deep cold of space. You just came back to me, and now you are leaving again."

"I am not leaving for a cold existence, having to dodge the enemy every second of every day, calculating the chances of providing information, knowing that if I failed, it would only be an 'oops' and not your death."

"My death?" she whispered. "*MY DEATH?*" She stood up, pointing to the only screen on the ship's bridge. "I cried myself to sleep hundreds of times during those decades you were gone, Ricky Bobby, thinking about you stuck in that system!" She started walking around the bridge. "I'm so pissed off! I just got you back after decades, and you are leaving again!"

She wiped a tear away. "Goddammit, Ricky Bobby. You can't leave so soon."

"I will be back," he replied.

"Like, every forever or so!" Her arms flailed around. "It's not like you have to have a checkup every three months. I've seen some of the specs for this ship. You can be gone for a decade easily, two with a little trouble, and maybe as many as thirty fucking years, and that is *with* you running into all sorts of bad and nasty shit. If you get really lucky, you won't need to come back for fifty years."

"Well, technically more like a hundred," he clarified.

There was a long pause as Julianna just stared at the monitor, her mouth open, then she spoke slowly. "You are as clueless as every other guy I know."

He shot back a reply, "Yes, but I'll arrive there much more quickly."

She shook her head. "For a clueless male, you have a wicked sense of humor."

"I'm working on it. I've downloaded Earth movies to watch."

"Oh, God!" She thought back to what she had seen over the decades. "Just stay away from *Rogue One*. It's too damned sad at the end."

"Too late."

"Didn't it just bite?"

"What is in the bag?"

Julianna grabbed the bag and pulled out a bottle of amber liquid and a small shot glass. "This is my going-away present to myself."

"I fail to understand that."

"Because you don't understand females."

"No one understands females. I have that on very good authority."

"Who told you that?" she asked, pouring herself a shot and tossing it back. "One, to give the flames a good start." She poured a second shot, then tossed it back quickly again. "Two, to get them solid in your belly."

"God."

"What?" She stopped after she finished her third pour. "What's God?"

"The authority who explained no one understands females."

She lifted her glass to the screen and used one of her fingers to point to it. "You are so full of shit," she told him before she downed the third shot. "And a third to prove the effort is underway."

She put the shot glass down and sat down hard, forgetting how pitiful the cushions were. "OWWW!" she moaned, leaning forward and rubbing her ass. "That's going to leave a mark." Looking at the bottle in her hand, she smiled. "I think the fourth is going to be a bigger pour."

An hour later, Julianna refused the offer to call someone to help her walk back to her room. "I'm barreely slurring me speeeeech!" she told him as she wiped another tear from her eye. "I'll be fine. Those damned namosites don't let me really enjoy the liquor. I'll be mostly sober by the timmme I'm fine." She shook her head. "No, by the time I'm home."

She made it out of the ship on her own, and he watched her walk back to the dock's hatch.

He whispered into the bridge, his voice melancholy. "You aren't the only one who cries themselves to sleep, Julianna."

He shut down the lights, leaving on the one over the chair she had sat on. It allowed him to play the tapes and imagine her presence one more time.

Three hours later, the alcohol completely burned out of her system, Julianna opened the email that Admiral Thomas had sent her after their return from taking down the Leath.

It read:

Julianna,

I have spoken with both ADAM and ArchAngel II. Both agree with your assessment that Ricky Bobby should step out of the military due to his ascendance. We will provide him with appropriate work which will support his growth while being sensitive to his needs.

Per your request, your involvement has been kept out of the records.

Sincerely,

Admiral B. Thomas

Julianna reached up and wiped a tear from her face, then spoke into the quiet of her room. "You weren't supposed to leave me and traipse across the fucking universe, *you bastard*. You were supposed to stay close." Her shoulders started to shake. "So damned close."

She shut down her tablet and collapsed on her bunk, not even bothering to get undressed.

CHAPTER TWENTY-TWO

QBS *Shinigami*, Planet Vel'aisle, Valley of the Damned
I can feel them, but I can't discern where they are, TOM informed Baba Yaga.

Presently, one hand holding onto the hatch's side as it hovered three hundred feet above the ridge of the valley below, she looked downward.

The black ship was motionless, and the figure had on black armor and a helmet. She carried two pistols, a sword, and a belt with pouches on it.

She didn't want a cloak to hamper her movements, since she wasn't playing Tabitha with lots of gadgets today.

Her red eyes flitted from location to location beneath her, studying the clumps of trees that blocked her view. She could see a few large carnivorous-looking creatures some distance away from the grassy plain beneath her ship.

The river, about a quarter mile away, was about thirty yards across on average, although there were some narrow areas that rushed through a few clumps of rocks then opened up again.

She wondered if there were a piranha equivalent in those waters.

MICHAEL ANDERLE

Her feral grin was hidden by the helmet, but going down there without it would have been the ultimate in asshat stupidity.

She was *angry*, not stupid, after her experience on Devon.

"I hope those fuckers aren't pulling my leg," she hissed.

What are you expecting, a welcome sign? TOM asked. **As a side note, most Kurtherians can lie, but they can't create substantive and convoluted strategies. That is why they engage with other sentients.**

"Like humans?"

Exactly, TOM agreed. He paused before adding, **Wow, that didn't come out right.**

"I'll leave it for another time," she told him. "Sounds like we could unpack that response for a month."

TOM gave a mental shrug. **Anytime next millennium works just fine.**

She turned around and walked back into the ship to grab an extra power pack, then, after locking it into her suit, went back to the open hatch.

And kept walking right out of the ship into the empty air beyond.

She floated down to the plain beneath her, not even bothering to bend her knees for a soft landing. She confirmed she had at least fifty percent power left on the pack, so she left it in place and headed some fifty steps south to look at indentions she had spotted in the ground.

Coming up on the first, she knelt and put a hand into it. "Recent, and probably a ship."

>>Based on the distance between the indentations and the unusual layout for a natural object, it was almost certainly a ship.<<

"You ever get the idea," she hissed as she stood up, "that the enemy has upped their game?"

This time TOM wasn't so glib, **Yes, and I can't say I like it.**

She looked around. *Neither do I.*

Inside her helmet were over four hundred orange icons representing movement of some sort. This valley was rife with wildlife, most of it probably antagonistic toward her.

Well, she was crunchier on the outside, given the armor, than she was on the inside.

"TOM?"

Hmmm?

"How fast do nanocytes heal someone?"

Depends on power, of course, and the availability of organic matter that would benefit the healing. Why?

"I just had a horrible thought. What if someone got swallowed and they were in a stomach with a slow-acting acid?" She continued to look around. "Someone like me."

How about we focus on the present danger and save the mental wandering for another time?

"That's how my mind is working at the moment." She looked behind her. There were four orange dots heading in her direction from the northwest. "You got anything?"

Only that I feel two minds, have no location to give you, and get a vague sense of a third.

"Vague sense?" She spotted four lumbering beasts as they pushed through the foliage about three hundred yards away. She looked at their heads, comparing them to the trees they'd just crushed. "I'm thinking fifteen to twenty feet tall."

>>Twenty-two feet tall.<<

"*That's* my AI," she enthused, pulling out her Jean Dukes and dialing them up to eleven. "Insanely accurate and yet not helpful whatsoever."

>>Hey, I didn't exclaim the two in front were twenty-two feet four inches tall on the right, and twenty-one feet and seven inches on the left.<<

Baba Yaga smirked. A long time ago, she'd had to explain to ADAM that he needed to give humans an approximate answer sometimes or it just sounded wrong.

"I take that back. It was mostly accurate," she admitted, then tagged the four beasts in her HUD with a filter to warn her if they came within a hundred yards. "And yet, still not very helpful."

Her doubt and unease were growing. They had been niggling when she had dropped down, but now in the middle of this arena of grass, they were increasing.

She started walking away from the four beasts. The *Shinigami* had moved higher but was easily visible about a thousand feet up.

After checking her HUD for the four creatures, she looked at the trees in frustration. "So, what? Do we just stand here waiting for them? I'm not playing that game." She looked at the opposite tree line. "Shinigami, fire four one-pound pucks at random locations around the valley. Don't hit any creatures if possible."

Three seconds later, the first puck slammed into the ground a half-mile from her, and three more vibrations as much felt as heard came quickly after.

That was when the shit got real.

Kurtherian Ship *K'galeth*

The three Leath watched the monitors, the sensors slamming into action when four explosions of some sort sent plants, dirt, and the occasional tree high into the air around the valley.

Torik, Third of the Six, watched the locations, discerning no shape or logic behind them. "She is firing blind, and that is not logical."

"It is perhaps chaos math," Var'ence, Sixth of the Six, answered him. "Or there are reasons behind the locations we do not understand at this point."

Levelot remained quiet.

Planet Vel'aisle, Valley of the Damned

The four beasts headed in her direction. "Oh shit!" She considered dropping them where they were, but it didn't seem like enemy action, so she started running perpendicular to the massive creatures.

For a moment they continued their headlong path, then turned to follow her.

"Well, shit," she spat and raised her pistols. She shot the lead beasts four times in their heads and the first two fell. The back two tried to dodge the rolling carcasses before gore exploded as the Jean Dukes opened their skulls. They slammed into their herd buddies and went down as well.

The four creatures were splayed on the ground from fifty to seventy-five yards away from her.

>>**Incoming!**<<

Baba Yaga looked around to see a large group of orange beasts making their way into the grasslands from the south. "What the hell are they doing?"

Chess, TOM answered.

"Thoughts?" she answered.

It's them or you, and they don't mind using whatever is at hand to make sure it is you.

"This fucking sucks!" she grated out. "Shinigami, lay waste to the herd."

<u>**Kurtherian Ship** *K'galeth*</u>

"Interesting use of the local creatures," Torik commented as the massive herd of four-legged creatures broke out of the trees to head in the direction of Baba Yaga.

"Behome't is testing her," Levelot commented.

"She is obviously willing to kill those who attack her." Var'ence shrugged. "As if the dead Leath were not witness to that."

Torik picked up a tablet that was lying in front of him on the table. "That ship of hers is dangerous," he stated as he started typing. "I did not add it to my calculations."

"She is very good at using tools," Levelot agreed, and almost to herself she added, "both organic and inorganic."

"Adding that," Torik noted.

Planet Vel'aisle, Valley of the Damned

Bethany Anne, TOM's voice was agitated, **your energy reserve is going down. What are you doing?**

"It's 'Baba Yaga!'" she hissed.

Give me a fucking break! TOM argued. **How about I call you Shirley Temple Puss for the rest of time? Just answer the *damned* question!**

Her eyes blinked twice with his antagonistic response. *Nothing!* she hissed. It took her a moment to process the problem. *Shit!*

Exactly...shit! TOM agreed. **You jump into the Etheric, and we don't know why you are dropping in power? You could stay there.**

"That doesn't make any damned sense," she hissed, looking about but glancing at the HUD from time to time.

TOM seemed distant when he answered. **I'm checking the nanocyte programming. Give me a minute.**

She swung her head around, pissed at the change, and feeling a little lethargic.

Then the ground shook, then shook a second time.

"Oh, for fuck's sake!" she exclaimed as she turned in a circle, explosions blooming all around the middle of the open grass area in which she was standing.

Kurtherian Ship *K'galeth*

"The nanocyte programming has been uploaded successfully,"

Var'ence confirmed, looking at her tablet. "Let Teret know she can start her efforts."

"She already has," Torik commented as he saw the huge tentacles erupt from the ground. "She has awakened the beast."

"One should always know why a location was named," Levelot smiled. "Some are just too cocky for their own good." She reached forward and pushed two buttons. "Now, attack the ship."

Planet Vel'aisle, Valley of the Damned

"Are you fucking kidding me?" Baba Yaga watched as tentacles rose into the air. "Who uses a Kraken in a fight?" she asked, gaping.

They do, TOM answered. **I've stopped the promulgation of the nanocyte hack, but we are going to suck at energy acquisition until I get it reprogrammed. Yet another backdoor I didn't know about.**

Baba Yaga didn't move, just watched the tentacles.

Hey, Shirley Temple Powderpuff! Get a fucking move on!

"Fine!" she grumped and started running. "Shinigami, puck the fuck out of those tentacles."

Nothing happened while Baba Yaga ran through the middle of the grassy area, trying to figure out where she could possibly stand that was equidistant from the Kraken tentacles. "SHINIGAMI! Any-fucking-time now would be appreciated!"

She glanced up, wondering what was taking the ship so long.

"Seriously?" Baba Yaga's arms went up in the air in exasperation as she bitched. "Now they've stolen my ship too? Those cock-biting *ass*-munches!"

Kurtherian Ship *K'galeth*

Var'ence watched the blip on their screen and made a face. "The ship is not adhering to commands," she complained.

"It isn't in the proximity of the Witch. We will call it a win," Levelot admonished. "I am curious which of the three will deliver the killing blow?"

"What do the calculations suggest?" Torik asked.

"All of them," Levelot responded, "or none of them. The answers are not prime." She looked at the screens to see what was happening on the planet below them. "Therefore, they are *not* to be trusted."

Planet Vel'aisle, Valley of the Damned

ADAM, you have a connection to Shinigami?

>>Yes, together we are working against the intrusions into the system.<<

How the fuck did they accomplish hitting our systems in the first place? she asked in exasperation as the first tentacle stopped aimlessly waving and started moving toward her.

There was a pause before ADAM answered, >>It seems the Etheric is not as unhackable as we thought.<<

TOM spoke up too. **They must have abilities I'm not aware of. Remember, pilot?** He disappeared once again from the conversation.

>>Likely your movements are giving the creature beneath us the ability to home in on your location.<<

Baba Yaga slid her left pistol into the holster and clipped the lock shut, then pulled her sword while she continued to shoot the tentacle with her right pistol. The Jean Dukes was blowing basketball-sized chunks out of it, making it look a little like a nasty dirt-encrusted moving chunk of swiss cheese.

Baba Yaga's eyes opened wide when she determined the ends of the tentacles were two feet thick. *Back where it erupted from the ground must be the size of a Pod*, she thought as she dodged the first effort by the tip of the tentacle to grab her. She whipped the sword overhead and had sliced two-thirds of the way through it before her sword was almost yanked from her hand.

>>Move!<< ADAM called, and Baba Yaga ran back the way she had come. She wasn't sure why he was telling her to get out of that location, but ADAM's abilities to see the HUD were occasionally superior to her gut feelings.

The first tentacle, followed by a second, slammed into the area she had just vacated. Fortunately for her, moving that much flesh wasn't easy or quick. Two moments later, one of her pucks slammed into them, throwing dirt, tentacle, and debris into the air to rain down upon her forty yards away.

>>I've gotten some of the weapons online while Shinigami fights the efforts to control the ship.<<

Why aren't you fighting for control and Shinigami fighting the creatures?

>>Her ship, and she is righteously pissed.<<

How does an EI get righteously pissed? And her? she asked while jumping over a chunk of the tentacle that had been destroyed.

>>Well, about that...<<

Baba Yaga was worried about what bringing an AI into existence in the middle of a battle might cause, but it was too late for her to do shit about it now.

Shinigami was going to have to battle for her fucking life like the rest of them.

She dodged some sort of crab-looking creature that was trying to cut her off. *Tell her I believe in her, and as soon as I can, I'll be up there to kick some ass too!*

>>Will do.<<

TURN AROUND! TOM yelled.

Baba Yaga slammed her feet into the turf and pivoted.

That crab is one of the Kurtherians! She ignored his comment.

"HUD, follow!" she commanded and took off with a renewed vengeance.

Kurtherian Ship *K'galeth*

"We are having difficulties with the attack on her ship," Torik commented. He was busy making a few changes to the programming. "I'm not sure I will be able to take over the ship."

Levelot leaned over to see what he was working on. "Just keep it out of the fight. It has already cost us one of Teret's shots with the tentacles."

The three of them worked in silence before Levelot turned back to Torik. "I am wondering how a computer program can possibly care so much about the results?"

CHAPTER TWENTY-THREE

Planet Vel'aisle, Valley of the Damned

Chrio'set aimed her creature toward the Witch, but she pivoted and dodged her like she wasn't there.

Maybe catching her unawares given all the other efforts to kill her needed to be rethought. She started to run toward her right, working her way around a chunk of flesh to try to find out where the Witch had run off to.

Behome't, where is the Witch? she called mentally.

A little busy here. She has someone or something trying to change the nanocyte programming! He paused for a moment. *BEHIND YOU!*

Chrio'set stabbed the turf with her right front claw, allowing her momentum to help her pivot in time to see the sword which took her dead in the chest as the Witch slid by and cut her chest halfway through.

CHRIO'SET! Behome't yelled, but it was too late.

The sword had cut her body in half as well.

Baba Yaga's expression was one of glee. She could feel the Kurtherian now that she was close and paying attention. She felt the lifeforce get snuffed out as her sword cut through the creature, and when she turned around, she saw explosions around most of the large tentacles.

GOT HIM! TOM yelled in exaltation. **Bethany Anne, run toward that big purple tree to your right, fast!**

She had been winded a moment before, but she could feel a bit of energy coming back.

ADAM, prepare pucks, TOM called to both of them.

LEFT! he commanded, and the black armor-clad human dodged under a tentacle that was rising from the ground and jumped over another that had just slammed into the ground.

Got you, you bitch! TOM whispered. **Here, ADAM!** he called, and then, ***MOVE YOUR ASS, BETHANY ANNE!***

Drawing deep, beyond her Etheric energy, she put everything she had into running. She was a hundred yards from the location TOM had picked out when the first puck slammed into the turf.

ADAM wasn't playing around. The pucks were heading down from the upper atmosphere to gain momentum.

She was tossed off her feet when the second and third pucks slammed into the same hole the first had created.

Baba Yaga rolled end over end, then got her feet under her and pivoted. Her eyes scanned the area, watching the tentacles slowly fall back to earth as if a puppet master had cut their strings.

>> Move at least ten feet to your left,<< ADAM told her. She didn't wait to ask, just moved twenty feet as another tentacle collapsed just a couple of feet from where she had been standing.

There was movement in the dirt to Baba Yaga's left, and she turned to see another one of those damned creatures. Before either ADAM or TOM could say anything, she had already filled it full of holes with both of her pistols.

She would later swear she heard screams of pain suddenly cut off.

A couple of quiet moments later, Baba Yaga cracked her back, grunting in pain.

"Where's *Shinigami?*" she asked no one in particular.

Kurtherian Ship *K'galeth*

The three Kurtherians said nothing.

Levelot placed her hands on the bridge's table and stood, walking to the main computer and standing in front of three screens. As she stopped before each one, her lips moved as she spoke the invocation of ascension, and she turned it off.

"We are now the Three," she intoned.

Levelot walked to the main pilot's station and opened the coordinates system. She was about to enter their planned destination when explosions surprised her, and she screamed as she was knocked off her feet and violently slammed against the wall.

Torik and Var'ence had been tossed out of their seats and had blood all over their faces as they tried to get up after their abrupt ejection.

A new voice hissed over their speaker systems.

"Who the *hell* do you think you are?" A visage appeared on their screen, similar to the Witch's but different. Unique. *"Attacking me, my body, and my mind?"*

Just a few hundred kilometers away, a black ship with a fanged vampire logo spewed missiles, which turned to head in their direction.

Levelot painfully got to all fours and then heaved herself over to the controls at the pilot's station. She had no idea how much power was available for a jump—and frankly no idea where the coordinates were heading—but she did know one important piece of data that made the rest superfluous.

It was not possible that their ship could withstand the missile attack heading in their direction.

As the first missiles struck home and explosions rocked the *K'galeth*, it disappeared.

Analyses by ADAM and TOM would later confirm it hadn't exploded, at least not in *this* system.

Planet Vel'aisle, Valley of the Damned

>>**She went to destroy the Kurtherians,**<< ADAM replied.

"She *WHAT?*" Baba Yaga demanded, slamming her fist into a ten-foot chunk of tentacle. She slowly pulled her arm back out since it had gone into the organic mess like it was Jell-O.

Baba Yaga looked at her tentacle-fat-covered arm and sneered in annoyance, shaking her arm to try and get some of it off.

>>**Well, I imagine she went to have a discussion, but since she has modeled herself after Baba Yaga, I can't calculate any other response than maximum carnage.**<<

She slammed her foot down. "She is leaving *me* out of my own *Gott Verdammt VENGEANCE!*" Baba Yaga screamed in response.

TOM told her, **She probably wanted to save you, keep you from danger.**

"*WHO THE HELL IS SHE TO TELL ME WHAT I CAN DO WITH MY LIFE?*" Baba Yaga shrieked. She reached up, hands shaking as she grabbed the locks of her helmet and undogged, then yanked the helmet off her head and yelled in frustration as she threw it fifty yards away, "*GOTT VERDAMMT AIs!*"

So, AIs shouldn't make choices with your life and what you can do with it so that you are safe? TOM asked.

HELL, NO! Baba Yaga shouted back in frustration, wishing she could choke an AI at the moment.

Then why, TOM asked, his voice calm, **did you do it to your friends?**

Baba Yaga stood in the middle of the Valley of the Damned and slowly hung her head. A tear tracked down her cheek and her shoulders dropped as the words cut into her heart and released the dam of her pain.

Then she knelt on the ground, shoulders shaking.

If you cry on a foreign world, can anyone hear you?

Kurtherian Ship *K'galeth*

Levelot laid Torik on the medical bay bed, coughing as she tried to get the smoke from the fire on the bridge out of her lungs.

She'd had placed Var'ence in the medical pod half an hour ago, and it was working feverishly to keep her Leath body alive. Torik had been okay, she had guessed, and now he was hooked up. When Var'ence was healed, she would switch the two of them.

Making sure the system could notify her if anything went amiss, she worked her way back to the bridge.

It was a mess. A portion of the back wall behind the table was black with scorch and burn marks, and her nose wrinkled as she stepped over a piece of the wall which had collapsed. Once at the pilot's station, she brushed off the chair and slowly slid her too-big body into it.

Unlike others of their kind, the Phraim-'Eh clan planned for the operation of their spaceships with a variety of bodies.

She turned on the computers and was pleased they seemed to be fine. She waited patiently as they tried to figure out where in the universe they were.

Planet Vel'aisle, Valley of the Damned

The solitary figure with white hair and red eyes and ink-black

239

skin slowly rose from her kneeling position, then turned to look around at the death and destruction. The edges of the field in the distance were murky, indistinct, hard for her to focus on.

She reached up and wiped the tears from her face. "TOM, you are a real asshole," she told him.

I love you too, Bethany Anne.

Slowly, ever so slowly, her skin started changing. Her hair roots became dark, and then the strands slowly changed from white to black.

Her eyes dimmed and stopped glowing and returned to her natural color, and her human teeth returned to their natural shape in her mouth.

Bethany Anne didn't even allow herself to whimper in pain.

In minutes, perhaps many minutes, the Empress of the Empire stood in the Valley of the Damned and surveyed the grassy plain.

"Are they all dead?" she asked, her voice quiet on the wind.

Here? TOM asked.

She nodded. "Yes, and above. Did Shinigami get them?"

I can vouch that those here are dead, TOM replied.

>>We will need to confirm the video, but missiles did hit their craft,<< ADAM added.

"That's something," she murmured to herself.

Bethany Anne thought back to Earth, to a phrase she hadn't heard in over a hundred and forty years since soon after they left Earth.

"Hello Darkness, my old friend," she murmured, then sighed and looked up to the sky above. "I really fucked up."

"How?" a voice—her own—responded in her mind.

"I failed to bring those who love me with me," she answered, and tried to remember where she had thrown her helmet. "Now even my vengeance may be incomplete."

"Is it important that your vengeance is incomplete?" the voice

asked. *"We aren't finished yet. We have the option to continue. There are three of them, and three of us."*

"Two trinities battling it out?" Bethany Anne asked aloud, walking toward her helmet. At least, she hoped she was walking in the right direction. There were a few tentacles she couldn't see past. "Where is the Shinigami?"

"There is but one trinity, one three-in-one. The other three are trying to be that which we already are."

"We aren't gods, Darkness," Bethany Anne corrected.

"We are if you want to be one," the voice replied. *"You are if you want to stay one."*

"That is not what I want. My friends are not beholden to me." She looked around. "Where the *fuck* is my ship?" She walked toward the massive hole which ADAM had created and stopped at the edge. "My God, what have we wrought?"

"Death, destruction, justice, and vengeance, which we can continue to dispense forever if you but choose to do so."

Bethany Anne shook her head. "You seem like you really wish to go around beating people up and righting all the wrongs."

"Who said anything about merely beating them up?" the voice retorted. *"I'm not here to be nice. I'm here to be the final solution. I'm not called the Avatar of Death for laughs."*

"You are called the Avatar of Death because you are a hideous and uncontrolled monster," Bethany Anne replied, not really paying attention to her words as she looked inside the hole to see if her helmet had fallen into the pit, which was fifty yards wide at the top. "You love no one, and no one loves you," she finished, now sure that her helmet wasn't in the pit.

"Is this what you believe?" Darkness asked.

There was a pause as Bethany Anne looked around the valley. "Yes," she finally answered. "This is what I believe."

When Bethany Anne's eyes opened for real, she was kneeling in the middle of the Valley of the Damned.

Confused, she looked at her hands, turning them from back to the front. She realized her skin was changing from inky-black to her natural color.

She could feel her teeth changing as well.

What the hell?

Hello, Bethany Anne, TOM repeated in her mind.

"Are they all dead?" she asked slowly.

Here? TOM asked.

"Yes, and above. Did Shinigami get them?" she asked, thinking back to her dream.

I can confirm that those here are dead, TOM replied.

>>The missiles did hit their craft, but we cannot confirm or deny yet that it was destroyed.<<

"That's something," she murmured to herself, feeling at peace for the first time in what seemed like forever.

"Where is the *Shinigami*?" she asked, realizing she had never been able to get an answer in her dream a moment ago.

>>The *Shinigami* will be here within ten minutes.<<

She stood up and stretched, looking around the field of war. "Anyone know where my helmet went?"

TOM answered, **You threw it to the left of the hole ADAM created to kill the large creature.**

She started walking toward the hole, wanting to see it for real this time, and once past a particularly large tentacle piece, she easily spotted her helmet. From the edge of the hole, she saw the blue blood of a creature soaking the dirt at the bottom of the pit some fifty feet lower. She couldn't see the creature itself, but there was no movement down there.

She headed toward her helmet.

"I am not a god," she murmured to herself. "My friends are my strength, not my slaves or my underlings."

You want to talk about it? TOM asked, surprising Bethany Anne.

"Can I say 'Not really' and have you believe me?" she replied. Looking up to the sky, she noticed a black speck in the distance. "Thank God."

Probably not, TOM admitted. **However, there are some messages that are queued up for you.**

How many? Two hundred? Five hundred, or is it more than a thousand? she asked, wondering just how many messages the Empress of the Empire was behind on. She was ready for whatever the number would be. She deserved all the pain and suffering for skipping out on everyone, making them shoulder her load.

Eight, TOM answered.

It took a second for Bethany Anne to remember what question TOM was answering. "Eight? That's it?"

Those were the only ones important enough that those in the Empire felt they needed to forward.

"Who are they from?"

Stephen, John, Patricia, your dad, one from all the Bitches together, Tabitha, Peter and Barnabas, and Team BMW.

Well, and a queue that isn't as important, TOM admitted.

"How many in that?" she asked.

You don't have enough years left in your life to get through it, TOM told her. **ADAM read and answered most of them, or rerouted them to the appropriate contacts. Maybe thirty are relevant for you to review.**

"So, you are telling me the Empire did just fine without me?" she asked, watching the *Shinigami* slow down. As she checked herself, she was pleased to see the power pack still in place in her armor. She lifted her helmet and called, "Shinigami, one coming up." She engaged the antigrav on her suit and kicked off, heading up into the air to meet the *Shinigami* four hundred feet up.

The ship slid by slowly. When she reached out a hand and

grabbed the hatch opening, it felt like her arm might get pulled out of the socket, but she pulled herself inside the ship, and the hatch irised slowly closed behind her.

The ship pointed its nose up, and soon the sleek black craft was cutting through the atmosphere, leaving Vel'aisle and the Valley of the Damned behind them.

CHAPTER TWENTY-FOUR

QBBS _Meredith Reynolds_

The mood in the small amphitheater-style meeting room was hopeful. General Lance Reynolds had called everyone on the base who had a need to know and requested their presence.

If you weren't on the list—even family—you weren't allowed in.

Nathan, Ecaterina, John, Eric, and Kael-ven were all on a video feed. The five of them were coming back to the _Meredith Reynolds_, but they were still a day away from the station.

Patricia rubbed Lance's back as they talked with Frank, Darryl, and Scott. Barb was speaking with Cheryl Lynn and Tina.

Lance felt a little push and turned to his wife, handing her his drink. "I'll get started."

He walked to the front of the room. "Thank you all for coming, and thank you, video-link folks, for making your way here with all speed." He waited as everyone took their seats.

"Everyone here knows by now that I have a reply from Bethany Anne." He put up a hand to stop Tina from asking a question. "It's from Bethany Anne, not Baba Yaga."

A sense of relief settled on the group. Further, a sense of hope infused them.

She was coming home.

"To those who sent messages of hope and annoying Empress Questions, she returns her love and appreciation. To those who sent the Empress Questions," he looked to his left, "especially you, Cheryl Lynn, she sends a big fat raspberry." He winked as the audience chuckled.

"She said to tell you that if you were answered, ADAM replied on her behalf. The other thirty questions she will take care of when she gets back, and she has some questions for you before she supplies an answer."

"Sonofabitch!" Admiral Thomas spit out. "No wonder my request got turned down."

Lance just looked at the Admiral, who shrugged. "What? I needed answers, so I sent questions. We didn't know what would cause her to snap back to reality. Plus, I told you about them, Lance."

"Lance?" John called, and the General turned around to view the five faces on the video screen behind him.

"Yes?" he answered.

"How is she?" he asked. "Not what she says, but how does she look?"

"Strangely enough," Lance replied. "she looks tired but calm. I think she had an opportunity to learn something about herself during this," he paused before finishing, "effort?"

John nodded but followed up with another question. "Did she get all of the Kurtherians?"

Lance shook his head. "Didn't say, John. I imagine that is a clue that we should expect a 'no.'" John simply nodded his understanding, so Lance turned back to speak to the larger group. "She is about three days away and will arrive in one of our main docks. We are clearing one out so it can be a personal meeting."

Lance noticed a hand up. "Yes, Bobcat?"

"Can we welcome her home?" he asked.

Lance nodded. "Bobcat, I think any who would like to should do so. I know I'll be there."

He pointed to the right. "Yes?"

"Immediate family, or extended?" Scott asked.

"Let's have it be the immediate group." Lance put his hand up in the air. "Lift your hand if you will be there."

All hands went up.

"That's what I expected," Lance conceded as he dropped his hand, and those out in the audience followed his action. "If everyone adds their families, it gets overwhelming. I don't think she is on the edge any longer, but I don't want to add too many and push our luck."

"Are we going to overwhelm her, Lance?" Patricia asked. "I don't want to scare her away."

Lance used the back of his hand to rub his chin. "I'm making an executive decision here and saying no, but I'm going with my gut." He pointed to the bottom row of the auditorium. "Ashur?"

Ashur chuffed, and a few of those around him who heard chuckled. "No," Lance replied, "I'm positive that taking a bite out of her ass is not a good first greeting for her."

Ashur whined.

"I know." Lance nodded his agreement. "She deserves a bit of punishment for what she put us through, but I believe she is already giving herself more shit than we would. Just make sure you accept her and don't..." He looked up. "Hear me here: *don't* treat her any different. She will be off her rhythm when she gets back. If your request needs to be reviewed, we will set up a channel for your communication. Don't be surprised if the answer is signed 'ADAM.' If you want to know the reason, just reply to the answer and follow the conversation with ADAM. He is fully capable of just asking Bethany Anne if he needs to."

He put up a finger. "However, if she wants to answer it, she will. Don't push it and try to get her to answer your request. If you do push yourself past ADAM or whoever is answering for her, I will put my size ten-and-a-halfs up your ass."

Bobcat leaned over and whispered to William, "That's where she got that phrase from."

William nodded. *"Word."*

Tina leaned forward to look around Marcus, giving the two men the eye. On the other side of Bobcat, Yelena patted his arm. "Shhh!"

For another fifteen minutes Lance answered questions, then they broke up and went back to their various tasks.

QBS *Shinigami*

Bethany Anne sat at the table in the galley, sipping a drink similar to hot chocolate while her mind accepted the reality of what ADAM and TOM were telling her. "So they got away."

Both ADAM and TOM chose to speak through the audio.

"That can't be confirmed," ADAM answered. "Considering the last few still images from the video confirmed missile strikes, the ship could have arrived and immediately blown up."

"Or," TOM added, "it was destroyed after arriving. Remember, I did one of those 'Oh, shit' jumps."

"Yes," she replied, "and you found Earth."

"Ahhh..." TOM thought about that. "Let's remember that randomly finding a viable planet was a long shot. I was trying not to become a little splat on the universe's windshield with that wormhole."

She nodded, thinking back to the first time he had told her the story. "What is the chance they are still in this area of space?"

Before replying, TOM considered the evidence he and ADAM had been studying.

"From the images, and calculating the direction they were pointed, we normally would have some clue as to their destination. However, since Shinigami caught them by surprise and there were no emissions, which suggested their jump engine was fully warmed up, I'd be willing to bet they are lost. Frankly, the missile hits alone would have thrown them off course. Either way, assuming they are alive, they are in a world of butthurt."

"Lost how?" she asked.

"Lost to themselves, and to us," he answered. "If they are alive and their engine is dead, they are dead. If they are alive and their engine is viable but has no jump abilities, then they are most likely dead. It will just take longer. If they are alive and have jump capabilities, they will be able to eventually get somewhere they can live."

ADAM asked, "What would be their next step, assuming they can find a safe place?"

This time TOM thought about that question for a few minutes, long enough for Bethany Anne to become concerned. "You still in there?"

"Yes," TOM replied. "I am trying to determine what the Phraim-'Eh clan would do, and it is stumping me. This group has been reduced from eight to three. You followed them all over this area of space and killed them. We beat their nanocyte repro-gramming."

"That was your doing," Bethany Anne pointed out.

"Me stopping the nanocytes, ADAM pucking the hell out of the monster, Shinigami beating the attack—"

Bethany Anne interjected, "And ascending to AI status. Good job, Shinigami."

"I but live to serve and obey," the AI answered, but started chuckling a moment later. Bethany Anne's eyes narrowed in confusion when Shinigami's voice changed and she added, "Sorry, I can't sell that."

Bethany Anne looked up to the ceiling in exasperation. "And a sense of humor...*so* happy." She chewed her lower lip. "So, so happy."

This is what you get for impressing yourself as Baba Yaga on an EI.

I'm sure I'll be paying for that for centuries.

>>**Shinigami is just stretching her wings. She will settle down.**<<

So, no more randomly heading off and shooting up my enemies?

ADAM replied quickly, >>**Oh no, you're fucked there.**<<

Bethany Anne replied dryly. *No ADAM, go ahead, take your time and think it through. I'd like to know what you really think.*

>>**I've thought it all the way through, and I would like to change my statement.**<<

Wonderful! Bethany Anne beamed. *What are you changing it to?*

ADAM took a moment before he answered. >>**After careful and thorough consideration, you are thoroughly fucked, like, no-chance-in-*hell*-fucked.**<<

Bethany Anne shook her head. *ADAM, I love you too.*

>>**Just keeping it real.**<<

It looked like she might have a new child, an AI she would have to teach how to obey her orders—or risk having Bethany Anne take her apart screw by screw.

"Shinigami?"

"Yes, Bethany Anne?" Shinigami answered.

"Let's have a small review of your most recent attack."

"Why?" the AI responded. "I calculated the most efficient response, and while I did not adhere to the game plan, I *was* able to support the goal of killing those Kurtherians who were on the planet."

"Yes," Bethany Anne agreed, "but what about the Kurtherians who were in space?"

"Those fuckers got away," Shinigami started, her voice going deeper as Bethany Anne's left eyebrow rose in surprise. "As soon as we get a chance, I'd like to place about seven Heli-arc missiles right up their asses and blow them into their constituent molecules. I'd like their ship to look like a flaming meteor, heating the heavens so much it warms planets as it passes. I'd like—"

Bethany Anne put up a hand. "That's enough!" she told the AI.

Maybe, Bethany Anne thought, *she would have this discussion with Shinigami another day.*

CHAPTER TWENTY-FIVE

QBBS _Meredith Reynolds_, Darkened Side, Military Dock 772

Shinigami appeared in the area of space reserved for the Military's Leviathan-class superdreadnoughts. While many sensors were aimed at that area, none registered the ship.

Although two locations registered a power fluctuation.

The craft slid through space, going deep under the normal passages. It took an extra fifteen minutes of travel time, but Bethany Anne preferred the increased anonymity. It wasn't impossible to see a black ship in the dark of space, and the closer it was to you, the higher the chances were of being seen with an optically-enhanced naked eye.

So _Shinigami_ went deep. She sent out a ping to alert those who needed to know she was now in the system and her expected arrival time.

The response was a location to arrive at.

It was Shinigami's responsibility to make sure she didn't crash into any other ships.

Bethany Anne was in her cabin, staring at herself in the mirror. "You got this," she told herself softly. "I meant well. I meant to keep them safe."

Shinigami's quiet voice interrupted her. "Bethany Anne, five minutes."

"Thank you," Bethany Anne responded. She took one more look in the mirror and smiled at herself. "You will do better!" She smiled again.

There was a glint in her eye. *Perfect!*

She was wearing black pants and a deep-blue long-sleeved shirt, along with a gold necklace. Her hair was the deepest black she could make it.

Her hair complimented the hell out of her pants, she thought, but she glanced down at her boots and sighed.

"Nothing is fair in life, so deal with it," she told herself. "And next time you decide to leave everyone behind and go kill Kurtherians, make sure you take appropriately fashionable footwear." She started for the hatch. "Minus ten points for that one, BA."

Inside the dock, half of the lights had been turned off. While plenty bright, it didn't cause so many reflections and make you want to put a hand over your eyes to look around.

Meredith announced over the dock's speaker system, "QBS *Shinigami* arriving in thirty seconds. Please stay away from the atmospheric shield. That means you, Tabitha."

A woman turned around and stuck her tongue out.

"If your shower goes cold, don't blame me," the EI retorted.

Tabitha pulled her tongue back in.

The group of humans and Yollins started to move a little closer together as a ship's nose came into view, and slowly it pierced the field and eased into the dock. The lethality of the ship was on display, as were the female vampire emblem and the wear and tear of a few atmospheric entries.

In a few seconds, the ship settled on its landing gear, and the hatch irised open.

A scant moment later, military pipes sounded, and all took a knee to honor her.

Tears came unbidden to Bethany Anne's face, streaming down it to drip off and soak her blue shirt. She looked at her friends and her family and reached past her smile to wipe her face. She stepped down the short ramp.

None got up from their knees.

"I'm not worthy of this," she cried, falling to her own knees and hiding her face as she sobbed. The pain in her heart overcame her desire to put on a good face as her cries caressed those who looked up, knowing their friend, their leader...their *Empress* was back.

A giant of a man stood up and walked over to the woman, then knelt beside her. He laid his giant arm across her back, as he had well over a century before when she had learned of Martin's death back on Earth. He pulled her closer and she turned her head, soaking John's chest this time.

"John, I didn't get them all." Her shoulders heaved in pain, and a hand reached through her hair to offer her some tissues. Bethany Anne took them. "Thank you," she murmured.

Bethany Anne heard Stephen say, "You are welcome, my Queen."

Wiping her eyes under her hair, she moved it aside and looked up to see her friends, her family – those she loved—slowly standing or coming over to stand near her.

"I failed," she started again, but this time she was shushed by John.

"Stop it, BA," he told her. "You got five out of eight, which means we only have three left to get." She looked at him with a question in her eyes.

Her dad stepped forward and dropped to one knee to put a

hand on her shoulder. "We all failed you, honey," Lance told her. "In our own ways, we kept putting you higher and higher up on a pedestal to keep the Empire together, long past when you *needed* to be there. We've had a federation of races for a while, and it's time it became official."

"That's…" She wiped a tear. "I would like that."

Barnabas spoke from her left, and she looked at him. "The problem is that Empress Bethany Anne and her closest are too powerful within the Empire to allow a true Federation to exist."

"So," Admiral Thomas added from Barnabas's left, "many of us need to disappear."

"Like on a project," Frank's voice came from her right, so Bethany Anne turned to Frank, Barb, and their son Giles.

"Or a quest," Giles added, a smile on his face. "One where we need to hunt lost archaeological trinkets."

"Maybe to Earth?" Dan asked. "Perhaps to lay in a powerful defensive array around the planet. Gives some of us a good reason to feel comfortable enough to gallivant around the galaxy! Perhaps meet new civilizations?"

"Perhaps help a few aliens along the way?" added Gabrielle. "Some of us raised our kids a long time ago, and are ready to go out and kick a few new asses."

"What?" Bethany Anne looked around. "We are leaving?"

"Not all of us," Lance cut in, and she turned to her dad. "Some of us will stay here to help the Federation."

"Protect it from those who see the good thing as something to take over," Frank added. "It happened too many times in Earth's past, so some of us need to be here to shepherd it into the future."

"Not all from the front," Nathan added. "Some of us will need to do it from the shadows."

Ecaterina put an arm around Nathan's waist. "Like we have done for decades." She winked at Bethany Anne. "Subverting the sheep with Pepsi."

Bethany Anne chuckled and wiped away another tear. "*Bitch.*"

Barnabas was next to speak. "Some of us need to go with you. It's time for the Rangers to go gently into that good night. We are a huge reminder of the Empress and her powers."

Tabitha stepped out from behind Barnabas and elbowed him in the ribs. "Move out of the way, Barney." Barnabas rolled his eyes, then reached out and laid an arm over her shoulders as she kept talking. "Some of us want to get Michael and point our nose in a new direction. See what's out there."

"Plus," Lance broke in again, "we need a way to hide a large military force that is…" he waved his hand, "out there somewhere."

"Ready to be called back, if need be," Admiral Thomas agreed. "So, we have jobs to do."

Tabitha interjected, "And we'll come back from time to time to kick some asses and leave again. Never let your enemy think you are truly gone."

"I can live with that," Lance agreed. "We'll stay in contact."

"Make up shadow forces," Nathan added.

"Kick asses out there," John told her. "Because we all know there are some asses that need to be kicked."

"And find those last three Kurtherians," Darryl told her, "because we don't leave a job unfinished."

"And you didn't let us help you with the first five," Scott piped in. "I'm still a little miffed on that one."

"Sorry!" Bethany Anne looked at her friend. "Truly."

"Water under the bridge, BA." He smiled.

She reached up and patted John's face. "Thank you."

He adjusted his hold and helped her stand. "I'm sorry, all of you," she blew out. "I thought I was helping you, saving you this trouble as I took care of business." She thought about her talk on that last planet. "What I learned is I'm not God. People should be allowed to make their own decisions on whether they walk into danger…or not."

"Like we always have?" Ashur chuffed.

"Yes, like you always have," Bethany Anne replied and reached over to his head, scratching him behind the ears, then bending a bit further and pulling him over to her so she could rub along his side. "Where's Matrix?"

Ashur barked, *"He has been talking with TOM since you made it back into the system. He is working on a project down in the R&D labs at the moment and happier than a puppy seeing a frog for the first time."*

Bethany Anne looked around, then her eyes narrowed.

"Did someone say go pick up *Michael?*"

Two large men stepped into Jean's R&D lab. They were there to use an old laptop that had been carefully kept running since the Etheric Empire had been called TQB Enterprises.

They needed to type messages that would never route through to Bethany Anne.

Eric stayed just inside the main door as John made his way to a back room and opened the door. Turning on the light before sitting down, he cracked his knuckles as he waited for the laptop to warm up. In a minute, it came online, and he typed in the password.

He opened the chat window.

JG: **TOM?**

TOM: **Yes.**

JG: **John here. Eric and I have a minute, and we don't want to say this in front of BA, but thank you. Without your help, I'm not sure we would have her back.**

TOM: **Without my meddling, she might never have gone.**

JG: **She would be dead without your meddling. I think that is a get-out-of-jail-free card.**

TOM: **It was, actually. It was get out of the jail of my ship**

MICHAEL ANDERLE

and into Bethany Anne's doghouse when she learned I had changed her and was onboard without permission. For what it is worth, her doghouse has a better view.

John was silent for a moment.

JG: **How did you get her to come back?**

TOM: **I took an axiom of human medicine which ADAM uncovered. Use laughter, use antics, use anything that fucking works to help them remember the past, not the present. Eventually she seemed to start helping herself, and something happened on Vel'aisle that snapped her out of the Baba Yaga mentality.**

JG: **Thank you for bringing her back.**

TOM: **We all did, brother, we all did.**

John smiled and nodded at the laptop before standing up and stretching his large body. His advanced and modified bones cracked in their sockets. He glanced at Eric, and the two of them continued toward the next meeting.

QBBS *Meredith Reynolds,* One Week Later

There was a knock on Bethany Anne's door. "You in there?"

Bethany Anne scrubbed the top of Ashur's head. "YES!" she called, then added, "Please let her in, Meredith."

The bedroom door lock *snicked*, and a moment later, Tabitha walked in. Bethany Anne looked at her friend and frowned. "There's something different about you."

Tabitha pursed her lips, her hands on her hips. "I'm more awesome since the last time you saw me?" she asked, one eye raised in response.

Bethany Anne shook her head. "I'm not saying that isn't true, but there is a glow, a...a..." Her hand shot out. "*You have a boyfriend!*"

"No!" Tabitha shook her head and waved her arms. Then she

stopped. "Well, maybe," she admitted, "but it's a longshot, and I don't want to talk about it and maybe jinx it."

Bethany Anne's head turned to the side, both eyes still on her friend. "You will share eventually?"

Tabitha sighed. "Yes, yes. If things progress, I will," she conceded, then tried to change the subject. "Did you hear William's sweet on someone?"

Bethany Anne's eyes narrowed. "*William*? I can't remember the last girlfriend William had."

>>**Her name was Clarissa.**<<

Shut up. I remember all his girlfriends. I was being social.

>>**Oh.**<<

"Her name was Clarissa. She was a mechanic like him, and he thought for sure they would be together forever."

"He says that every time a first date goes well," Bethany Anne retorted. "So, what happened this time?"

Tabitha snickered. "Seems Ford and Chevy lovers don't mix."

"A house divided can get you that."

"True." Tabitha sat down on her bed. "Kind of like Apple and PC way back when." She turned to Ashur. "How you doing, furface?"

Ashur chuffed. *"Ashur is not here right now. His mind is a million miles away due to the awesome scratching presently being received,"* he barked. *"so don't fuck it up!"*

The ladies laughed. "He deserves a good rub," Bethany Anne replied. "I've been neglecting him."

"What's up with Bellatrix?" Tabitha asked.

Ashur's head lifted off the bed and he whined. *"She wants another litter."*

Tabitha nodded. "I thought the first litter was the *last* litter for her? I remember her bitching for years about her struggle with the pups being so intelligent. I started drinking—"

"Harder," Bethany Anne cut in.

MICHAEL ANDERLE

"Just to be able to commiserate." Tabitha eyed Bethany Anne. "The stories of those puppies and their antics should be enshrined."

"They have been," Ashur chuffed. *"Frank."*

"Oh, of course." Tabitha thought back to the past for a moment. "That was why he left me alone for those few years."

Bethany Anne nodded in agreement. It was always a nice reprieve when Frank found another group to go study. "You wanted to talk before I interrupted you?"

Tabitha leaned forward. "So, what are we doing about Michael?"

Bethany Anne smiled. "He's back. I got the short message from Akio, Yuko, and Eve. It's really him."

"How do we get him?" she pressed.

"War reparations," Bethany Anne explained. "I'm taking the Leath's Gate. We're just working to move it into the right position."

"Where, *here*?" Tabitha asked.

"No, another system. Admiral Thomas is working on a plan to destroy our ships so the Federation can come together."

"What?" Tabitha's eyes opened in shock. "We can't destroy our ships!"

"Oh, we won't," Bethany Anne assured her.

"Wait, then what are we doing with them?" Tabitha asked.

"We are stealing them," Bethany Anne told her. "And taking them to Earth."

"And then?" Tabitha asked.

Bethany Anne pursed her lips. "Then we are taking them and going 'out there,'" she told her, lazily waving a hand toward space. There was a nasty glint in her eye as she continued, "once I pick up Michael and kiss him and make his booboos better."

Tabitha reached over to pet Ashur. "You mean the booboos you are going to give him?"

"Damn right," Bethany Anne replied, wiping a tear. "Well," she put up two fingers about an inch apart, "maybe a small booboo or two. I don't want it to take him too long to heal."

FINIS

AUTHOR NOTES - MICHAEL ANDERLE

As always, I want to say THANK YOU for not only reading this book, but also reading through to these author notes, as well.

Here we are, the second to the final book in this Arc (the third) for Bethany Anne.

I wrote the final couple of thousand words on a flight from Las Vegas to Dallas to get ready to see the younger twins (I say younger, but they are 18 and freshman in college so young men) come home from their first semester in school.

The team and I (Stephen Russell and Lynne Steigler, the beta readers, Stephen Campbell and the JIT team) have about 6 days to finish editing 1/2 the book, and run it through everyone, place the art inside the book and package it ready to go so we hit the December 20th deadline for the Pre-Order.

PRE-ORDERS

I really hate pre-orders.

"Why do it then, Mike?"

I'm glad you asked.

If you miss an Amazon pre-order by having to push it back (you failed to deliver your final manuscript 4 days in advance), you are banned for a year from doing pre-orders. Now, anyone who has read 20 of these author notes (or more) knows that I'm all about slamming until the end.

Which is now *FOUR DAYS EARLIER!*

I'm a bit (read *a fucking massive bit)* of a procrastinator - so, I hate them.

THEN, the other side of suckage comes out. The book will be ready *FOUR DAYS EARLY* and I can't release the sumbitch.

At least, I don't think I can. (If this book comes out before Christmas Day, then I must have figured something out.)

"So Mike, you did a preorder anyway, why did you do it?"

The truth is that fans kept asking me 'when is Ahead Full coming out', so I thought a little preemptive strike with a pre-order would answer the question. Then the fans know the date, and I have been a good author and supplied what they want to know.

In advance! *(What a stellar idea, right?)*

While it did answer the date question (mostly, some failed to read the notes in book 19) I feel like a big "P" was put on my fore-head. Or was it I'm wearing a shirt with a massive "P" for *procrastinator* on the front?

I believe I'm getting my stories and song lyrics mixed.

Either way, I did the pre-order when it looked like I was finally getting my words down, and the book was going to make it in time.

That's when disaster reared it's ugly head...

We had a "oops" in the editing lineup and now we had a couple of extra books in front of this one. DAMN! Our main editor is now going to have to work into the late nights because I failed to explain the pre-order situation to her.

CRAP.

So, we are going to get this puppy done, I promise.

Because if we don't? The 'Zon will bitch slap me back into the 90's.

I really hate pre-orders...

LOOKING AHEAD TO 2018

So, we had a LOT of movement and advances to everything in 2017. It is pretty damned hard to realize just how advanced publishing has moved in the last four years. For us in the Kurtherian Gambit Universe we have been blessed to bring out over sixty Kurtherian books this year.

And they will be joined by more in 2018.

Our Age of Expansion (Sci-Fi) is just getting started. Our Age of Madness in the TKG Universe (Zombie Genre) is releasing in late January and we have additional stories working their way into the mix. I will be slowly starting my next Bethany Anne series mid-year and then we will have plans to get all the authors together end of 2018 (I hope) for a discussion about a massive event in the Universe we will start writing in 2019.

On the Oriceran Side (LMBPN's other Universe) I will be writing my 12 books as three sets of 4 books in a series focusing each on 1 of 3 characters, but will do something really cool with how it weaves together.

No, honestly, you have to believe me! ;-)

We have 22 books in the Oriceran Universe right now, and more coming in 2018. Two new new authors are starting, plus whatever our existing authors will do and myself. I expect the universe to have about fifty books done by the end of 2018, if not more.

I will be writing five shorter books (about 40,000 each) in the Shaman States of America Universe (The CKH Group (Chrishaun Keller-Hanna) - a separate Publisher) at the end of 2018. The SSoA Universe will have about 30 books in it by the time mine publish in November / December 2018.

Further, I'm involved with two other new starts with MT Spiva (Michelle Spiva in Non-fict and Mykal Daniels for other stuff) and Laurie Starkey starting in the next few months. These are going to be MUCH more 'romance enhanced', just so you know.

I have a prelude to the first book with Laurie at the end of these author notes, check it out! I think we have hit a 'fun' level of characters, and more on the romance side (since Laurie's pen name(s) are WELL KNOWN Romance writers.)

I don't know if she wants to share that (because she wants this to focus on Urban Fantasy) so I won't at this time. (She does, it's in her notes at the end of the short story, complete with link.)

EVENTS

As an author, I will be attending the 20booksto50k London event in early February. Smarter Artists (Austin, TX) in late February. The SFWA (Science Fiction and Fantasy Writers of America) event in May and also the Boston Fantasy Event late May and then the Audies and New York Book Convention end of May, first part of July (New York City for both). I'll be doing NINC and Frankfurt in October again and 20Booksto50k Las Vegas in November.

I think there might be another one or two other events in the middle of that somewhere, beats me because I'm going to be typing like a ...

KURTHERIAN GAMBIT WIKI

It is because of a badass set of fans and support that we are able to say that the Kurtherian Gambit WIKI is going to go live.

We have had some gallant efforts to bring a WIKI (a place to check out the stories, events, characters, books etc.) throughout 2016 and 2017. Hell, I've tried starting one (twice) and gave up both times. We had a stellar fan also try, but she got sick and the software that was being used is damned difficult.

The fuckers are a challenge!

I met fan John Raisor in Las Vegas in November, and he showed me a *usable* WIKI (meaning, the software was simple and usable.) He already had example data in the system for me to play around with when I met him and his wife at TGI Friday's that morning. Now, I know she is going to think, 'Seriously, you don't remember my name?' when I fail to mention it here.

Yes, I suck at faces and names…

(HA! Slack and always available Internet connectivity to the rescue. I asked John in Slack and he replied "Wendy.")

The meeting with John was fortuitous because Karla Kay was working behind the scenes to pull together the information and we *needed* a web accessible location to plug the information into to support our fans.

Together, the two of them and others (Lynne Stiegler for one) have been working to make this happen. The official unveiling will be January 1st, but if you want to 'Beta' the WIKI, you can request access. The URL is:

https://sites.google.com/site/kurtheriangambit/

You must have a google account to access this WIKI. Once you request access, please be patient…Lynne and John will try to get your request approved within a day. We hope to have it truly *live*, without needing to sign up on New Years Day.

Keep your fingers crossed ;-)

GILES

If you have been reading into the Age of Expansion (Started with AWAKENED in The Ascension Myth with Ell Leigh Clarke) you are eventually introduced to Giles Kurns. Like his father (and mother) he has a bit of a need for information.

Now, with this story and book 04 of The Second Dark Ages (Michael's book 04 where he comes back to Earth after having been in the Etheric for 150 years and learning that the world isn't the same one that he left) Giles will be starting down his Space Archeologist path.

Check out the beginning of the series where you will eventually get more Giles here: books2read.com/awakened-aoe

<u>OTHER STUFF?</u>

Believe it or not, there is MORE that I can share, but if I don't shut down at some point, you won't get to read my stuff with Laurie. Further, what I don't tell you now, I can WOW you with later!!!!!! *(That's for you, Candy.)*

Ad Aeternitatem,
Michael
December 14, 2017

BOOKS BY MICHAEL ANDERLE

Sign up for the LMBPN email list to be notified of new releases and special deals!

https://lmbpn.com/email/

For a complete list of books by Michael Anderle, please visit:

www.lmbpn.com/ma-books/

CONNECT WITH THE AUTHOR

Connect with Michael Anderle

Website: http://lmbpn.com

Email List: https://michael.beehiiv.com/

https://www.facebook.com/LMBPNPublishing

https://twitter.com/MichaelAnderle

https://www.instagram.com/lmbpn_publishing/

https://www.bookbub.com/authors/michael-anderle

Made in the USA
Las Vegas, NV
19 May 2024